HIS CHRISTMAS BOX

HIS CHRISTMAS BOX

Julian Fane

CONSTABLE · LONDON

First published in Great Britain in 1995
by Constable and Company Limited
3 The Lanchesters, 162 Fulham Palace Road
London W6 9ER
Copyright © 1995 Julian Fane
ISBN 0 09 474310 X
The right of Julian Fane to be
identified as the author of this work
has been asserted by him in accordance with
the Copyright, Designs and Patents Act 1988
Set in Monophoto Poliphilus 12pt by
Servis Filmsetting Ltd, Manchester
Printed in Great Britain by
St Edmundsbury Press Ltd
Bury St Edmunds, Suffolk

A CIP catalogue record for this book
is available from the British Library

To

MARK WYNDHAM

Contents

Festivities

CHRISTMAS fell on a Friday that year, and as Willo Todd left London for his country house on the Wednesday he did not immediately receive a particular letter which dropped through his letter-box on the Thursday morning.

The address in town of Captain (retd) Willoughby Michael St John Todd M.C. was 25D Edgware Mansions, London W2 7BD. The Mansions were ponderous redbrick terraces of purpose-built Edwardian blocks of flats, facing each other across a narrow street and located just off the east side of the northern end of Edgware Road. 25D, on the fifth floor, had a sitting-room and bedroom, both small, a kitchenette and a cupboard-sized bathroom. It was reached either by stairs flaunting a runner of threadbare Turkey-type carpet or by an alarmingly creaky old lift.

Willoughby Todd, known to his friends as Willo or Will, had resided here mid-week for thirty-odd years. It had not seemed old-fashioned, cramped, cheap and tawdry when he moved in, and now he was used to it. Despite his fifty-six years he could still climb the stairs without too much effort.

On Wednesday 23 December he was woken at eight o'clock by Mary Cole knocking on his bedroom door, entering, placing a cup of tea on the bedside table, pulling back his curtains vigorously and saying: 'Good morning, Capting.'

Mary not only insisted on calling him by his rank in the army, but also on mispronouncing it. Long ago, when she started to clean for him, he told her he was not her Captain and certainly not her Capting, but she took no notice and in time he followed suit. For that matter, later on, when he said he and his flat did not require an hour of her attention every five-day week throughout the year she simply ignored him. Rain or shine, minor indispositions notwith-standing, undeterred by advancing years and the journey from Cricklewood, and without regard to the financial aspect of things, she knocked on his door at the same time, eight sharp, brought him tea and collected his clothes to valet them.

His response to her greeting was a groaning question: 'What's the weather like?'

'No sign of a white Christmas yet, Capting — grey and drizzly.'

In due course he opened his eyes and drank his lukewarm tea. He would have liked to stay in bed and snatch a bit more sleep: he had stayed out late the previous evening, or rather got in early in the morning — and not so early at that. He also wished he had not been reminded that Christmas was coming.

Dutifully, typically, having arrived at this negative stage of his cogitations he arose and went into the bathroom, shaved and bathed, and donned his comfortable country clothes also wearable in town, blue Oxford cotton shirt and bow-tie, cream-coloured cavalry twill trousers and brown loafers, and long and loose Lovat tweed jacket. The smell of coffee and bacon frying sharpened his appetite and improved his mood. He stepped in his light-footed way into the sitting-room, where the tray-table laid for breakfast and boasting a copy of the Daily Telegraph stood in front of his armchair. Mary popped her head round the kitchen door to check that he was ready and waiting and brought in the food, scrambled egg and bacon, a rack of toast, coffee and hot milk.

He ate, she talked — the routine was unvarying.

'Have you done your shopping, Capting?'

He shook his head and obligingly volunteered the complementary cue: 'Have you?'

She fixed him with her brown eyes magnified by spectacles and subjected him to the rigmarole of her list of Christmas presents: bedsocks for her sister with whom she lived, a retired nurse named Biddy, and even humbler gifts for the friends and acquaintances whose life stories she recounted.

He finished his breakfast and asked her: 'Where's the gold watch I'm expecting to get from you?'

Mary, who never saw his jokes, responded to this one as if to a signal to make his bed and tidy up the bathroom.

Willo moved from the armchair to the chair by the desk and wrote out a cheque for Miss M. Cole for a hundred pounds, sealed it in an envelope and deposited the envelope on the kitchen table.

Back in the sitting-room he picked up the newspaper, skimmed through it, yawned, stirred himself restlessly and summoned Mary.

'I'm not going to the office – I'm due at Tollworth at one o'clock,' he informed her.

'Yes, Capting.'

'I'd better buy presents for my damn grandchildren – what do little boys like nowadays?'

'Pens are always welcome, or a torch.'

His boredom took the form of an abrupt change of subject: 'You'll find your Christmas box in the kitchen.'

She thanked him and said: 'I've posted your gift to The Court.'

'That's wrong of you, Mary. I've always told you not to waste your money on me.'

'I could say the same to you, Capting.'

'Oh – I've got pots – it's my fun to chuck the stuff around – you ought to be saving yours for your old age.'

No doubt because she was already far from young, Mary was amused by his advice and showed her ill-fitting dentures as she laughed.

He continued: 'My cheque'll cover this week's wages. Now I'm off – I want to get to the shops and out of them before I'm trampled to death by women shoppers.'

'When will I be seeing you again, Capting?'

'Next Wednesday – in a week, God willing – I plan to leave Tollworth on the Tuesday. Listen, don't you dare spoil your holiday by fussing over the flat while my back's turned.'

In the hallway she helped him into his three-quarter-length overcoat made of more cavalry twill and handed him his battered brown trilby. She wished him a safe journey and a merry Christmas, sent her regards to Mrs Todd and everybody else who would be at The Court, graciously received his very best wishes for the happiness and health of herself, her sister Biddy and her cat Madam, and shut the door.

He chose to go down the stairs, he distrusted the lift, and stopped in the front hall on the ground floor to study his reflection in the mirror framed by encaustic tiles. He was six feet tall with a youthful figure. He removed his trilby: his black hair going grey at the temples was fine and flat, his nose crooked owing to a breakage at school, his complexion ruddy and his expression keen. He was the image of a probably military, probably sporting, certainly well-heeled

English gentleman. He replaced his hat, tipping the brim to obtain the pre-ferred jaunty angle, and stepped out into the December morning with a con-fident air.

His first call at the Toy Department of Selfridges was fruitless. After five deafening and indecisive minutes he concluded that he would give William and James Milsom, his grandchildren, money: let the blighters choose their own presents. On second thoughts, money would solve most of the problems of his shopping. He cashed a big cheque at the National Westminster Bank in Portman Square, and proceeded southwards via Grosvenor and Berkeley Squares to Old Bond Street. He still had presents to buy for his wife and his mistress.

He ended up with a Gucci scarf and an antique enamel patch-box bearing the legend on its lid: Forget me not. The former present was the matrimonial one; the other was to be gift-wrapped and delivered by hand to Mrs Gloria Deane, 18 Avebury Flats, Grosvenor Terrace, W.1.

He returned to his flat at eleven. Mary had departed, leaving all in apple-pie order. He made two brief telephone calls.

His side of the first ran as follows: 'Bad moment? . . . Thank you for last night, darling . . . Well, I'm sorry too, you know that . . . But you're going to Jane and Dick for Christmas Day, aren't you? . . . I'm back on Tuesday with any luck . . . No, no, I'll be there – eight o'clock at your place . . . Happiest Christmas, sweetie . . . Until Tuesday, goodbye.'

The other went: 'Barbara? . . . Are you all right? . . . Yes – just leaving – see you soon – goodbye!'

He then stuffed the bag containing the Gucci scarf into his attaché case, locked up, descended the stairs two at a time, walked round to the garage he rented in Edgware Mansions Mews, and in his two-year-old red Mercedes 190 drove off and eventually on to the M4, leaving it at Exit 15 and taking the cross-country road to Tetbury and to Tollworth beyond.

It was half-past twelve. He could not be bothered to garage the Merc. The village street or rather the road through the hamlet was empty. He climbed out, pushed through the greenish-white picket gate under the clipped yew archway, stepped along the flagged path, unlocked the front door, put his case on the cir-cular hall table and hung his hat and coat on available antler coat-hooks in the cubbyhole beneath the staircase, negotiated the moth-eaten green baize serving-door and called: 'Barbara?'

There was no answer, but dishes clattered in the kitchen.

His wife was cooking.

'Hullo, my dear,' he greeted her, advancing as if to give her a kiss.

She turned away from him and said: 'How I hate Christmas!'

He had been feeling just as she said she did. But he reacted with inward annoyance to her customary killjoy attitude.

Of course she was reproaching him for being her husband and a minor plutocrat, for working in London and saddling her with housewifely duties in Tollworth, for having two daughters by another woman and one son-in-law and a pair of grandchildren, who were all coming to stay and would soon have to be entertained and fed, and for never having understood her or made her happy, except for a few mad months in the year they married.

To the last of these subliminal charges he might have snapped back: 'Same here!'

Instead he replied cheerily: 'Melanie and Prue have promised to help with the housework. Don't keep dogs and bark yourself. That reminds me — where's Tray?'

Tray was Barbara's Tibetan spaniel.

'He's in the garden,' she now said, making an obvious effort to be civil and turning to Willo with a wan smile, ready to submit to his kiss.

He pecked her cheek without establishing contact elsewhere.

'I've been doing the mince pies,' she added in an excusatory tone. 'I will get the girls to lend a hand when they arrive. What about lunch? Will you find sausages acceptable?'

Sausages were just the job, he answered. And he would leave her in peace and get himself organised. And eating in the kitchen would suit him to a T. And he was jolly glad to be home.

His gladness was not a lie; nor was his sorrow, as expressed to Gloria Deane a couple of hours previously, because he had to spend Christmas with his family. Willoughby Todd was truthful temperamentally, training and principle apart — he was born forthright. And the truth was that he would have had good fun in London with Gloria; also and equally that The Court, its dear old bricks and mortar, and being there again, meant a hell of a lot to him.

The house was originally Tudor — certain tiny mullioned windows at the back proved it — and Todds were lords of the manor of Tollworth in those days, and administered rough justice in their Great Hall or Court. As time passed it was altered almost beyond recognition inside and out, losing its top storey at some stage, getting a sort of face-lift in the Georgian style, adding rooms and subtracting them, gaining bathrooms and central heating. It stood in the centre of the present village, which consisted of fifty odd dwellings on either side of a quiet country road, opposite the Post Office-cum-general store, behind the yew hedge already mentioned and a strip of unsatisfactory lawn, and was completely covered with creeper, red Virginia creeper in the autumn.

The so-called front rooms on the ground floor were dark because of the hedge; they also faced north-east. The rooms in question were the large one with the ping-pong table and the study, Willo's lair, which, together with the entrance hall, had probably once been part of the Great Hall. The drawing-room was in the south-west corner, the dining-room adjoined, and the domestic offices straggled away towards the stable yard. The outhouses were more numerous than the reception rooms of the main inhabited house: there were sheds for firewood, saw-bench, central heating boiler, disused electricity generator, painting equipment, furniture storage, gardening tools, mowing machinery and potting. The garage contained the bicycle that Barbara rode, and a tangle of rusty children's bikes and trikes, and an apple loft above. The garden had some uneven lawn, a herbaceous border against the high wall of the kitchen part, and half a dozen gnarled fruit trees in an area called the orchard. Upstairs, on the first floor, were eight bedrooms and three bathrooms.

The interior was chock-full of evidence of occupation by a single family for donkey's years. Willo's first wife Minnie and his second Barbara were linked in spite of themselves not only matrimonially, but in addition by their trying in vain to stamp their personalities upon the decoration of the rooms. They were equally defeated by ancestral forces, by the number of portraits in oils, watercolour, charcoal, pencil, silhouette, wax, by the furniture that had always fitted into such-and-such a place, by almost every item that had sentimental significance or was hallowed by the tender care of generations going back to the dawn of time. The past of The Court, the history of Todds, probably helped to propel Minnie on her revolutionary flight into the arms of the pop musician Jack Max, and onward to achieve a happier landing with her second husband, Christopher Miller-Boyd. Barbara reacted differently: at least in the decorative context she retreated into the fastness of her bedroom, banishing the four-poster and the black oak cupboard and the tattered needlework curtains sewn by maiden aunts, and introducing the exceptional elements of space and light.

The front hall remained as it was in the days of Willo's father, Colonel Jack Todd, and indeed his grandfather, the notorious hunting parson Reuben or Reuby Todd, whose nickname was sometimes spelt Ruby in consideration of his complexion. The cream colour of ceiling and walls had turned to burnt umber; but it was mostly and mercifully obscured by black pictures, by a dusty line of whips and switches with which bygone horses had been encouraged to do their bit for equestrian Todds, by coaching horns, a barometer, a defunct grandfather clock, and by coats of all descriptions and trilbys, caps, boaters, sun-hats hanging from those antlers of deer stalked and shot by Todds out for bigger game than their foxy namesakes. On the central table were a Visitors' Book, a tarnished silver inkwell and a variety of pens, a railway timetable and a list of forthcoming Meets of the Beaufort Hunt, and one pile of junk mail and another of letters addressed to Willo.

He picked them up and carried them into his study before lunch on Wednesday 23 December. They were not important, except inasmuch as they were after his money: none was to be compared with that which was making its way to his London address.

He lingered in his worn leather desk chair nonetheless: he loved this room. It was like a temple dedicated to Todd rather than God. Above the book-shelves it had oars which had rowed some forebear to his university Blue. It had school and army group photographs, and silver cups and rosettes won by the efforts of the dead, and in and out of glass cases stuffed souvenirs of fox-hunting runs and fishing exploits, and the hoofs of favourite horses converted into match-holders, and deeply sat-out armchairs lit by angular lamps with faded green silk shades; and it was further sanctified by the odour of the cigar smoke of yesteryear. From wives, from children, it had often sheltered Willo.

But he wanted to see Denis Willett, his gardener, handyman and friend, who might be knocking off early today. Denis chose which hours he would and which he would not work, and was inclined to justify the receipt of his weekly wage by digging the garden at five in the morning or by moonlight.

Willo found him in the potting shed. Denis seemed to be a survival from another age, a peasant out of Thomas Hardy's books, or, if he had been less genuine, an actor imitating rustic innocence. He was thickset, apple-cheeked and approximately clean-shaven, and wore a soft tweed hat.

'I was hoping to see you before I left, Mr Todd,' he proclaimed in his inim-itable West Country accent. 'I'm going to Tetbury this afternoon to buy my missus her present.'

'What are you giving her, Denis?'

'I don't know – a fat turkey or a new TV – something or other I want, that's what.'

Willo laughed and Denis continued: 'I'll be in with the Christmas tree and the holly tomorrow morning, and then I've said I'll take the bus into Bristol, so my wife can buy me something nice. And we're stopping with my brother in Bristol till Sunday.'

In that case, Willo said, he would distribute his Christmas Boxes not on Boxing Day but on the Monday, another holiday, when he hoped Denis would look in to collect his.

'I'll be pleased to,' Denis replied. 'I aim to work here and make up my time on Monday – I don't hold with holidays, and I'll have had enough of the wife by then.'

Willo managed not to say that he already shared the latter sentiment, and bracing himself re-entered the house by the back door and the kitchen.

The salient points of his conversation with Barbara over the sausages without mash were as follows.

She asked him: 'Do we have to have Josh to lunch on Christmas Day?'

Josh was the Reverend Joshua Kemball, Willo's best friend and fellow-officer in the army, who had gone into the church in early middle-age and by chance become the vicar of the parishes of Tollworth, Measham and Snathe. He was a widower and lived at the Rectory over in Measham.

Willo replied: 'Our parson's had his Christmas lunch at The Court since God knows when – but I suppose I could tell Josh not to eat much.'

'It's no joke – feeding eight people isn't funny.'

'Oh well, Josh is usually good for a laugh . . .'

Her next question was asked in a more conciliatory tone: 'Was your week satisfactory?'

'Not bad. What about yours?'

'Not bad,' she echoed him mockingly. 'But I don't like to think of your eve-nings in London. I won't believe you sit and eat bread and cheese in that horrid little flat. I mean it's not as if you were a reader,' she concluded this disagreeable speech, bemoaning not for the first time his lack of intellectual interests.

Willo smiled and munched sausage. He was pretty sure that Barbara would not want to prosecute her inquiries into his urban solitude in case he should inquire into hers. He nonetheless changed the subject: 'By the way, did a parcel arrive for me from Mary Cole?'

[16]

Barbara said yes, and that as it was covered with Christmas stickers she had put it with the other presents to be opened on Christmas Day.

She pursued: 'You'll probably like Mary's present better than mine – she always gives you those babyish fruit jellies, doesn't she? My present's dreadfully dull, but at least it won't rot your teeth. I find you the most difficult person in the world to give a present to – I suppose you're the man who has everything, or almost.'

His reassuring murmurs were cut short by her afterthought in the postal context: 'Oh – we've been invited to drinks at Waddington on Christmas Eve – the grand invitation card had "Bring the family" scrawled on it in vulgar red ink.'

The Ellerys were rich people who had recently bought and moved into Waddington Hall, the most stately of homes in the neighbourhood.

The Todds argued over this invitation, Willo saying he was longing to meet the Ellerys and to see what they had or had not done to Waddington, Barbara countering that she loathed typical moneyed vandals such as the Ellerys seemed to be, and that Willo's sister Amanda, who also lived in Tollworth with her huge family, would be bound to suggest a get-together on Christmas Eve.

'You know how it upsets Mandy if we don't make the pilgrimage to Shoe House and bow down to Theodore and praise their hopeless children,' she warned.

At last it was decided that he would telephone Mandy and try to fix a meeting that did not clash with the Ellerys' party, which Barbara reserved the right not to attend.

Further seasonal issues were debated, meals, liquid refreshments, church services, when the house-guests would arrive and depart, and so on.

Then Tray whined at the drawing-room french window, begging to be admitted, and Willo rose with relief to let the dog in. But Tray was like his mistress; Willo was cringed from and barked at for his pains.

The union of Willoughby Todd and Barbara Jameson always was unlikely.

His first marriage to Marigold Fenner-Wells, otherwise known as Minnie, could be called predictable. He was Tollworth's finest son, she was the prettiest flower of Snathe. He was still in the army, a uniformed hero of the Suez Expedition, winner of the Military Cross, and an upstanding nice-looking slim and humorous twenty-three-year-old; and she was a black-haired blue-eyed bubbling nineteen.

[17]

The Fenner-Wells family were relatively new arrivals in Snathe: Willo did not meet Minnie at children's parties. They caught a first glimpse of each other at the annual summer fete at The Court when he was seventeen and she was thirteen. Then he joined up and she grew up, and six years later they were included in a tennis afternoon – not quite a tournament – at Waddington Hall, organised by the Waddingtons who were still living there. The sun shone on that day in every sense. All the gilded youth of ten square miles of Gloucestershire had been invited by elderly and benevolent Sir Humphrey and Lady Waddington, whose only son had fallen in the war – the host and hostess and their staff were probably nostalgically indulgent. There were two super tennis courts, and flower and kitchen gardens and folly-filled grounds to explore, and the lake for boating, and a tea to end teas; and Willo and Minnie fell in love as they wandered through the long June dusk while swifts and bats kept them company and the lit windows of the great Georgian house shone out like beacons of hope.

Their courtship was impetuous. She was supposed to be too young to wed, but her passion or wilfulness moved mountains of doubt; and how could impoverished Mr and Mrs Fenner-Wells, who had two younger girls to marry off, seriously object to a match that was brilliant in the eyes of the locality?

The young couple observed their wedding vows to begin with, especially the one referring to bodily worship.

They soon had issue, Melanie Mary in 1961, Prudence, who was always Prue, in 1963. But Minnie was not cut out for motherhood, she was too flighty, too keen on fun and games.

Moreover in 1963 her father-in-law, Colonel Todd, aged seventy, fell ill and died in the following year. Minnie was horrified by the prospect of becoming the lady of the manor of Tollworth. She and Willo had been living in rented accommodation in Tetbury: her mother-in-law Muriel, as soon as she was widowed, suggested an exchange – she would remove herself into their house, so that they, her son, daughter-in-law and two grandchildren, could take possession of The Court.

Minnie bolted. She could not be bothered with or tied down by any of it. She had grown used to parties and being the life and soul of them, to travel and laughter and flirting and non-stop treats. The round-the-clock chores of the nursery, and the threat of starring in future only in the Women's Institute and Mothers' Union, frightened her into the indiscriminately open arms of Jack Max, who was the exact opposite of her clean and clean-cut husband.

Willo did not try very hard to get Minnie back. He might have been too proud to do so, or perhaps he realised they had reached the point of no return of absolute satiety with each other. Besides, it was obvious that for one reason or another she was not going to settle down or, as she would have said, bury herself alive at The Court. After she had finished with Jack Max, and although or because she was at a tempting and dangerous loose end, he insisted on divorcing her.

She remarried soon enough. Christopher Miller-Boyd could and did gratify her every whim, financially at any rate, which may have accounted for the durability of the union. Willo, however, argued that Christopher's charm was mainly nominal. In droller moods he would say: 'Minnie was born double-barrelled — Fenner-Wells never could come to terms with Todd — one word and a single syllable at that — she was always lost without her hyphen — and the name Miller-Boyd seemed to point to the promised land — she knew where she was and who she was when she again had two barrels to bless herself with.'

The Todd girls were in the legal custody of their father. But they were largely brought up by his mother and a nursemaid. Willo, following his divorce, set to work in London with, or rather for, Anthony Haden, a friend or acquaintance from their Harrow School days, who had financed a small publishing house specialising in military and sporting texts. And Minnie, although she had access and no other children, confined her affections for Melanie and Prue to disruptive telephone calls and occasional spoiling weekend invitations to the Miller-Boyd place, Charbrooke Park in Northamptonshire.

In 1980 Muriel Todd died. Willo realised his daughters needed responsible adult supervision. He determined to spend more time at The Court. He was anyway sick of bad books and his love affairs that were also a waste of time and energy.

The consequence or the side-effect was Barbara Jameson.

A new bookshop had opened in Tetbury, calling itself The Studio and giving itself other airs by putting pricey coffee-table books about avant-garde art in its window. One Saturday morning Willo, whose work was meant to include promotion of the products of Anthony Haden Ltd, tried to interest the bookseller in a copy of *Fox-hunts of the United Kingdom* by Sir Horace Mabberley.

He had failed to notice a discrepancy, not promising from his own commercial point of view, between *Fox-hunts* and most of the wares already on display. He was not observant, nor was he a snob – if he had recognised any sort of snobbery he would not have stooped to be influenced by it. He therefore marched into the shop in his friendly way and received a reserved, not to say supercilious and chilly, greeting from the young woman behind the counter.

Barbara was thirty at the time. She wore her straight brown hair in an up-to-date version of the pudding basin cut, eschewed cosmetics and had sharp features and a somewhat sour expression. The sartorial look she affected was that of the smart yet classless intellectual: loose black garments and third-world black espadrilles. Her clothes defied the ocular lustfulness of the opposite sex, yet in vain: or was it on purpose that her robes managed to hint at the delights of her slim tense figure?

Willo introduced himself and produced *Fox-hunts*.

She laughed at it or at him as if involuntarily, because he was presuming that she would buy or sell tripe of that sort.

He joined in, laughing with her, he refused to be snubbed, and leant on the counter and explained that her shop was empty because she did not stock books on the two subjects that might induce the readers of Tetbury to reach for their purses, fox-hunting and sex.

'The answer's still negative,' she snapped.

'Never mind,' he replied, unabashed. And where did she come from, he inquired, and why had she alighted at Tetbury?

She answered his questions with a snarly reluctance that he found provocative.

A few days later he returned to the charge and elicited the information that she was trading at a loss and feeling lonely in her new surroundings: she had sunk nearly all her money in the shop and the accommodation above it. Her story was that having qualified as a librarian she had had jobs in suburban libraries in London and trouble with arty and crafty men; and not long ago both her parents had died, leaving her well-to-do and giving her the chance to start her life all over again, doing something different somewhere else. As for Tetbury and its inhabitants, her idea that she liked it and them was undergoing a reversal.

His native optimism was intrigued by her trenchant chippiness. He had never known a woman so clever or pretentious, and was impressed or at least inquisitive. He was half-drawn to her differences from his other women; that she also half-repelled him was perversely attractive. She was a sort of no man's land, or a trap baited by the mysteries of her personality and physique.

During his fourth Saturday morning visit to the Studio she asked him to steady a ladder which she was about to climb to fetch a book from a top shelf. In the course of this manoeuvre he dared to caress her and was rebuffed by what sounded like a curse: 'Oh no, not that!' A week later she relented: she offered him a cup of coffee in her office behind the shop, directed him to a chair, without any preamble sat on his knee, and when she had put a note in the shop window saying 'Back in five minutes' became his mistress.

Sex simplified nothing between them. More often than not she made out that he was taking her against her will. She sneered at love and never would say she loved him: rather, she seemed to hate him for wanting her attentions. She was inclined to refer to their relationship as 'dirty work' and 'getting his oats'; and although she was no respecter of marriage he was cognisant of the fact that she resented giving herself to him for nothing much in return.

The other side of the medal of her prickly contrariness was the excitement she brought to intimate exchanges. He could not be sure of her, or of what might be her fancy, or when she would fancy it. She had something of the quality of an acquired taste, or indeed a drug: he desired her more and was disgusted by her, and was increasingly dependent on a habit he wished he could break.

They were weekend lovers for six months or so. She was prevailed upon to visit The Court, where she met Willo's children, and she stayed odd nights at Edgware Mansions.

He was embarrassed by her socially. Her class was not quite his, her manners were awkward: he did not introduce her to his friends. And she was losing her power to surprise him, and they had one or two pointless scratchy quarrels.

But Melanie was nineteen and Prue seventeen. They had lost their granny and must need the guidance of an older woman, he thought, who would hold the fort while he continued to earn a crust in London – their mother was not to be depended on.

He proposed along these lines to Barbara Jameson.

Her reply was to murmur derisively: 'Talk of a *mariage de convenance!*' Then she accepted him.

After lunch on the aforesaid Wednesday prior to Christmas, Barbara Todd hurried up to her bedroom to watch an Open University programme on TV.

[21]

She was not formally studying the Eng. Lit. course; but she followed it in order to coach and generally assist her friend Roger Byle, who was trying for the second time to get a degree.

In the eyes of Willo, Roger, a poet in his later twenties, unpublished, unemployed, unhealthy and living with his mother at Snathe, was a lame duck and a bit of a joke. But ever since Barbara had met Roger five or six years ago she had taken him all too seriously. He seemed to be a replacement for her bookshop, which was sold soon after she married, and to offer an outlet for her literary aspirations. No doubt he shared her jaundiced views of life in general and Tetbury in particular, and corroborated her opinion that she deserved better than to be the wife of an uncaring philistine who treated her as his children's nanny and his housekeeper. Roger Byle, privately nicknamed Byle the Vile by the disrespectful Todd girls, could also have provided Barbara with the services she had ceased to require from her husband soon after marrying him. But considering that she, now aged forty-six, was grey-haired and wrinkled, with bosom and hips that had gone to pot, and Roger was spotty and delicate and at least limp-wristed, Willo spared his imagination the unpleasant task of contemplating their sexual conjunction.

'What's on today?' he had asked Barbara as she stumped upstairs to the refuge of her bedroom, which sported a television set.

'Minor Jacobean dramatists,' she retorted with venom.

He exclaimed, 'Good God!' and she scorned and pitied his limitations with a speechless glance.

Proceeding into his study he framed the unspoken retort: I may be stupid, but you're not as clever as you think you are, you'd be happier if you were, and for that matter Byle the Vile's a flop with nothing to show for his nearly thirty years.

But as usual he came to the conclusion that Roger was a blessing in disguise inasmuch as he tethered Barbara to The Court and the protection of Todd property, and instilled in her sufficient guilt to stop her poking her nose into his own extra-marital doings.

He sat in his green leather-covered desk chair. He thought of Denis Willett: after only three hours at home he – Willo – had had enough inclusively. It was a boring old story: he just suffered a sharper than usual pang of dissatisfaction with his life – with both his country and his town lives – and his career, if it merited such a term. Yet when Gloria invited him to spend Christmas in her company he had shied away from that revolutionary prospect with undiplomatic certitude; and he had been pleased to refuse Anthony Haden's invitation to see the new year in at Havinton Hall. He now regretted the additional fact that he was not in the mood for a peaceful post-prandial nap, and, metaphorically shaking himself into better humour, he prepared to take a walk.

Tray was waiting for him in the hall.

He addressed the dog thus: 'I know, I know, you want a walk too – but I can't be seen in public with a Tibetan lapdog – you'd ruin my reputation – oh to hell with it – you win, come on!'

They went by way of Church Lane, and back by Beech Coppice and across the fields to The Court.

Barbara was still upstairs. He made himself a mug of tea and retired with it into his study to write and address a dozen Christmas cards for delivery by hand, to put money into envelopes, draw numerous cheques and clumsily wrap up the Gucci scarf.

At six Barbara reappeared – Josh Kemball was calling with his carol singers at six-thirty. They signed some joint cards, then between them mulled the wine and set out the glasses for the adult singers and chocolate bars for the children. Josh and the Tollworth verger William Fawl, known to the friends of his less religious youth as Juggy Fawl, and a party of about fifteen arrived at the customary hour of six-thirty and crowded into the garden. Willo opened his front door and he and Barbara stood in the doorway to be sung to – it was a mild dry night; and afterwards they invited everybody in for refreshments.

The Todds, alone again, chatted flatly over cold ham and cheese for supper, and watched nonsense on TV in the chill drawing-room until they said good night.

He slept in his dressing-room not very well. He had not liked to grouse about the food, but actually cheese at night always gave him bad dreams.

He was up early, expecting Denis, who, true to form, rang the doorbell at seven-thirty. Together they moved furniture in the drawing-room to create space for the eight foot high Christmas tree, and afterwards distributed holly in the usual places, and hung mistletoe from the overhead light in the front hall.

In the course of their activities Willo inquired: 'What did you buy for Mrs Willett in Tetbury yesterday?'

Denis replied with a chauvinistic wink: 'A propagator for our greenhouse – she'll like that.'

'Your greenhouse, you mean – and who'll be using the propagator?'

'I'll be giving her a hand with it.'

'Poor Mrs W.!'

'She'll be poorer this afternoon, when she's bought me my present in Bristol.'

Breakfast for one was laid in the dining-room by Peggy Sparks – Barbara had already ridden on her environmentally friendly bicycle to the shops in Tetbury. Peggy was Barbara's age and kindred spirit, and lived up to her surname: she was a redhead and rustic feminist, married with militant reluc-tance to a mild-mannered and certainly long-suffering farmworker called Les. She brought Willo his scrambled egg and bacon as if she hoped they would choke one representative of the male sex: which took the edge off his appetite.

The Christmas cake arrived at ten-thirty, borne indoors with almost reli-gious solemnity by Florrie Twill, the septuagenarian daughter of Mrs Twill, who had made it and iced it despite her ninety-two years. Mrs Twill had been cook at The Court once upon a time, and lived rent-free in the cottage in Tollworth which had once belonged to Ruby Todd's butler, Grayvener by name: Victor Grayvener retired and died there, and then left his home in trust for the usage of members of the family of his former employer. Willo and his parents had always wished Mrs Twill lived somewhere else; she was the most troublesome tenant, she broadcast her attitude to Honeysuckle Cottage by changing its name to Beggar's Roost, she complained perennially to Willo rather than to the Grayvener trustees that it was too small and too primitive, yet would not hear of the abolition of the outside privy or the thatched roof, and swore that a water closet would be installed over her dead body. She also fanned the flames of unneighbourly feelings by her treatment of Florrie, a harmless sort of village idiot, forced to share her mother's bed at night and in the morning ordered out to empty her mother's potty over cars displeasingly parked.

But again Mrs Twill had exercised her immemorial right to produce the Todds' cake, and to be received with it and her daughter ceremoniously at The Court. She was a shrunken personage with a nose almost as sharp as her tongue, bespectacled, dressed in her best and on two sticks. Florrie was twice her size and given to nervy giggling. Willo received them and, apologising for the absence of his wife needlessly, since Barbara was not popular with the village people who soon found out that she only cared for them in principle, he led the procession into the drawing-room and requested Peggy to bring in the tray of coffee and biscuits. The cake was deposited on a table and admired, although Xmas shakily inscribed in pink icing was spelt with an extra s, and they sat down.

Willo had reason to regret his opening statement which no doubt put ideas into Mrs Twill's head: 'You're looking fighting fit.'

'That would be a miracle if I was, judging by the hardship I put up with,' she retorted.

'What's wrong, Mrs Twill?'

'What's right, I say – Beggar's Roost is wrong – I shouldn't be a beggar at my age, nor have to roost like a fowl – not after cooking for your family, Mr Willoughby, and carrying my cross through life.'

She gestured angrily with her head towards Florrie, who was much amused.

The familiar catalogue of complaints was aired in the next half-hour. Willo listened to it patiently, interjecting occasional jokes, which were about the only utterances that Florrie did not laugh at. The telephone came to his rescue: he promised that money for the cake would be included in Mrs Twill's Christmas box, and wishing her a merry Christmas and many of them, which conven-tional valediction sounded cruelly ironical in the circumstances, he fled into the study and shut the door.

The telephone call was from his elder sister and only sibling Amanda, Mandy so-called, who was married to the retired clergyman Theodore Wriggs, and the mother of six, whence the name of the Wriggs residence, The Shoe House.

'When did you get down to Tollworth?' Mandy demanded, and hurried on reproachfully in her bossy and brassy voice: 'I bet you've been here for days and never rung me, you beast.'

He laughed and replied with more tact than honesty: 'I only arrived late last night. How are things, Mandy?'

'Could be worse, I suppose – Theo's stone deaf and sliding downhill visibly, and Desirée's brought mumps back from school – and the boys say they could kill her. When are we going to meet?'

'That's a good question. I'm sorry for Desirée, but don't want to ruin my chances.'

'Oh you men – honestly! – you're too ridiculous – even Theo's worried in case he catches the disease.'

'I think it's high time Theo slid downhill in that way too – he's been too potent by half in my opinion.'

[25]

'You're telling me,' Mandy commented, and they both laughed.

'Anyway,' he resumed, 'what had you in mind?'

'Are you going to Waddington this evening?'

'I'm hoping to.'

'Theo says we're in quarantine and mustn't, which is just so boring for everyone. He doesn't like to be left alone in the house, and he's terrified of being with the mumpy one. Are you busy tomorrow evening?'

'Why?'

'You don't have to sound cagey. I thought we might come across after tea and give you our presents and ring our bells for you, provided the weather's fine. We wouldn't cross your threshold, don't worry, we won't infect you – but it would be something to look forward to.'

Her plan was agreed. He felt chronically sorry for his sister, who had been an unattractive child, had loved and been loved by the wrong men, entrusted her patrimony to a confidence trickster, and ended by marrying their grand-father's curate. In the last months of Ruby Todd's life and ministrations to his parishioners, Theo Wriggs lived at The Court, and years later he proposed or was proposed to by the unmistakably mature woman he had met during his youth and her childhood. They made an ill-favoured couple, Mandy big and coarse, Theo bald and bloodless; but the Almighty blessed their union in His mysterious way with child after child and ever less money. The Wriggs off-spring were now grown-up, except for Muriel, sixteen, and Desirée, twelve; but Jim, Alice, Cathy and Peter never seemed to earn a penny, Theo's pension was a drop in the ocean, and Mandy, good soul that she was, continued to turn the screw on the sympathetic conscience of Willo, who had kept his part of the family fortune intact and was lucky and rich.

'My present for you is really a disgrace – sorry,' she warned him. 'But I don't have to tell you why.'

He winced and said: 'You know I'll do what I can for you.'

She ended by calling him a kind brother.

A minute or two after ringing off he was relieved to hear the front door open and the voice of Prue.

She was not so plain as her Aunt Mandy, nor so pretty as her sister was and her mother had been, and she had no obviously noticeable look of her stylish father. With her rosy cheeks and indeterminate features she bore a resemblance to her great-grandfather Ruby Todd; but she wore spectacles. Her character was gentle and diffident, she had survived her disconcerting childhood, and she had one of those slow sweet transfiguring smiles. Prue was now thirty. For the last eight years she had been in love with, and blinded to the charms of potential husbands by, John Seward, a married man, who kept her dangling on the end of the telephone, on unkept promises and meetings at his discretion. She lived in a basement flat in Cretton Road in Cirencester and worked in a kindergarten school. She motored home in her Mini to Tollworth for most weekends, and had never missed a family Christmas.

'Dad?' she called, and he strode out of the study and embraced her almost under the mistletoe.

'Thank God you're here,' he said; 'I've had Mandy on the telephone and the Twills for coffee! You wouldn't like a little walk before lunch, would you? I must get out of the house, and I've a few Christmas cards to deliver.' He was arrested by the idea that dogged his relations with Prue, the idea that he was treating her as badly as he thought others were, and exploiting her amenability. 'No,' he contradicted himself, 'probably you don't want a walk at all – you've only just arrived – you tell me what you'd like to do.'

'A walk would be fine – honestly, Dad – don't worry. How are you?'

They walked along the village street, delivering cards through letter-boxes.

Willo loved Prue, and believed he was loved by her. But it was an unsatisfying sort of love: self-consciousness, which spread from him to her or vice versa, was never quite overcome. It was a love marred by shyness, and the shyness was complicated and exacerbated by her protracted adulterous affair, which he thought and she knew that he thought destructive, and they did not talk about. Paradoxically three or more were better company than two in their experience. Yet they clearly shared a wish to be alone together, or, perhaps, to try again, and not to be disheartened by having to stick to the surface of things, almost to small talk. And they always had laughter to fall back on.

Yes, she was well, she said, and Christmas at The Court was her favourite treat: she could not understand why Barbara made such heavy weather of it. What was the latest news of Byle the Vile? She referred to her sister Melanie and brother-in-law Edgar by their surname and asked when the Milsoms were arriving. No, she declared, far from being sick and tired of children, with whom she worked daily, she was longing to see William and James, Melanie's boys.

Willo told her about Desirée's mumps. Desirée's Christian name always tickled the Todds: it was inaccurate considering her galumphing undesirability, and twelve years ago had no doubt been chosen defiantly by parents aged sixty-six and forty-four who already had a litter of five.

Father and daughter were acquainted with most of the village people and kept on meeting them, which fragmented their dialogue.

He mentioned the Ellerys' do at Waddington between tea and supper: 'You're invited — what about coming with me?'

Prue hedged: who would be staying at home to put the little ones to bed?

He knew he was no match for her unselfishness, also wondered whether she might prefer to be with her nephews.

Had she heard from her mother, he asked.

Prue laughed and answered yes: typically, that is to say unexpectedly, she had had a call from a cruise ship in the West Indies the previous evening — the Miller-Boyds had decided to spurn their stately home in Northants and celebrate their festive season in the sun — and apparently were welcomed aboard by 'White Christmas' blasting out on loudspeakers.

They returned home. Barbara, having spent four hours in Tetbury ostensibly shopping but surely communing with Roger Byle, was calmer than she had been. Stepmother and daughter of the house, who had always got on fairly well, cooked lunch between them, and afterwards slung Christmas cards on strings and put up paper decorations. Their labours, and Willo's nap in the study, were interrupted by the noisy entry of Melanie and company at the inconvenient hour of two forty-five.

William and James giggled and wrestled, Melanie shouted at and Edgar tried to pacify them, Tray barked and ran out through the front door and into the street pursued by Barbara, Prue made soothing noises, and Willo had to pretend to have the party spirit.

Melanie's marriage to a poor but biddable insurance agent, motherhood and thirty-two years of age had not done damage to her good features and luminous complexion: she was not so sensitive as Prue. Her hair was black and fine, like her father's, her eyes were brightly blue; but her eyes were too round and monkeyish to satisfy experts in the field of female beauty. She had been an awkward child, demanding and jealous; in her late teens she chose to consult a psychiatrist, who persuaded her to write hateful letters to everyone who was fond of her or had been trying to remain so; aged twenty-three she married Edgar on the rebound and because she was pregnant, possibly with his assistance; and since then had

[28]

been inclined to blame all and sundry for the disappointing situation in which she found herself.

Willo said how nice it was for the family to be reunited, to the hypocrisy of which remark, designed to encourage, Melanie sharply drew attention: 'But you hate kids, Dad.'

Then she warned Barbara that children caught horrible diseases from dogs, and Barbara snapped back at her: 'Only if mothers let their children eat dogs' messes.'

Edgar was asking where he should park their car and if he should lock it, and was harshly ordered not to fuss by his wife.

Whereupon Prue offered to take William and James into the garden for a game of football, and Melanie hissed a nasty old insult at her with a two-faced smile: 'Thanks be to St Prudence!'

Willo intervened authoritatively or with the almost irrational irritation his firstborn stirred up in him: 'Come along, Melanie, I'll carry some of this luggage up to your rooms. You lead the way.'

William and James were to have the run of the nursery, which still contained the toys of generations of Todds, and to sleep in the night-nursery. The Milsoms would have the West Room, the nearest guest bedroom to the nurseries, while Prue was in the garret she had been moved into at the age of ten to separate her from her hostile sister.

In the West Room Melanie dumped her plastic bags and subsided on the bed, announcing in tones of reproach: 'You know my life's ghastly, don't you, Dad?'

He had heard it before, he could have dished out a spot of routine sympathy, instead he felt bound to argue the point: 'Edgar's a decent chap, and you've got the children, who I don't hate, as a matter of fact. A lot of people wouldn't say no to your life.'

'Oh don't preach, Dad! It's easy for you to look on the bright side – you get away from Barbara every week and have a ball in London, you've no commitments and no money worries. Edgar's driving me round the bend – I'm turning into a drudge – and I'd bolt if I had anyone to bolt to – I'm not Mummy's daughter for nothing. There – never say I didn't tell you what I aim to do at the earliest opportunity!'

'Is money very tight?'

'What do you think? Edgar should start selling hot cakes – he gets no bonus this year – we'd be on the breadline if it wasn't for my pathetic little nest-egg.'

[29]

'The present I'm giving you ought to help a bit.'

'I'm sorry to say your presents go nowhere fast. You're out of touch with what it costs to raise children and not to sink for the third time socially.'

'Oh well,' he commented, unable to exclude the grudging note in his voice: 'I'll help more – as much as I can.'

She shrugged her shoulders and asked in her reproachful manner: 'Where's my make-up case? Did you leave it downstairs?'

'I don't know – I'll fetch it in a minute – I wanted to tell you that we've been invited to drinks with the Ellerys this evening. Are you interested?'

'Oh my God!' she burst out. 'I'd just adore to see Waddington again – but I've promised to decorate the Christmas tree with the boys – Edgar made me swear I would – oh hell! I can't ever do anything pleasant. Is Prue going with you?'

He saw the danger signal of her jealousy and had the presence of mind to say no.

At this point Edgar blundered in with more luggage, asking: 'Melanie, where do you want me to put these things?'

She gave him a sharp answer, and Willo left them to it.

Later that afternoon he managed to have a snatch of private conversation with Prue.

'Have you had further thoughts about Waddington?'

Her reply was cautious: 'What's everyone else doing?'

'Melanie's put out because she can't come, she's got to decorate the tree with Edgar and the boys.'

'Perhaps I'd better stay here and help.'

'Are you sure?'

'Will Barbara go with you to Waddington?'

'You must be joking. Barbara considers the Ellerys are scum, she wouldn't soil herself with their money. But I'm perfectly happy to go alone.'

'Well then – I think I'll stay here.'

'That's nice of you – at least your sister won't be able to make a scene because you're stealing a march on her. But listen, darling, there's something else I wanted to ask you. Are you all right for money?'

The two of them, standing in the doorway of the study and speaking in undertones, were embarrassed by this unwontedly personal question and could not meet each other's eyes.

'Oh good heavens, Dad – yes, I think so – why?'

'It's your Christmas present – I'm just going to get it ready.'

'Oh I see – thanks – but you don't need to do anything special – I seem to manage, Dad – and you have the expense of me when I'm home for weekends.'

'That's my treat – and it's cheap at the price.'

They both laughed, though Prue was blushing too.

William and James came to the rescue in a sense, claiming Prue's attention and allowing Willo to say he was busy and shut his study door.

But he had to emerge at teatime and once more engage in the battle of family life.

At six he was able to retire to his dressing-room to change into a grey flannel suit, and at ten past he could relax in the Mercedes, his company car, courtesy of Anthony Haden Limited, and drive through the peaceful night to Waddington.

Willo enjoyed the party. He had not exaggerated too much when he said he would be perfectly happy at it. He took an instant shine to Max Ellery, a compact smooth-skinned man with unflinching liquid brown eyes and a hospitable humorous manner, and Mrs Ellery – Maude – who was taller than her husband, carelessly elegant and classlessly friendly; and he approved of the evidence not so much of the house having been done up as prevented from falling down. Again, it was not the atmosphere of wealth that he temporarily basked in; rather of good organisation, or the encouraging idea that the Ellerys' lives – and his own so long as he was their guest – ran on oiled wheels. He was glad to exchange Christmas greetings with neighbours, and almost forgot to remember that Waddington was partly responsible for his ill-fated first marriage and consequently or to some extent for his second.

The rest of the evening at The Court might have been worse for Willo at any rate: he exercised his old-established right to wash up the supper things in his own way and by himself in the pantry, and, having watched television with his undemanding son-in-law, while the women stuffed the turkey and skirmished in the kitchen, he pleaded tiredness and said good night to everybody and went to bed.

But the early morning of Christmas Day seemed to him a nightmare. He was woken at an unearthly hour by William and James shooting each other with cap pistols. Before he finished shaving he had received complaints about Melanie from Barbara, and from Melanie about everybody and everything.

The boys whined and then blubbed throughout breakfast; there was half a quarrel over the time it would take to roast the turkey; the Gucci scarf did not go down well with Barbara, who said with some truth that it was too smart for her, and Willo knew he would not be seen dead in the tie she gave him; and he wished his daughters had not spent so much money on, respectively, a framed photograph of his grandchildren and a pair of patent Japanese slippers, and that they had been less busy and more appreciative of his generous cheques. He considered his best present was Mary Cole's fruit jellies, the majority of which were immediately devoured by his family. His only comfort at this stage of the Christmas story, if not his joy, was quietly to clear away breakfast and lay for lunch for eight, counting Josh Kemball, in the unoccupied dining-room.

At ten-thirty he escorted the Milsoms along the village street to Matins in the tiny Cotswold-style church: Barbara was an atheist, and Prue had again volunteered to stay at home and carry on with the cooking.

He sat right at the back on the traditional Todd pew or bench between the font and the bell rope, which was now being pulled energetically by Juggy Fawl. His sister Mandy and her crew were in front, and they exchanged nods and smiles; and he nodded at other members of the congregation of roughly fifty souls. The effect of the preparatory harmonium music discoursed by retired schoolmaster Alick Mowbray was ruined as usual by the tolling of the tinny church bell.

Silence fell at eleven, broken momentarily by the moo of a cow. Josh entered through a side door from the vestry, a shed tacked on the altar end of the building. He announced a hymn number and the service began.

Willo felt increasingly somnolent. The practicalities of being a husband, father and grandfather, and putting on a show of patience and tolerance, were an unaccustomed strain. He swayed sleepily even as he sang, and subsided with gratitude into the attitude of prayer, which gave him a chance to close heavy-lidded eyes. He began to be afraid he would sleep through the sermon and disappoint his old friend, although Josh would laugh off such a comment on his preaching.

The text of the sermon was a phrase from the passage included in numberless funeral and memorial services: 'For now we see through a glass darkly.' There was no pulpit in Tollworth Church – the parson had to deliver his address from the low step in front of the altar; therefore Willo could only see Josh's face over the heads of parishioners, his heavy countenance reminiscent of Roman emperors, still dark hair, mild blue eyes beneath slightly drooping eyelids, and russet complexion.

Willo grimaced at William and James in hopes of keeping them quiet. But he was not sure that even Josh's probable re/hash of the nativity story would guarantee his own attention. Like his father before him, he had always paid his dues to religion, the dues he owed as much to his reverend grandpapa as to God. What he had faith in was mainly tradition, and in the beliefs dating back to the year dot of men and women much cleverer than he was. On the other hand, although he could appreciate, for instance through the medium of Josh, the advantages of living by and for Christian teaching, he was secretly bored to bits by going through the religious motions.

Josh was saying: 'The stable in Nazareth wasn't a patch on the stables round here. It would not have been full of architect/designed stalls with thick fresh straw underfoot and luscious bran mash in the feeding/trough. Fox/hunting was not the done thing in Palestine – we mustn't imagine the stable where Jesus was born resembled that palace for equine quadrupeds at Badminton House.'

The congregation tittered: despite Josh's popularity in the parish, as else/where, some people were not sure if or when he was joking. But Willo's amusement made him more wakeful and receptive. He began to follow Josh's theme, which was – in a nutshell – the difference between now and then. Life eludes forecasts, our hopes are dashed, our expectations and assumptions prove erroneous, whatever we are used to is bound to change, the argument proceeded; and by the same token, of course, hope can be fulfilled, we can find what we were looking for, miracles do happen. Josh's advice, his remedy for living, in a manner of speaking, was never to think you know all the answers.

He summed up: 'That's easily said, I agree. It's a counsel of perfection. If I'd popped into the stable in Nazareth on that evening two thousand years ago, I would have been extremely surprised to see a baby in the manger, and even more so to be informed that He happened to be the son of God. We can imagine how today's streetwise media people would react to the news of the birth of our Saviour: with scoffing and blasphemy. But truly intelligent men and women, I guess and suspect, never forget that what is theirs can at any moment turn into what was theirs: they watch and wait with wise humility for the acts of God and tidings thereof. For the rest of us, Christmas is – amongst other things – a reminder of the mistake we probably would have made in

Nazareth, and of the ever-present possibility of change, external change for better or worse, change of mind, change of heart. While we were children or on the childish side, it never dawned on us that sooner or later we might see through a glass darkly, but now, now we do, if we do, we at least have experience of the changeable nature of reality. Although we can't and we shouldn't presume to judge God, we must be grateful for the changes He instigates, which always give us the chance to recognise Him.'

The final hymn was sung and the congregation blessed, and Willo said to Melanie as they joined the queue leaving the church: 'I'll hang around and walk home with Josh — why don't you go ahead?'

Melanie for once agreed and headed homewards with her family in tow.

Willo sat on a gravestone until Josh in tweed jacket and grey flannels, but wearing a clerical collar, joined him.

They strolled along the village street, talking in the disjointed manner of friends able to understand what was not and did not need to be said.

'Sermons like that won't do, they stop a man having forty winks,' Willo observed.

Josh replied: 'Don't blame me — the word "fox" wakes the dead in Gloucestershire.'

'My grandfather buried parishioners on hunting days with his muddy boots on while the verger held his horse.'

'How's Christmas turning out for you?'

'I don't know, Josh — I'm too old for it — I don't seem to be pleased with anything much at present — and I shouldn't be grumbling — sorry! I suppose you're having your own sort of Christmas rush?'

'Yes.'

'Too much of a rush?'

'No — far from it — what changed for me was my luck.'

Willo got the point: Josh was referring to the death of his beloved wife Clare, their unlucky years of her suffering, followed by his decision to take holy orders.

'No — more good judgment than luck — you knew what you wanted to do and you did it,' Willo said. 'I've really no cause to grumble — my health's okay, and I've always had enough money — and I must apologise again for gassing about myself — but the fact is I've drifted through my life, and I'm beginning to feel sorry.'

'All is not lost yet,' Josh commented.

'Perhaps not, according to your sermon. I wonder when I'm going to see through a glass darkly.'

They both laughed, and Josh inquired, referring to Melanie: 'How's my god-daughter behaving?'

'She tells me she'd like to leave her husband.'

'What do you tell her?'

'I try not to tell her to shut up and pull herself together. Edgar's a damn good husband – and it's not his fault that they're somewhat strapped for cash. Melanie's always had big ideas – her trouble is that she's impatient to inherit from me – she sees herself in my shoes, writing cheques with my money and ruling over the village.'

'What about Prue? Is she okay?'

'I hope so – God knows, as you'd say. She's my good angel. Incidentally, your looks don't pity you. I take it that you flourish?'

'Thanks be – and thank you for feeding me today.'

They had reached The Court.

Josh's arrival, lunch, his early departure, the Queen's speech and the next few hours passed in that way which has no history, happily or, to be more precise in the circumstances, without mishap.

In the early evening the front door was knocked upon heartily. Willo summoned everyone, opened it and revealed Mandy, standing with a handbell in each hand in the garden, booming greetings and wearing her dirty old anorak, and accompanied by five of her children. The three eldest, Jim, Alice and Cathy, respectively twenty-two, twenty-one and twenty, were also handbell ringers. The other two, Peter, seventeen, and Muriel, sixteen, carried long sticks from the ends of which glass jars containing lit candles were somehow appended. Theo Wriggs had been forced to stay at home and dare to do his paternal duty for Desirée.

The sky was clearing, stars were visible over the yew hedge, and there must have been a moon shedding a silvery radiance. The moon-glow, the candle-light and the shaft of golden brightness from the open door of the house, illumined the concentrated faces of the musicians, who had immediately struck up a rendering of 'While shepherds watched their flocks'. Peter and Muriel tried to hold their sticks steady in between grinning at their cousins, and Willo and his family crowded together in the doorway to get a better view of the performance.

At the conclusion of the first carol, after the clapping and congratulations

[35]

died down, regrets about the mumps and the quarantine were aired, and the basket containing Mandy's presents materialised. She handed out at arm's length the prettily wrapped little packets, undoubtedly containing the fudge or the truffles she made at home, the butter in which was apt to be or to go rancid, and received in return Willo's handful of sealed envelopes and an extra gift of some sort from Barbara. They all exchanged thanks and again wished one another a happy Christmas.

Then the jangling metallic measured notes of 'Silent night' rang out.

And it struck Willo that the heart of his blustering gallant sister was in the right place, and her children, annoyingly penniless though they were, but always having exams or vital interviews to contend with, not to mention youth, inexperience, love, sex, were a decent lot and might one day become the salt of the earth. Moreover, he unexpectedly thought, catching sight of the distinctive profile of Melanie and the homely smiling countenance of Prue, he should and he would stop being negative and begin to count his blessings.

Whether or not because of Willo's fonder family feelings and so on while the handbells lent new meaning to the old carols, and in a sense rang out Christmas, the next and last three days of the holiday were relatively peaceful.

His daughters thanked him in their different ways for their presents. Melanie, who could only show her nicer impulses in a physical manner, volunteered an embrace that was almost too close for comfort and called him a generous old brick. Prue tried to return his cheque, saying it was far too much and he probably needed it more than she did, referring to the expenses of life at The Court, especially at Christmas-time. He pleaded with her not to talk nonsense and not to give the money to her sister or her nephews – immediately anyway – and they laughed and exchanged a shy kiss.

Barbara deigned to wear the Gucci scarf, although she managed to negate the satisfaction of the donor by complaining that the quality and obvious cost of the luxurious thing shamed her. Mandy rang to say thank you for his largesse. She boomed and, roaring with laughter, let on that her children had stopped her calling him their fairy uncle. She said Desirée now had a neck like a bull, and recalling the diseases they had shared in youth she proceeded to reminisce with wistful nostalgia about the good old days.

But when Willo asked her if she was happy she retorted: 'Of course I am. Aren't you?'

Saturday passed, and Sunday after the early service at Tollworth Church. On the Monday morning, Willo's Christmas boxes in the form of more sealed envelopes were given to Denis Willett, Peggy Sparks and Florrie Twill. The latter, coming round to call on her own, excused her mother by communicating with many a giggle the somewhat nauseating news, in view of the privy out of doors at Beggar's Roost, that Mrs Twill had been laid up in bed with a bad stomach since Christmas Eve. Envelopes also awaited collection from the kitchen by the milkman, postman, travelling fishmonger and butcher, and refuse collector.

Willo plus two large and two little Milsoms then joined the long queue of cars crawling towards the Meet of the Beaufort Hunt at the Kennels at Badminton, and eventually the crowd of spectators. William and James had wanted to see the fun, and Melanie had persuaded their grandfather that it was his duty to accompany them. Even the return journey of eight miles to Tollworth took an hour.

After lunch Edgar Milsom ventured to say that he wanted to get home to Sprocketts and prepare for work on the following Tuesday morning. For so asserting himself he was embarrassingly and unreasonably squashed by Melanie, who despised him for being poor but would not help him to get rich. Not until four o'clock was she ready to cooperate with her husband, making it punitively clear that she was reluctant to leave The Court.

Prue, before her departure, agreed to take a stroll in the dusk with her father. And Willo, by not quite being able to see her or be seen, was encouraged to ask a question about her relations with John Seward.

'Are you still fond of him?'

'Oh yes.'

'Is he good to you?'

'He does try to be.'

'But you meet other people, don't you?'

'Yes, lots, Dad – mostly under five – I mean the children in the kindergarten.'

He laughed and said: 'You know what I meant?'

'Yes – I'm technically a free agent – I'm not married to John.'

He persisted: 'Forgive me, darling – one other thing – don't forget how much you love children, will you? Now I'll change the subject.'

Later, when Prue had said goodbye to Barbara and was being seen off by

[37]

Willo, she told him through the window of her Mini: 'Please don't worry, Dad – and please take care of yourself.'

He went indoors and locked the front door for the night. Barbara had retreated to her bedroom, and he thought he could hear her speaking on the telephone. The house was strangely quiet: it was too empty, it was too big for nowadays, he reflected yet again, and he entertained his recurrent fancy that it was haunted by the ghosts of forebears who had once crammed into it, and by the echoes of the laughter of absent youth. All the same, apart from one or two minor squabbles, Christmas had not been too bad. Although he had denied that he was unhappy to Mandy, copying her defensive denial, in fact none of his house-full of adults was exactly happy: but perhaps they had all been inspired by handbells playing carols to rise above their discontent.

He shut his study door and sat at the desk of the head of the Todd family and household. On a scrap of paper he began to do sums: one hundred pounds to Mary Cole, hundreds to Denis, Peggy and Mrs Twill, twenty pounds apiece to William and James and to the six Wriggses, ten to each of the service people, the milkman and the rest, and a thousand to Melanie, to Prue and to Mandy. He totted it up: he had disbursed three thousand six hundred pounds, not counting the costs of his presents for his wife and his mistress, or the expenses of food, wine etcetera. His total outlay for the month of December, including the bills for Edgware Mansions as well as The Court, might be in the region of five thousand. Spending at the same rate for a year would require sixty thousand: but luckily Christmas always was an open drain for money.

He believed he could afford it. That he was not absolutely sure was due to two factors: his ineradicable lack of grasp of money matters, and secondly his always having had a sufficiency, as the old-fashioned euphemism put it.

His financial history was short and sweet. When he finished his schooling he lived on his army pay and an allowance from his father. At the age of twenty-one he came into the money set aside for him by his maternal grandparents. Colonel Todd considered it bad form to discuss money, except with professionals, but as the executor of the large sum in question he deigned to say to his son: 'Invest in Lloyd's!' – which advice was followed. Then Willo inherited a small fortune from his parents. He consigned it too to Lloyd's, and was made even more comfortable in the economic context by Anthony Haden, who paid him handsomely for doing almost nothing.

His income at the present time in round figures, Willo thought, was as follows: fifty thousand a year from Lloyd's Insurance Market, give or take a few thou, and fifteen from Anthony. In addition he had a spot of available capital, his two cottages in Tollworth plus the use of a third, and The Court and its contents.

He thanked God for his money, not in a miserly spirit but because it enabled him to carry on the family tradition of helping people. He had given Melanie a damn good dowry and put money aside for her children's education, and for Prue he had made a hefty contribution to the purchase price of her flat in Cirencester. Barbara had money of her own, the proceeds of the shop in Tetbury she had bought and sold, and frowned on his filthy lucre even as it paid for the luxury she enjoyed. He had always tried to be, and hoped that within his capabilities he was, generous. In the fullness of time, the distribution of his estate in accordance with his will would solve the material problems of his dependants.

In the mood induced by assessing his securities and security, he impulsively drew yet another cheque for two hundred and fifty pounds in the name of the Reverend J. Kemball, and put it in an envelope addressed to Josh together with a note, saying: 'Dear old boy, Distribute to any deserving cause or anybody as you see fit. No thanks, please. W.'

Time passed. He had a bite to eat with Barbara in the kitchen, and after watching TV on his own went to bed.

On the Tuesday morning he kissed his wife goodbye in a fashion – the fashion in which she bore his kisses – and drove up to London, garaged the Merc, called at 25D Edgware Mansions and opened his letters.

The only one that did not look like a bill he left to the last.

It was from his Lloyd's agent Desmond Simcox, and it ran: 'Dear Willo, I can't tell you how I'm hating to write this letter, especially just before Christmas. But I feel I mustn't delay. I've heard ominous reports about several of the Syndicates in which you have an interest. Information is hard to come by at this stage; nevertheless I feel it's only fair to warn you of severe shocks in the pipeline. Can we meet at your earliest convenience? Please ring me. I am so frightfully sorry. Yours ever, Desmond.'

Finance

WILLO Todd did not like it.

On the other hand he had an equable temperament, and had received alarmist epistles from Desmond Simcox before. He remembered that in his experience Desmond was a pessimist and fusspot, recently jumping to gloomy conclusions about one Syndicate after another, and that to date, or at least for the sixty-odd years of the Todd father-and-son investment in the insurance market, Desmond had been proved wrong.

They were friends as well as business associates. Desmond was his contemporary and had been his own and Josh Kemball's fellow-officer in the 10th Lancers in the fifties. Following demobilisation, he had gone into the Lloyd's agency Alleyn and Co., which soon became Alleyn and Simcox, and, in association with Willo's accountant Arnold Waters, had taken care of everything. He had a good head for figures, and was a nice chap. But, the apologies in his letter notwithstanding, Willo thought he might have waited to write or post it until after Christmas. The timing and the disagreeable contents of the communication were on the insensitive side.

Willo refused to panic and saw no reason to. At the back of his mind was the idea that not to ring up in a rush would serve Desmond right. He also suspected he would have to telephone all over the place including the Simcox country house in Lincolnshire, Shilley Grange in the village of Shilley, in order to run Desmond to ground.

Besides, he had better things to do. He read the letter once more: what on earth did Desmond mean by 'severe shocks', and indeed by putting such a melodramatic phrase in his letter? Willo felt more irked than anxious, and went to change into his blue London suit.

The bedroom was claustrophobic after the relatively wide open spaces of the rooms of The Court. He really should buy a bigger and better flat, either not up so many stairs or in a block with a trustworthy lift. But if he did so, it would accommodate Barbara; and if Byle the Vile were to bow out of her life, she might turn her back on Tollworth and want to be with her husband in London.

He donned his overcoat. On impulse he retrieved Desmond's letter and folded it into his wallet, then left and locked up the flat. In Edgware Road he hailed a taxi and asked the driver to go to St James's Street.

The office of Anthony Haden Ltd was in Babel Yard, reached via an inconspicuous ill-lit alley at the lower eastern end of St James's. The yard itself was minute, dark and damp. Several small old edifices looked out – euphemistically speaking – on it. Willo unlocked the front door of one, sorted the Anthony Haden mail from letters and packages scattered on the floor and addressed to the half-dozen commercial organisations based in the house, and proceeded up a rickety staircase to the two connecting first floor rooms. The outer office was for visitors and had a desk and secretarial equipment for the use of Jenny Webster, who came in on Monday, Wednesday and Friday mornings of ordinary working weeks. Beyond was the more luxurious room with a red carpet and two leather-topped antique desks, the less imposing of which was Willo's.

The place was cold. Nobody else seemed to be in the building. He tore open envelopes and glanced at the contents: mostly offers of books searching for a publisher, some cheques from bookshops, a couple of unsolicited typescripts, and the proofs of *Nip and Tuck*, the autobiography of the veteran sportsman and daredevil Lord Plewes, who was sponsoring the publication. There were also letters for Anthony addressed in the same handwriting: probably by his latest love.

They irritated Willo, although he was in no position to disapprove. They lent confirmation to his suspicion that Anthony only kept the firm going so as to receive communications from women who were not his wife Helen. He wished he could stop Anthony rubbing him up the wrong way. They had known each other too long – or was it too well? It was somehow galling to work in a business that did not mean business, which was almost designed to lose money, and was just a rich man's toy and tax dodge.

Had the time come to resign? Why should he still slave away at non-profit-making non-books for an absentee boss and playboy? But this train of thought ground to a halt joltingly: his pay from Anthony was handy, and might help

[41]

to absorb the 'severe shocks' speeding in his direction according to Desmond Simcox.

He reached for his telephone and pressed the button that rang through to Havinton Hall.

Perry, Anthony's butler, answered.

Willo wished him a happy new year.

'Thank you, sir. May I return the compliment?'

'Thanks, Perry. Is Mr Haden about?'

'He was going out shooting, Mr Todd. Will you hold on, please, while I try to catch him before he leaves?'

Five long minutes elapsed.

Perry returned to the telephone and said: 'Mr Haden asked me to apologise, sir, but he was in a hurry and couldn't take your call. He wondered if you'd ring back some other time.'

'Oh – all right. Do you know if Mr Haden means to be in London this week?'

'I understand that he'll be staying here at Havinton until after the weekend, sir. But you never can tell with Mr Haden, not for sure.'

'I agree. Goodbye, Perry.'

Willo paced the floor of the office for a few minutes, trying to control his dissatisfaction with Anthony and, for many different reasons, in general, then made a second telephone call.

He began the ensuing conversation: 'It's me,' and continued: 'I missed you too – I couldn't wait to get back to London . . . No, no, not only London – I couldn't wait for this evening . . . I'm sorry, I thought you wouldn't have too bad a time with Jane and Dick . . . You got it, did you? You liked it, did you? I chose it mainly for the inscription – no, I didn't forget you either . . . You don't need to give me anything – except the nicest present of all . . . Thanks, sweetie . . . I could get to you around five . . . We'll have dinner wherever you choose . . . I'm in the office – same here, same to you – goodbye.'

It was now twelve-thirty.

He walked from Babel Yard to the Bachelors, a luncheon club in a base-ment in Duke Street that made a point of catering for its members on days and for periods such as Christmas week when other clubs closed.

A dozen or so men sat at the communal table upon which twenty-five places were always laid. Willo was acquainted with several, exchanged greet-ings with the company, and chose the chair next to someone he had known vaguely for years, the stockbroker and *bon viveur* Nicholas Laithwaite, a bachelor in fact as well as in clubbable terms, now nearing retirement age.

They chatted together.

Willo was at first amused by Nicholas' cynical account of the services he rendered his clients.

'Oh yes, I have a few clients left – and thanks to me they all enjoyed their turkey and plum pudding – they could afford their Christmas fare because I've obeyed the first and last rule of stockbroking – which is to lead a rich and varied social life and hardly ever speak to would-be investors, let alone execute their orders. You'd be amazed by the eagerness of the general public to play ducks and drakes with its savings. By not giving my clients the chance to back their bright ideas I refused to allow them to ruin themselves: when they wanted me to gamble with their money, I was gambling with mine at Ascot or Newmarket, or hunting or shooting or fishing, or sleeping late at home or having extended lunches, or anywhere but on the receiving end of a telephone. Half my services consisted of being unobtainable; the other half was to invest in the safest simplest dullest ways. As a result my clients may not have made fortunes, but they ended up in profit rather than loss, and remained my friends rather than my foes. And I've done as I please for getting on for fifty years without anxiety or guilt.'

This monologue ended by jarring on Willo, and prompted his question: 'Nicholas, tell me, do you hear any gossip about the situation at Lloyd's?'

He could have done without the reply he elicited: 'I used to advise my clients not to believe in the existence of money for jam, and therefore to steer clear of Lloyd's. The Lloyd's principle of unlimited liability is admirable, no doubt – but why make one investment that puts all your other investments at risk? Anyway – no, I've heard nothing new, bad or good. Why do you ask?'

'I just wondered.'

'Are you a Member, Willo?'

'I am, and my father was before me. He did well, and so have I up till now.'

'I congratulate you. I shouldn't have spoken as I did – apologies! In fact I have many friends who swear by Lloyd's, and by being Members have lived much more comfortably than they otherwise would have done.'

'That's my story too.'

'Well – I've heard no sinister rumours – so I shall confidently wish you another happy new year.'

*

Willo rang the doorbell of 18 Avebury Flats, Grosvenor Terrace at five o'clock that afternoon, and was admitted by a blonde woman wearing a pink satin ankle-length garment, part negligee part dressing-gown – Gloria Deane.

She was forty, or said she was. Her figure was still good in a sturdy style, but make-up could not conceal the puffiness of her face. She had an easy smile and scarlet fingernails.

Her flat was in one of the few local authority blocks in Mayfair: she had wangled it somehow and paid a minute rent. Her means of subsistence were various: occasional payments of alimony from the husband of her youth Roly Deane, an uncertain income from her official job of interior decorating, presents from her sister Jane Hodges and her brother-in-law Dick with whom she had spent Christmas Day, more presents from admirers, and money she made from time to time by keeping a sharp eye on the main chance.

She opened the door warily and shut it in a hurry. She was careful not to mix with her fellow-tenants: she did not want them to see her in her finery or draw compromising conclusions from the number of her obviously well-heeled male visitors. But in her own hallway she threw her arms round Willo's neck and pressed herself against him.

'Hullo, lovey,' she said with laughter in her voice and slightly forced excitement. 'You're a sight for sore eyes – I've been having such a dismal time.'

She led him by the hand into her brightly lit sitting-room, which had a double-bed in a partly curtained alcove, and connecting doors into the bathroom and kitchen. The other room, which might have been her bedroom, she had filled with cupboards for her clothes and called her office.

'Let's have another look at you.' She swung him round, and they embraced again. 'It's just so nice to see you!' she exclaimed. Her negligee had parted in front, revealing her underwear, and she giggled and said: 'Sorry, pet. What can I give you, a cup of tea or something a bit more interesting?'

Willo had known Gloria for just on four years. He had been her lover for the same period of time since he had ended in her bed a few hours after making her acquaintance. She was the younger of the two children of a Northamptonshire squire and military man – a colonel like Willo's father, a Colonel Thompson – and his well-connected wife. The elder child Jane had followed in the family's respectable footsteps, marrying Dick Hodges, a scion of the land-owning class, when she was twenty-two, and bearing him two boys. Gloria had more spark: at the age of seventeen she eloped with Roly Deane, who turned out to be a burglar and was soon in prison; divorced Roly, became a good time girl, had a succession of protectors, figured in various scandals and probably drove her shame-faced parents to take refuge in their graves; and shortly before meeting Willo began to look around for a home to retire to.

For the first few months of their affair he had as it were led her step by step up his garden path, and she entertained high hopes of stealing him from drab and frigid Barbara and becoming his legal consort. But his feelings for her took on an ambivalent character: while loving her for being such a change from his wife, unpretentious, happy-go-lucky, warm, basic, he was put off by her coarseness, disingenuousness, self-seeking disposition and promiscuity. He loved her for the transparency of her motives, yet wished she would neither demand monetary favours almost with menaces, nor leave the diary lying about in which he read the names of unknown men she was having dinner with.

Their relationship subsided into more of a convenience: she was his mid-week haven, he provided her with the necessary in the form of evenings out and subventions of one sort and another. They used the word love lightly, and so adapted terms of endearment as to extract the sting of sincerity from them — lovey, for instance, and sweetie; while the sighs summoned by references to their living together happily ever after were merely polite. The contract each was a party to, although it was unspoken and unwritten, bound Willo to respect her freedom to try to improve her prospects, and Gloria to recognise his family commitments or, perhaps more accurately, his preference for sticking in the mud.

The gift she offered him that was more interesting than a cup of tea was sex. He chose, or was guided by the forceful signals of the state of her dress or undress to choose it. His virility was unimpaired by time, and her sensuality was backed up by her inclination to be reassured.

Yet even as they sought to please each other and in due course succeeded, he was aware that by making love to her now he would not have to do so later on and would therefore get a reasonably early night, and her thoughts straying from the task in hand were that she was repaying him for the Bilston enamel box and, at once, putting him in a good helpful mood and a sparkle in her own large blue eyes.

Afterwards they lay on the bed in the alcove, chatting amicably. She complained of the smugness of her sister Jane who had everything she wanted, and of the expense of being the recipient of Jane's hospitality at Christmas and

[45]

having to buy presents for every member of the Hodges' household. He regaled her with fanciful accounts of Barbara's kinky passion for Byle the Vile and the possible circumstances in which they studied the Jacobean dramatists together.

'Oh by the way,' she said, 'I took it on myself to book us a table for tonight at the Savoy – in the restaurant, where it's quite sparky in Christmas week and we might even shake a leg – is that all right? There's always a waiting-list for tables, so we could easily chuck if I've tired you out. But it would be fun, wouldn't it?'

He thought immediately of the costs involved and the letter in his wallet, and wished she would surprise him by not taking advantage of his gratitude and good manners.

'Fine!' he replied with a smile that he knew was perfunctory.

'Is there some place you'd rather go to?' she asked, adding in a pettish tone: 'I've told you we could chuck.'

'No,' he contradicted her with a hint of asperity. 'Haven't I told you it was fine?'

'Okay,' she said, as if she meant: no need to be nasty about it. 'Anyway – I wouldn't mind a bath before I change – what about you, lovey?'

Their next exchange of note occurred in the bathroom.

He inquired: 'Have you got any plans for Thursday?'

'Next Thursday?' she said. 'It's new year's Eve, isn't it? Are you free?'

She was pretending to be thrilled by the prospect of his freedom, but he guessed that her questions were asked in order to gain time.

'I should have suggested our seeing the new year in together long ago. But it would be nice for me if you could manage it.'

'Same here the other way round,' she enthused. 'I have half-accepted to join a party at the Morrisons' – but I don't see why I shouldn't take you along – it's a big do, and you know Billy and Tina Morrison, don't you? I could give Tina a tinkle and see how the land lies tomorrow morning. Actually, why I only half-accepted the invitation is that I've simply nothing suitable to wear for that sort of quite grand occasion. It might be better if I wriggled out of going and we had dinner quietly here.'

'No – I won't spoil your fun – that's definite – don't worry about me.'

'Oh but I do – I will! The trouble really is my frock.'

'Buy one on me!'

'What?'

'I'll give you a frock,' he explained, feeling he must make amends for his mean reaction to tonight's dinner at the Savoy, and remembering that, for the moment, there was no proven reason why he should start to economise.

She thanked him with kisses and promised him faithfully – that is, untruth-fully – that she never would have been a bore about her clothes if she had dreamed he would cough up so magnanimously.

A little later, after he had handed her a cheque for three hundred pounds and they were sipping martinis in the sitting area of her living-room, in the course of transferring the contents of her day-bag into her evening one she extracted from the former his Christmas present, the Bilston box, and showed it to him.

'You see I obey orders and don't forget who gave it to me and how fond I am of him – I carry it everywhere with me,' she said.

He expressed gratification, but observed: 'I wonder if that's wise – bags are apt to get pinched.'

'But it's like my lucky charm.'

'Luck can run out,' he countered, thinking again of the letter from Desmond Simcox.

'Why?' She regarded him wide-eyed. 'Do you mean my box is too valuable to take risks with?'

'The police would say so if your bag was stolen.'

'What's it worth, for heaven's sake? You shouldn't be spending all this money on me. Is it worth a hundred?'

Eventually he admitted that he had paid some four times the figure she had mentioned.

She volunteered more demonstrative thanks, then had to retire into the bath-room to re-do her lipstick.

When she returned, he yielded to impulse and produced Desmond's letter: the talk of money kept on reminding him of it, and he hoped for a comforting reaction from Gloria, who was as shrewd financially as anyone and had friends in high places in financial institutions, bankers, stockbrokers.

She read it slowly; and as he watched her she blushed, or at any rate blood suffused her face and neck.

'What's wrong?' he queried.

'When did you get this, Willo?'

'Only this morning, although it was written before Christmas.'

'Have you spoken to Desmond?'

'No.'

'God, you're a cool customer! I'd have been on the phone to him two minutes after reading his letter.'

'He's done it before, you know, panicking and getting me worked up unnecessarily.'

'How involved are you in Lloyd's, lovey?'

'Up to my neck – Father was too. Lloyd's has been really good to both of us. What's your worry, Gloria?'

'Why should I worry? You must ring Desmond though – Johnny Bartholomew's been saying bad things about Lloyd's for ages, and he's a full-blown underwriter, he works there.'

'All right – I'll talk to Desmond tomorrow – but let's just celebrate this evening – can we, sweetie?'

And he asked for another of her expertly mixed martinis.

The next morning in Edgware Mansions Willo woke with a cup of tea on his bedside table and a thumping headache. Mary Cole was drawing his curtains and bidding him good morning in such a loud voice as to suggest she was having to repeat herself.

'I didn't hear you come in, Mary,' he mumbled.

'No – you were far away. Nearly a new year, Capting!'

'How near? Don't tell me I've been asleep for two days and two nights,' he said.

She failed to see his joke and voiced her customary exit line: 'I'll be getting your breakfast, Capting.'

He regretted drinking and eating so much the previous evening, staying so late at the Savoy, dancing and probably making a fool of himself, and over-doing everything as he always seemed to in Gloria's company. He felt older if not wiser, and poorer. He felt unwontedly depressed. His home life, his working life, his love life, they all lacked savour. Of course he was damn lucky to have a mistress sixteen years younger than he was; but in the unfavourable light of sexual repletion he saw ever more clearly that Gloria gave away nothing much. The stickiness of her fingers for money put him off. He could not believe her or trust her. At the same time he wanted her, and to some extent depended on her.

What a muddle, he thought as he shaved with a shaky hand; what was the

[48]

point of partial cohabitation with Barbara, and paying in various currencies for Gloria's kisses, and taking Anthony's shilling for massaging his ego?

Willo's breakfast was black coffee.

When Mary scolded him for wasting the egg she had cooked, he pleaded a hangover.

'That's not like you, Capting,' she said.

'Perhaps it is,' he replied.

Mary then treated him to an almost hourly record of her activities with her sister Biddy over Christmas: their numerous attendances at church, the sermons they had listened to, their elevenses with friends and almost every mouthful of their meals.

He bathed and dressed and escaped her by hurrying off to the office.

He walked through depopulated streets. The rooms were again empty: Jenny Webster would not be coming in until next week, next month, next year. He ought to ring Gloria to thank her and be thanked for yesterday, he knew it. Instead he picked up the proofs of *Nip and Tuck* and began to read. The dullness of the book, the quietness of the building, his tiredness and aching head were soporific. The telephone woke him.

It was Gloria.

She said: 'You don't sound like yourself, lovey.'

'Don't I? Sorry — I'm okay,' he fibbed.

They spoke of the wonderful time they had had: which might have been the refrain of a song they had sung for four years.

'Listen,' she said, warning him that she was about to explain why she had tracked him down and to impart unwelcome information; 'New Year's Eve is kind of difficult — Tina Morrison's got even numbers and can't fit anyone else round her dining-room table — and she won't let me off the hook — so sorry, lovey.'

'Think nothing of it,' he replied. 'It's my own fault, I should have asked you earlier — you were bound to be booked up.'

'What will you do that evening?'

'Probably go down to The Court and make a long weekend of it.'

'You'll quite like that, won't you?'

'I always like the old place. What about you? Where will you be over the weekend?'

'At the Pennants' — I told you.'

'Oh yes. Can we make a date for next week?'

'Well — there was talk of my staying on for a few days at the Pennants — could I possibly ring you on Monday, say, to let you know plans and things?'

'Do!'

'Lovey, are you sure you're okay?'

'Just a bit hungover, otherwise fine.'

'But our evening was bliss, wasn't it? It was for me at any rate.'

'Absolutely!'

A tiny pause ensued. He was impatient to conclude this pointless conversation, but sensed, drawing on past experience, that Gloria had some other snippet of bad news to communicate.

'Oh yes, my pet, there was something else I meant to say. Have you been in touch with your Lloyd's man?'

'No, not yet.'

'I mentioned his letter to Tina — I hope you don't mind — but she's like a grave for secrets, and Billy Morrison's a big noise in the City — and she whispered to me that Billy's advising everyone to steer clear of Lloyd's and pull out if they can. That's all. I thought I should tell you.'

'Thanks very much.'

'You're not cross with me, are you?'

'No — certainly not — I'm grateful — grateful for everything and I'll ring Desmond right now. Happy new year, sweetie.'

'You do love me, Willo?'

'You know I do.'

He did not ask her if she loved him.

'Happy new year,' she said.

He wished he could be less suspicious of Gloria and her motives. Yesterday he had a nasty feeling that she was not so keen on him after reading Desmond's letter, and today he had received the impression that, should he be unable to pay in full for her affection, all he could count on were marching orders. Her prevarications about Thursday evening and next week boiled down to giving him notice that she intended at least to wait and see.

He shook his head to try to clear it. Gloria's advice was counterproductive. She had instilled in him not an urge to learn the worst or the best from Desmond, but a novel element of apprehensiveness. He did not feel equal to discussing Lloyd's business, the intricacies of which he had never understood and had left to the professionals, let alone to receiving the slightest shock.

He returned to the proofs of Lord Plewes' book. It was too bad to attend to, and he was too distracted to drowse over it. The time was eleven-thirty: the Bachelors Club would not yet be open for lunch. He thought of telephoning through to The Court to tell Barbara he would or could be with her for New Year's Eve after all; but she would be certain to have a plan with Roger Byle, he had licensed her to make one by telling her in repressive terms that he would be staying in London until Friday. He paced the floor indecisively.

At twelve, labouring under a sense of obligation and surrender, he rang Alleyn and Simcox. An answerphone gave him the message that the office was closed until Monday the fourth of January, and a telephone number for use in emergency.

Obstinately, although he guessed the number belonged to Shilley Grange, where Willo was loath to disrupt Desmond's holiday for such a trifling matter, he rang it.

A young girl answered – one of Desmond's three teenage daughters.

'Is that Mr Simcox's house?'

'Yes, it is.'

'Can I speak to Mr Simcox, please?'

'Who is it?'

'Mr Todd – Willoughby Todd.'

'Hold on, will you?'

She sounded uncertain; but Desmond, who must have been standing near or listening on another instrument, came on the line.

'I'm so glad it's you, Willo – I can't take every telephone call – and I've been hoping to hear from you – I was beginning to be afraid you might not have got my letter.'

'It arrived after I'd left London before Christmas. I found it waiting for me yesterday morning – it didn't seem to need an urgent reply. Anyway, how are you? How was your Christmas?'

'Thanks – all right – and yours?'

'Yes, thanks,' Willo returned either ungrammatically or uncommunica-tively. 'What's the score, Desmond? What are these problems we're looking forward to or not looking forward to?'

'Can we meet, Willo? I'd rather we met and talked things over.'

'Yes, sure – have lunch with me one day – what about next week?'

'This week would be better if you could manage it, or as soon as possible. I'll come to London, or I could come to Tollworth – I'm driving all over the shop to see people. You suggest a time and place.'

[51]

'What about lunch tomorrow, say at the Bachelors?'

'Sorry – my book's full from dawn to dusk tomorrow – I'm seeing clients in about six different counties – friends, like yourself. But Willo – just on the off-chance – you don't happen to be free for dinner in the evening, although it's New Year's Eve?'

Willo said he was and accepted an invitation to dine at Desmond's flat in Pimlico Gate near Victoria Station.

'But won't you be too tired after dashing about all day?'

'That's not important, that doesn't matter. It's good of you to have taken my letter calmly, Willo – I appreciate it. See you at eight o'clock tomorrow at Flat 15, Pimlico Gate – and thanks again!'

Willo replaced the receiver, feeling agitated as well as liverish. Desmond's appreciation of his calm was out of date – menacing questions now mounted up: why was Desmond in such a hurry to hear from him, talk, meet? What was it that mattered enough for Desmond not to want to spend New Year's Eve with his family? How were his other clients responding to the letter he must have sent them – angrily, hysterically? If so, why – what did they know that Willo would be told tomorrow? And what was the exact meaning of 'severe' in the context, and what effect would the 'severity' have on his bank balance?

Willo rang the doorbell of Desmond Simcox's flat with reluctant punctuality.

Since speaking to Desmond some twenty-four hours ago he had had too much time on his own in which to regret their arrangement. Discussing business on New Year's Eve must be a mistake; surely no financial setback at Lloyd's, or indeed any crisis, benefited from panicky action; Lloyd's accounts were always rendered in the summer – and sufficient unto the day etcetera. Besides, he was not a close friend of Desmond's, and a long evening alone with him in his home – as distinct from the short lunches they usually had in bustling clubs – could well be a strain. To make matters worse, probably, Willo had been so put out by their telephone conversation that he had omitted to contact friends and had been bored and resentful as well as uneasy.

A foreign maid opened the door: Willo noted wryly that Desmond was unaffected by the hard times seemingly in store for his clients.

They met in a luxurious sitting-room with dining area, all thick Wilton carpet, crisp chintzes, multi-table-clothed tables groaning with knick-knacks, and pastel portraits of Desmond's wife and daughters.

He was – or had been – a smart smooth man, almost the stereotype of a City gent, in his thin suits and striking ties, his remaining hair well-oiled and brushed flat, and his rubicund countenance betraying the secret of his estate in the country where he had created a garden of note.

Now he was without the jacket of his suit, his braces showed, his tie was at half-mast and his crumpled shirt open at the neck. And his scant hair was disarrayed, and he had bags under his eyes.

Willo was taken aback to the point of alarm by these outward signs of adversity.

Desmond apologised for his appearance: 'I've just got in myself – forgive me for looking a wreck – I've been on the go all day and driven God knows how many miles.'

He made no move to retire for a wash and brush-up. Instead he poured out the glass of sherry requested by Willo, and a strong whisky with not much water which he half-consumed before they sat down in the yielding armchairs.

He began to voice more apologies.

Willo said: 'Hold hard! What on earth has happened – I'm still in the dark – can you tell me in words of one syllable?'

Desmond controlled himself with an obvious effort and replied: 'Yes – sorry! Yes – we're in for losses – you are, I am, because I'm a Name at Lloyd's too. Nobody's able to quantify the losses yet – but you can take it from me they're significant – and were completely unforeseen.'

'You've expected ruination before, Desmond. I know some of the Syndicates I'm in have lost money for two or three years, but other Syndicates have compensated by making gains. You're not crying "Wolf" again, are you?'

'I wish I was. Believe me! You're talking about the good old days. What's going on now is without precedent. You'll get the bill in June, and I'm giving you the longest possible warning.'

'But I've built up reserves to cope with losses. How much money is there in my reserves account?'

'A lot – you've been a Member for so long – you became one when your grandparents died, and were able to increase your underwriting limits following the death of your father and mother. Willo – I know you've questions to ask me, which I'll answer as soon as I can. But before we go any further, may I ask you something very important for you and your nearest and dearest, and for me? Please don't think I'm prying! Have you any resources – how shall I put it – out of reach of Lloyd's?'

[53]

'Cash, you mean?'

'Well – yes, cash, securities.'

'No – I've only got a few thousand in cash at the moment – I had to help one of my daughters and then the other – and Christmas doesn't come cheap – I've got the remains of the last cheque you sent me.'

Desmond's response to this statement was to rise from his chair hastily and wordlessly and help himself to another drink: thus, for some reason, reminding Willo of Gloria's inexplicable blush when she read Desmond's letter.

Willo was sparing rueful thoughts for the money he had splashed around in the last few days.

The maid now caused a diversion by entering the room, placing dishes on a hotplate on a sideboard, announcing dinner and saying good night.

Desmond, calling her Maria, thanked her warmly and wished her and was wished a happy new year.

'See you in the morning, Maria,' he said.

'Oh yes, sir. Good night – good night, sir,' she repeated, smiling at Willo – she was a dark-haired good-looking middle-aged woman with a dignified bearing.

After she had left the room and closed the kitchen door Desmond gestured with his head in her direction and spoke in an undertone: 'She's a wonderful person – she's been with us for eighteen years – her husband's a crock, he can't work, but she never complains. They're Portuguese.'

This inconsequential speech made Willo wonder if Desmond was or was getting drunk.

To humour him, and keep off the subject of money, Willo inquired: 'Does she have accommodation here in your flat?'

'No, downstairs, in one of the flats in the basement which we rent. But she's part of my family. Anyway,' Desmond rose to his feet and said: 'come and help yourself. Maria's cooked us some soup – onion soup, I think it is – then cottage pie. You drink red wine, Willo?'

At the table, before they had removed the lids from their bowls of soup, Desmond said abruptly as he pushed a toast-rack and condiments towards his guest: 'The point I was trying to make is whether or not you've transferred stuff into your wife's name?'

The answer was no – Barbara was an awkward customer where money was concerned and would never accept any sort of marriage settlement – although

[54]

she had a fair bit of capital of her own, she was against capitalism and liked to think she was the opposite of a capitalist.

Desmond commented in a gloomy and scarcely audible undertone: 'My God!' – and Willo laughingly burst out: 'Look – I'm an awful dunce when it comes to technicalities – can't we stop beating about the bush? What are you trying to tell me?'

'Four and possibly five of the Syndicates you're invested in are in trouble.'

'What's the damage?'

'The word is meltdown.'

'Meltdown!'

'They were amongst the best Syndicates in the whole market, Willo.'

'What happened to them?'

'Technicalities, you'd say – reinsurance problems, unbargained-for claims, vast damages dished out by American courts, and new illnesses and colossal storms and God knows what else.'

'These losses – what are they going to amount to?'

'I don't know at this stage – it's all guesswork.'

'You must have some idea – I wouldn't be sitting here if you didn't have some idea – come on, spit it out!'

Desmond picked up his soup spoon, replaced it, studied it, head bowed, and murmured: 'Everything.'

'What?'

'Everything plus.'

'What does that mean I'm liable for in figures?'

'More than I think you're worth.'

'I can't believe that.'

'You asked me to guess.'

'Please, a short answer, Desmond – am I bust?'

'Join the club.'

The silence was broken by Desmond retrieving his soup spoon and, probably because his hand shook, clinking it against a wine glass.

'Well,' Willo laughed, 'our soup must be getting cold.'

Desmond cried.

He did not boo-hoo; he just emitted a noisy sort of gulp, covered his eyes with a large hand, its back brown-spotted, and his heavy shoulders heaved.

Willo was astonished and embarrassed. He was mortified to realise how slow he had been in the uptake. Gloria must have blushed because she had the nous to realise what he in his blissful ignorance was in for — and what she would probably want to get out of.

To assist Desmond he asked: 'Is it as bad for you?'

Desmond raised his napkin to his face, mopped up and eventually jerked out: 'You're a brave man, you always were — I don't think I'm a coward — and I've no cause to complain — I've had my eyes open all along — but it's just got to me, being the bearer of such horrible news to one friend after another — and at Christmas — sorry, Willo! I'm no good at ruining people's lives. Sorry!'

'Do you want a drink?'

'Thanks.' Desmond reached for his glass of red wine. 'I've probably had more than's good for me already — but what's the difference? You asked me a question — you're kind to think of me — but I can only say again that I spread your money around amongst the top underwriters — and we're all in the same boat — and that's the answer to your question.' He drank, replaced his glass on the table, smiled across at Willo with bloodshot and red-rimmed eyes, and once more used his napkin as if it had been a face flannel, rubbing away tears. 'How can I say it to you,' he resumed in broken accents, 'when you're considering the position of yourself and your family? But forgive me — I keep on thinking of the Marias of this world, my Maria and our gardener in Lincolnshire, and no doubt your staff, who are probably going to get the sack and lose their homes and be worried stiff, and won't understand why, why well-meaning people like us are suddenly seeming to be so damned unkind. I feel for my wife, I do, and my girls who've been planning their showy weddings since they were children — ridiculous really, when there still isn't a husband in sight; but they've had loads of fun, they've had everything their own way, and now they'll have to see the other side of life. And they'll manage — we'll play fair and take the rough with the smooth — and you certainly will — and ditto most of my friends and clients. But I still dread having to face the poor people — and the people who will be poor — and to tell them, or be told, that I should have known better. Willo, thanks for listening to my tale of woe. I'll be myself in a couple of minutes.'

'Shouldn't you eat something — when did you last have something to eat?'

'Breakfast, actually.'

Desmond agreed to swallow a spoonful of soup, then retired to wash, and came back looking better, hair brushed and wearing the jacket of his suit. The two men ate the cottage pie, and later, adjourning to the other part of the room, began to discuss figures and prospects, passing documents back and forth.

At some stage Desmond said: 'Would you like to hear the new year rung in?'

Willo had not realised it was so late – his brain reeled from the impact of the negatives occurring to him – no longer this or that or the next thing, no more of this or that, nothing perhaps, and perhaps no one; but he supplied a lonely affirmative.

Desmond drew curtains and opened a window. The night was still and the view of roofs was moonlit. The idea of a moon somewhere in the sky, in its accustomed place, was comforting. Big Ben began to strike the quarters of the last hour of the old year, followed by the deep reverberating booms of midnight and the joyous outbreak of bell-ringing from Westminster Abbey and probably other churches within earshot of Pimlico Gate.

'I'm afraid we've hard times ahead,' Desmond observed.

Willo replied vaguely: 'Oh well – never mind!'

On principle, Willo Todd's father never spoke about money. How he agreed fair wages with his employees, let alone became a Member of Lloyd's or so-called Name, remained a mystery. Pounds, shillings and pence were for him the dirtiest of words, and his son inherited a touch of the same antipathy.

Three terse sentences had mapped out the latter's financial future. Colonel Jack Todd in the dining-room of The Court, having enjoyed a glass of post-prandial port with Captain Willo Todd, cleared his throat, recommended Lloyd's and added as he rose from the table: 'In my opinion Alleyn's a man to be trusted. Shall we join your mother?' Willo said yes and wondered who or what his father was driving at. A few months later he received two letters, one from his bank manager in Tetbury telling him that tens of thousands of pounds had been paid into his account by the executors of his grandparents, the other from Desmond, saying that his senior partner James Alleyn had been led to believe by Colonel Todd that his son had the means and the motive to join Lloyd's. Willo did not challenge these assumptions: he not only felt obliged to comply with the paternal wishes, he was also pleased to be relieved of the responsibility of ordering his own affairs. He managed to mumble to his father: 'Thanks for your kindness,' a speech as oblique and possibly as unintelligible as that from which he had benefited, and the ungentlemanly subject was closed. Willo, after the statutory lapse of time, began to pocket handsome annual dividends from his investment, and was therefore easily persuaded to entrust to Alleyn and Simcox

[57]

his share of the residue of family money he eventually inherited from his parents.

That he had the haziest idea of how the Lloyd's market worked, and what exactly his money bought, was due more to hereditary factors than to irresponsibility. Just as James Alleyn had measured up to Colonel Todd's high standards of honesty and reliability, so Desmond Simcox had passed all the requisite tests in the eyes of Willo. They had spent two years together in the army, and their regiment had taken part in the Suez Expedition in 1956. There were fellow-officers in the 10th Lancers, the Duke of Clarence's, who were sharper and better company than Desmond, but none with a straighter look or more common sense. He had behaved well in action and under fire, he was good with and to his men, and in the rough and tumble of military existence clung on to the notions of decency of civil-ised civilian life. When demobilised, he had studied to become a chartered accountant and then so impressed James Alleyn as to be made a partner in the old firm. Willo, who was not his father's son for nothing, reposed his fullest confidence in Desmond, and had not been disillusioned or dis-appointed in these last thirty-odd years. Their association was neither too friendly nor too professional, their discussions did not stray beyond general terms, and, in short, Willo had coined money without having to talk or bother his head about it.

If pressed, if forced to concentrate, he might have been able to explain that the attraction of Lloyd's was the chance of using the same money twice, by investing it in stocks, bonds and other assets, and by pledging it as collateral against insurance policies. He was so pleased with the rewards of his Membership that, when his parents died, he had no hesitation in entrusting the cash element of his inheritance to Lloyd's and topping it up with a percent-age of the value of The Court and its contents and its cottages. He was thus able to have and to hold his 'wealth', even to the extent of living in it, while it was also 'used' by selected underwriters at Lloyd's to generate and provide him with income from insurance premiums.

Lloyd's Members were entitled to some tax breaks into the bargain. The whole Lloyd's package, looked at from an optimistic point of view, was not far removed from attainment of the universal ideal, something for nothing. The fly in the ointment, or the wasp waiting in all the sweetness to sting you, was the contractual condition of unlimited liability. You were paid money if all went well, but you paid it if you were called upon to do so until your wealth was exhausted. To put it another way, you were bribed with promises and with privileges to risk bankruptcy and ruin.

Willo knew it. He had been warned verbally and in print, and appended his signature to contracts that committed him to honour Lloyd's tough terms by law. On the other hand he had reasons not to worry. Colonel Jack's experience as a Name had always been rewarding, at least to the best of his son's knowledge. Willo himself had never failed to receive fat annual cheques: he counted on them, he took them for granted. He had a sanguine nature: that he should ever suffer a serious setback at Lloyd's had not crossed his mind.

On New Year's Eve in Pimlico Gate, in a manner of speaking, he lost his financial virginity. It was as if his complacence or his squeamishness were swept away by the flood of tears so disturbingly shed by Desmond.

He had not appreciated, for instance, the legitimate size of the gap between money in hand and money at risk. He had been dimly aware that a Member's funds at Lloyd's could guarantee a larger amount of insurance business, the theory being that such funds would suffice to meet all conceivable claims submitted at the same time. He was now informed or reminded that his total liabilities could amount to a sum in the astronomical region of several million pounds.

He refused to believe it. But Desmond, after hurrying to clarify the point that he had referred merely to the relationship between cash in hand and underwriting limits, produced copies of letters addressed to The Court, which had not been carefully read.

Willo asked and hoped: 'You mean I'm not liable for millions unless the absolute worst comes to the worst?'

Desmond agreed: that is, he agreed that bad luck had to be piled on bad luck in order to cause a whole lot of Syndicates to lose vast sums of money simultaneously, and for a Name to have backed the Syndicates in question. Unfortunately in the present instance, he went on, he feared that coincidence seemed to have played havoc, and minimal warning signals had turned into widespread catastrophe.

Willo asked: should he not have taken out one of those stop-loss insurance policies? And should not alarm bells have been rung loud and clear by that old fool Arnold Waters, his accountant?

Desmond's answer was a trifle defensive: Willo was living in the past, in the golden age of predictability – nothing could stop losses which were without parallel, and many young as well as old accountants and experts had failed to anticipate the trouble in store.

Well – how had it happened, how could it happen, what happened next, and what was being done about it, and what was he to do?

Willo could not concentrate on Desmond's somewhat repetitive explanation, which surely boiled down to saying it was a nasty new world out there.

However, when Desmond concluded by promising to obtain final figures as soon as possible, since his clients would need time to prepare for the cash-call, Willo had to laugh: the joke was where on earth he was expected to find a million and more quid.

Another superfluous speech ensued: Members were legally bound to pay their bills within the specified period of three weeks – to break contracts and wait to be dispossessed by officialdom would just complicate the issue – and so on.

Again Willo's attention wandered, until Desmond said: 'You may have to sell up in Tollworth.'

He ought to have guessed – he could have put two and two together – how could he have missed perhaps the most important point of all?

He mumbled yes, and that it was late and he should be going.

Desmond promised to try to have accurate chapter and verse by mid-January at the latest.

Willo warned him: 'Don't ring me at Tollworth for the time being. I'll talk to my family when the picture gets a bit clearer.'

'Can I telephone your office?'

'No – I don't want Anthony dining out on my story – you can leave a message at the office asking me to telephone. Meanwhile I'm not leaping to any conclusions.'

'No – quite right – that could be another mistake – and you have an old family home with great sentimental value – but my personal preference is not to be caught short – I'm selling pretty well everything immediately, if I can.'

Willo said goodbye, and, having received more apologies and more thanks for his forbearance, was at last permitted to depart.

Out of doors, he breathed in the cool nocturnal air with relief. In army slang, he had had a basinful of bad news. He began to walk home to Edgware Mansions via Grosvenor Place and Park Lane.

Scepticism or a temporary inability to adjust to his altered destiny ruled his mental processes. He had looked or was beginning to look ruin in the face, but was not as disturbed as he perhaps should have been. The future might be bleak, and obviously worse for some of those reliant upon his money than for others. Yet life was usually neither as bad nor as good as one expected, he recalled. For the moment, now in the starry new year's night, he could not help noticing an involuntary and contrary spring in his step. The imminence of disaster seemed to have had a peculiar effect upon him: it was doing what nothing else had done for years, it was putting him on his mettle.

He woke with another sort of hangover, reiterating the thoughtless sentence: 'What a week! What a week!'

He remembered where he was, that he had not had much of a sleep, and why. Mary Cole, notwithstanding the Bank Holiday, had arrived as usual and was audibly in the kitchen. He groaned, not as he had before Christmas, not as he had last year and the years before that because he felt a little lazy, but with anguish. What was he to do about Mary?

He had been a grasshopper and wished he had been an ant. He had hopped blithely into Desmond Simcox's flat the previous evening, and, stranger still, more irresponsibly, hopped out as if in receipt of news by no means altogether bad. He could not reconstruct his reasoning. He did not like to think he was a feckless halfwit. He refused to believe it was all over bar the shouting – his moneyed life, his easy days; but Mary and her future recalled him to the realities of his possibly straitened circumstances. He connected her with Desmond's Maria, and Desmond's gardener with his Denis; and the problems he and Desmond might be going to have in common in respect of their faithful servitors – amongst others – caused his head to ache throbbingly.

'What a week!' he groaned.

Mary knocked and bustled into the bedroom, saying: 'Good morning, Capting – happy new year!' She put his cup of tea on the bedside table and began to open the curtains.

He pretended to be sleepier than he was, and mumbled: 'Oh yes – thanks – what's the weather like?' He drew the line at the hypocrisy of wishing her happiness in the new year.

She gave him a typically discouraging weather forecast in a cheery tone of voice: 'Spotting with rain, Capting, and looks like getting properly wet later on.'

Alone, he drank the tea and wondered where his considerable year's income had gone. He was sure he had not used all of it, he was not a prodigal spendthrift, yet had saved nothing to speak of. In other words he had no worth-while money to distribute to his dependants. Hypothetically, final free gifts might have softened the blow of his being broke.

In his bath he remembered that he was the father of two expensive daugh-ters. Prue had never asked him for a single penny; but she had let him help to buy her flat; and he was protective of her in every sense – how was he to protect her from poverty in future? Melanie was a different kettle of fish. He realised with a further sinking of his heart that, notwithstanding the arrangements he had recently made to pay for the education of her sons, she would not take kindly to the emptiness of the paternal purse.

A bad memory in connection with Melanie struck him. Some years ago he decided to sell a suit of armour packed in a coffin-like box and stored in the attic of The Court. When and how it had been acquired nobody knew, and it had never been assembled in Willo's lifetime and was beginning to rust; it was also supposed to be valuable, and he proposed to use the proceeds to renew the roofs of various garden and tool sheds. When Melanie heard him say that he was hoping to make a killing out of the armour rather than in it she was not amused. Her obvious displeasure conveyed an unpleasant message: that she was not in favour of her father selling any part of the property which she, as his eldest child, expected to inherit. She behaved almost as if she considered the armour was already and to a certain extent her own. Willo had not knuckled under to her impertinent, acquisitive, premature, un-sisterly and, from a per-sonal point of view, depressing attitude: he sold his armour and re-roofed his sheds. But now in Edgware Mansions, reminded of the episode, he did not look forward with equanimity to telling Melanie she was about to be disin-herited.

This morning he looked forward to everything, or nearly everything, with dread, his breakfast included.

While he toyed with his scrambled egg and bacon, Mary told him that she and Biddy were determined to have a week's holiday by the sea in the summer.

'We're thinking of Bournemouth,' she said, eyeing him through the thick lenses of her spectacles. 'We had our last holiday in Bournemouth – but that was when Biddy was nursing and bringing home a good wage – I expect we'll find the place changed – do you know it, Capting?'

No, he replied, recollecting that Biddy had retired at least fifteen years back, then deducing that the sisters had been too hard up for holidays ever since.

He interrupted Mary's description of the lodging house she had stayed in, and the bus she and Biddy had taken to the beach, to demand: 'You both get the pension, don't you?'

Mary was clearly startled by a question referring to the taboo subject of a woman's age, but allowed in cryptic terms: 'We manage quite well, Capting, what with my little job here.'

He wished he had not received her answer – he wished he had remembered that Biddy must be getting on for seventy-five and Mary for seventy – he wished to talk about anything except Mary's finances – but forced himself to seek further for reassurance: 'Your flat in Cricklewood – it's rent-controlled, isn't it? – and you can't be chucked out?'

Comfort was cold: Mary launched into a catalogue of the crimes of her landlord, the local authority, which, she grumbled, would not clean her windows more often than once a fortnight or redecorate her sitting-room when told to.

At the end of her recital he had to laugh. 'All I can say,' he commented, 'is that I wish I could have my windows cleaned and my sitting-room decorated buckshee. You wouldn't like to swap your flat for The Court, would you? No – seriously, Mary – you can't be evicted, can you?'

He regretted that question, too: he had to try to convince Mary it was without significance and he was certain she had nothing whatsoever to worry about.

He also had to lie to her to explain why he could not face his breakfast.

Half an hour later, when he had skimmed through yesterday's copy of the Daily Telegraph, he rang The Court.

Peggy Sparks came on the line.

'Is Mrs Todd around?' he asked her.

Peggy's brusque reply that madam had gone out bicycling conveyed the tacit accusation that he was to blame for madam not having a car.

'Tell her I'll be down for lunch, will you, Peg?'

More time elapsed – he was marking time – he was unable to decide what to do next. He shrank from ringing Arnold Waters and costing himself more distress and more money. Mary bade him a long-drawn-out goodbye. He lifted the telephone again and punched in the number of 15 Pimlico Gate.

Desmond's maid Maria said he was not at home.

'Oh – I see – could I leave a message?'

'Yes, sir. Who's speaking, sir?'

'Mr Willoughby Todd – I met you yesterday.'

'Hullo, Mr Todd. I have a letter here to post to you.'

'Have you?' He could not bear to think of the contents of the letter. 'Maria, the envelope is addressed to London, Edgware Mansions, isn't it? – I don't want to receive it in the country. Will you check, please?'

'Yes, sir.' – She set his mind practically at rest. 'What is your message, sir?'

'Oh – thank him for dinner last night – and say I'll ring him next week.'

'Is that all, Mr Todd?'

'Yes, thanks – goodbye!'

He wasted another half-hour, finally making a third telephone call.

'Perry, it's Mr Todd. Do you think you can find Mr Haden?'

The butler requested Willo to hold the line.

Five minutes passed. Willo thought of the expense involved. But after all his telephone bill could be regarded as the sprat to catch a mackerel. His job at Anthony Haden Ltd and his salary had assumed more importance than ever before.

'Willo? What's up?'

'Nothing much – I wanted to wish you a happy new year.'

'Is that all? Same to you with knobs on. But you've dragged me in from my greenhouses.'

'Oh – sorry. Did you have a good Christmas?'

'I can't remember – I suppose so. What was yours like?'

'Not bad. Are you going to be in the office on Monday?'

'Oh God! Do I have to be? I can't think that far ahead. What day is it today?'

'Friday – there's something I must talk to you about – and I've been reading the proofs of *Nip and Tuck* – the corrections are going to cost a small fortune – you'll have to persuade Lord Plewes to pay for them.'

'Well, I'm not sweating up to the office to touch Roger Plewes for an extra tenner. What else do we have to talk about?'

'I can't say on the telephone.'

'Why on earth not? Don't be boring, Will. I'll keep your secret.'

'Very likely! No, I can't. Shall I see you next week?'

'I don't know – it depends – what sort of thing are you refusing to tell me? It's not to do with publishing, is it?'

'No – it's personal.'

'That sounds slightly more tempting. Are you getting divorced?'

[64]

'No.'

'Have you got AIDS?'

'Not to notice, thank God.'

'Look here, keep it on ice for me. I've got a little friend ripening in the green-house — I'd better hurry back to her.'

Anthony rang off and Willo banged down the telephone.

His employer was impossible, he decided yet again, too rich by half, spoilt by money and therefore inevitably by women.

Willo's next thought caught him unawares: he himself had been rich — was he also demoralised?

He had a sudden yearning to be at The Court, to take refuge there, before it was too late.

He did not have the heart to ring Gloria, who would only probe into the Lloyd's business and show too much interest in his financial resources or lack of them.

His homecoming failed to lift his spirits. He found Barbara with Tray in the kitchen: the dog barked at him, and his wife drew away when he attempted to kiss her.

'I didn't expect you for lunch, even though it's New Year's Day,' she said reproachfully. 'I thought you could never get here till Friday teatime.'

'Oh well — it's meant to be a holiday, isn't it? — and there was nothing doing at the office,' he explained. 'Anyway, how are you?'

'Cooking now,' she retorted.

'You know I'm content with bread and cheese.'

'So you say,' she scoffed.

'What's the matter, Barbara — what have I done wrong?'

'You might have rung to wish me a happy new year.'

'Oh that!'

'Where were you on New Year's Eve?'

'Where were you? I was having dinner with Desmond Simcox.'

'And counting your shekels, no doubt.'

'No! Please stop — you could have rung me, couldn't you? But I'm not arguing.'

'And you could die in London and I'd be none the wiser.'

'Would that worry you?'

[65]

'What do you think? We are married – have you forgotten?'

'Oh come on, Barbara, let's make up even if you won't kiss me. I've had a hell of a week as a matter of fact, and don't feel like squabbling throughout the weekend.'

'My week wasn't exactly heaven. I was short of housekeeping money for one thing. You owe me nearly a hundred pounds for Christmas food and drink.'

'Isn't that a bit steep?'

'Certainly – I'm tired of telling you – it's extremely steep for one person to rattle round in a place this size for most of the time – and not particularly pleas-ant either. But if you want to play at being king of the castle, the least you can do is to pay the price.'

'Would you move house, Barbara?'

'What?'

He repeated the question.

She said: 'I thought The Court was sacrosanct, and you'd only leave it feet first. You've never asked me any question like that before.'

'What's your answer?'

'No – that's not fair – you must explain what you're getting at. I won't be accused by you in future of having forced the issue. Well?'

'Skip it, Barbara. I'll get my cheque-book. Is Prue coming over?'

'Yes, tomorrow morning. But why did you ask me the other question, Willo?'

'Why not? It's neither here nor there. Forget it, please! When are we eating?'

'One o'clock,' she returned. 'And don't be late – don't – I've an early appointment this afternoon and won't be back till six!'

He refrained from asking the obvious question, perhaps because he knew the answer.

At half-past one she duly wheeled out her bicycle and pedalled away in an adulterous direction.

Willo had an uneasy nap disturbed by Tray's barking, then went into the garden to talk to Denis Willett, who was sweeping up the fallen leaves on the croquet lawn. The sky was thickly grey and dusk seemed to be setting in pre-maturely.

Denis greeted him with the announcement: 'I'll need a new mower for the summer.'

Willo had hoped for a salty chat and to help with the leaves. Instead he allowed that the old mower was probably done for, that he would consider the purchase of a new one, and, having left Tray with Denis, hurried off as if urgently required elsewhere. Demands for money were getting on his nerves, and he was unwilling to enter into yet another commitment of any description, even including a commitment to walk the dog.

For the same reason he shunned the village street, where he might encounter neighbours seeking guests for social occasions or donations to charities. He dodged through Stink Alley, a sequestered path between houses and allot-ments, and plodded across muddy fields to Beech Coppice, preoccupied by a dilemma: whether or not to confide in Josh Kemball. To do so would be a relief, he would need to conceal nothing from Josh, and he would be sure to receive sympathy and wise advice. On the other hand a comparison of his wealth, however transitory it was, with Josh's poverty would be unavoidable and embar-rassing. Besides, his problem was mainly materialistic, so not quite the pigeon of Josh, who must have parishioners in more extreme situations to minister to.

Diffidence won the day: he gritted his teeth and returned to deal with the bills awaiting attention in his study.

Later that Friday evening he also did his duty by speaking to his sister on the telephone.

'Hullo, Mandy – how are you all?'

'Oh Will! Tell me how you are – we're past praying for.'

'Why? What's happened?'

'I told you not to ask – on your own head be it – Theo seems to be going down with our plague.'

'What do you mean?'

'Don't say you've forgotten we have mumps in the house!'

'Of course not. How is Desirée?'

'She's the least of it. Now I've two invalids to look after – and Theo's sick as hell, which is no joke at his age. I'm dog-tired, if you must know, and just hope I can stay on my feet for as long as it takes.'

'Poor Mandy – I wish I could help you.'

'Well,' she began in her scrounging tone of voice while he was biting his tongue, 'I don't suppose you'd let your Peggy come over here and give me a helping hand?'

'No – that's impossible – Peggy won't do a thing to oblige me – she loves Barbara and loathes me – and I can't order her about – sorry!'

'There's no need to be ratty, Will – you said you wanted to help – I don't see what you've got to be ratty about.'

[67]

'Look, can't you dig up a local body who'll come in and work for you – can't you ask around or put a card in the Post Office window?'

'Why are you so unimaginative?' she batted back in what might be described as a thunderous whimper. 'We're not all like you, Will, we're not all made of money.'

'Oh God,' he groaned. 'All right, I'll try to send you something, but you'd better get ready to use your imagination where I'm concerned.'

'What? Why should I?'

'I'm nowhere near as rich as everyone seems to think.'

'Maybe not – but you don't know what it's like to have so many children and never to be sure where the next meal's coming from.'

'Your children aren't my fault – but don't let's quarrel.'

'No – and it's not my fault that Father made such an unfair will.'

'You had your share, Mandy – and most of Mother's money – and gave it to that crook to invest – you frittered it away.'

He realised that he had levelled against her the charge of which he himself was guilty; also that she was whimpering again.

Contritely he added: 'I promise to do what I can for you for as long as possible.'

'Oh well, who cares?' she half-sobbed in catarrhal accents. 'I must go – Theo's thumping on our bedroom floor – and that's Desirée screaming for me – what a life! Take no notice of my grumbling – you haven't been a bad brother to me – keep in touch – goodbye!'

Willo had to take deep breaths and then pace round the house in order to recover sufficiently from this conversation to write a final cheque for a hundred pounds: his right hand had more or less stopped shaking, and he sought perverse consolation in the idea that the form of his relations with his sister would never be financially the same.

Supper in the kitchen with Barbara, which was reminiscent of meals eaten by foes in lulls in the fighting in the First World War, was not conducive to digestion; and Willo lay awake for most of the night, able neither to compose himself nor recover his sceptical attitude to Desmond Simcox's destructive prognostications. He counted not sheep, but the costs of his life-style, and speculated repetitively as to what if anything might be salvaged from the wreckage.

In the morning Prue arrived. He was waiting for her, greeted her at the front door, hugged her surprisingly tight, and suggested an immediate stroll – the weather had improved and was sunny and almost springlike. She said yes, how lovely, smiling up at him and studying his face with some concern.

No doubt he also surprised her by leading her through Stink Alley.

She asked him: 'Is all well?'

He hesitated – but could not do it – he loved her too much to add his burden to those already on her shoulders – her thirty years of spinsterhood, the inadequacies of her love affair – and therefore answered: 'I believe so – I hope so.'

'What is it, Dad?'

Her dear straightforward reddish face and the frizziness of her mousy hair seemed to make it impossible for him to hurt her, to deliver any sort of blow, let alone the home truth that he might have robbed her of her expectations.

'Nothing, darling,' he said.

'But you look pale – and why are we walking this way?'

'For a change,' he replied.

Belatedly he appreciated the double meaning.

Her glance at him was quick and sharp; but instead of inquiring into the cause of his brittle laughter she remarked, 'I don't think I like changes,' which made him wonder whether she too was playing the ambiguous game and referring to her fidelity to John Seward.

'No,' he murmured, agreeing with her and at the same time confirming his decision not to reveal the extent of the dislikable changes in the offing.

They walked on and reverted to safer impersonal topics – Mandy's plight, Prue's work at the kindergarten. They did not look at each other and the old upsetting barrier of constraint came between them.

Throughout the rest of Saturday his failure to trust her with his confession nagged at him, and he did not get or did not create a second chance to speak to her privately.

Again, that night, he could not sleep. He fretted over his unwonted insomnia on top of everything else, and feared he either was or would be ill. The bright side of life was effectively hidden from him on the Sunday morning. An uneasy walk to and from church with Prue, and Josh's superannuated deputy droning on in the pulpit, were no solace. Returning to The Court, as they opened the door, Barbara called out that Melanie was on the telephone.

He took the call in his study.

Melanie metaphorically rushed in: 'Dad, will you do me a favour? It's very important, and Barbara said you would.'

'What favour?'

'Oh please don't be so chilly and careful! William has to have his tonsils and adenoids out – our Dr Hopkins has recommended the operation and the specialist – and I just can't bear the idea of hanging around in a National Health queue . . .'

He interrupted her: 'How much, Melanie?'

'You needn't put it like that! All right – about two thousand pounds.'

'Good God!'

'You could contribute, Dad.'

'Could I?'

'You could contribute one thousand.'

'Thanks for telling me.'

'Why are you so cross?'

'Sorry – I can't talk now.'

The upshot of this conversation was that he marched into the kitchen, confronted Barbara and Prue, and rapped out in exasperated accents in a loud voice: 'I'm afraid I must leave you – it's business, an emergency, a meeting with Lord Plewes at two-thirty, he can't manage any other time.'

'But today's Sunday – and you'll have to have lunch – I've taken all this trouble to cook it – you'll have to have lunch somewhere,' Barbara burst out.

'Too bad. Prue can eat for two.'

'But you were speaking to Melanie. Are you going to pay for William's operation?'

'That's nothing to do with you, Barbara. Goodbye.'

'When did you know you were leaving? You might have told me! I didn't hear another call. What's going on?'

Her questions remained unanswered – he was already in the hall.

Prue had followed him: 'Dad, please tell me – what is it?'

'Don't ask for the moment, darling. Stay there! Goodbye.'

'You haven't got your night things.'

'I've more in London.'

He slammed the front door behind him.

In his car he was trembling so much that he could not get the ignition key into the keyhole. He had lost his temper or his head – Melanie's characteristically crude attempt to grab what was not hers was the straw that broke the back of his self-control – suddenly he could not bear the prospect of another meal served up with Barbara's acid sauce, or the difficulty of simultaneously fending off her hostility and trying not to fend off Prue's fond approaches. He had felt the whole weight of his house on his shoulders, as if the very bricks were reproaching him for betraying them and being about to sell them to the highest bidder – he had to run away, 'crawl out from under' in his slangy lingo, irrespective of the conventional shibboleths and whether or not he gave offence. He was more alarmed than the alarm he had perhaps left behind him; but his flight had seemed to be a matter of survival.

Gradually he ceased to drive too fast. All those damned demands for money continued to disturb his peace of mind – they seemed to have sprung like green shoots from the poisonous seed of Desmond Simcox's prophecies; but his present interest centred rather on his unusual reaction to them. He could not remember ever missing a meal for the sake of a quarrel or to avoid a quarrel. His behaviour was unprecedented – it must be connected with a stronger attachment to money than he had ever recognised, or else with some other latent tendency. The point that particularly claimed his attention was that it represented novelty.

And from his novel position things looked different. He was not happy – he felt unhappiness lodging in his throat and rumbling in his stomach – and realised that for a long time he had been unhappier than he thought he was. Granted, he had or had had blessings to count. But happiness was not exactly to do with material matters, a roof over his head, money for food, a wife of sorts, children, a spot of sex; and thinking otherwise was a mistake and a mixup of attitude and emotion.

Introspection was not Willo's strong suit. He was a man of action, who abided by the law and the conventions. But the strange ideas occurring to him in the car overruled his settled objection to delving into psychology and stuff like that.

No, he now realised, what he had been for an almost shaming number of years was comfortable. He had not bothered to try to be happy – he had been as lazy in his own fashion as Anthony Haden. Oh, there was always enough to do, putting in attendance at the office, motoring from country to town and back again, dining and wining Gloria and so on, but it was skating over the surface or, to use another sporting metaphor, shadowboxing. It was chasing and maintaining the illusion of a happy life, whereas it was actually a life that was merely full.

He felt tired: recent events, topped up by unaccustomed mental activity, were wearing him out.

But he was aware of a healthier stir of hunger. He began to wonder where he might get a bite to eat.

He stopped at the Membury Service Station on the M4 and after a reviving cup of tea and a sandwich drove on to London.

He spent the rest of the day at the Bachelors; back at Edgware Mansions, when he arrived there late in the evening, he disconnected the telephone; and early on Monday morning, before Mary Cole arrived, he went to the office, concentrating exclusively on what he could and should say to Anthony, given the chance.

He had to wait until after eleven o'clock.

Anthony breezed in wearing one of his blue chalk-stripe double-breasted suits, a silk shirt with cuffs showing gold cuff-links in the shape of a horse's bridle, a fifty-pound pale blue tie with white spots Windsor-knotted, and highly polished black slip-on shoes with a fanciful lace ending in two false acorns.

He had once been an engaging young man, tall, black-haired, toothy and chinless but lively and jolly. Then aged twenty-five or so he inherited Havinton Hall and the fortune made by his father. He instantly developed almost every trait attributed to new rich persons. He became flashy and purse-proud. He showed off and broadcast the prices he paid for his clothes, pictures, furniture and so on. He was extravagant and miserly, over-excited and bored. He married Helen, one of whose charms in his eyes must have been her inability to say boo, and set up as a publisher with an office in St James's from which he could mainly conduct amatory campaigns.

Now in his mid-fifties he looked the part he had elected to play. The whites of his eyes were yellowish, he had discoloured bags under his eyes, his full lips were creased and the lower one was apt to hang open, and his teeth were either badly stained or too good to be true. His previously lustrous black hair was thin, lank and grey. He was far from fit, he had some sort of liver trouble, he bewailed the fact that he was no longer always able to do the trick, and, judging by his telephone conversations from the inner office he shared with Willo, his liaisons had deteriorated into doing business with professional girls.

On the Monday morning in question he immediately used the telephone to ring up a girl he called Clotilde, although he had obviously never met her.

His end of the conversation included the following: 'Dine with me, my dear . . . We'll eat wherever you like . . . Give me your address – I'll come and fetch you round about eight o'clock . . . Yes, I've written that down . . . I can't tell you how much I look forward to it . . . Sweet of you, thank you . . . Until eight, goodbye!'

Then he grinned roguishly at Willo and advised: 'Never forget, variety's the spice of life!'

They chatted inconsequently until Anthony, lying back in his desk chair which had a reclining adjustment, inquired: 'What's this thing you wouldn't tell me?'

'Oh yes,' Willo began, and suddenly wished he was not going to have to reveal his possible dependence on Anthony, and was not on the point of making the well-known mistakes of pleading poverty and begging from a friend. 'Desmond Simcox has been on to me,' he continued lamely.

'What's secret about that?'

'He says Lloyd's is in a mess.'

'Thank God I never signed on the dotted line – Desmond tried to persuade me to, you know.'

'I did.'

'So you did, I remember. Are you heavily involved?'

'Quite,' Willo fibbed.

'Bad luck. But you'll have your reserves.' Anthony was losing interest. 'Where are the Plewes proofs?'

Willo said: 'I'm a Name twice over, if you know what I mean.'

Against his better judgment, he was now determined not, as usual, to make it easy for Anthony to brush disagreeable matters aside.

'I say – that's going it – I didn't know you had so much boodle to play with, Willo.'

'I haven't.'

'What?'

'According to Desmond I've lost it all.'

'You're joking – or he is.'

'No.'

'You can't have lost all your money – that must be an exaggeration. Desmond was always windy – nobody loses everything in Lloyd's – it's unknown.'

'Apparently not.'

'Well, I don't believe it for a second. You've got other money, haven't you?'

'No.'

'Don't be silly – you must have!'

[73]

'Everything I own seems to be forfeit.'

'You don't mean The Court?'

'I think I do.'

'My dear old boy, you'd better be sure! You can't let them chuck you out of The Court – it wouldn't be right.'

'No.'

'What beats me is how you got in so deep, and why. Who told you to do such a damn-fool thing?'

'My father first – then his agent – then Desmond – but I take the responsibility. Lloyd's has paid out tons of money over the years – I can't be ungrateful to Lloyd's or to my advisers.'

'Weren't you worried about the unlimited liability?'

'No, not very, hardly at all. I was never liable. The money always came my way.'

'Lucky old you! Now it's the day of reckoning.'

'Yes. It seems to be.'

'Well – chin up! Fancy you taking such a risk – I never would have thought it – I imagined I was the gambling man – you're meant to be the one to keep me on the straight and narrow. You've brought me out in a sweat, Will – there but for the grace, and the rest of it. Hadn't we better try to turn an honest penny? Where's *Nip and Tuck*? Can we really publish a book with that half-baked title?'

'Anthony, what do you think will happen here?'

'God knows.'

'Sorry to ask – but obviously work's begun to look different from where I find I'm standing.'

'I can't say, Will. We're both getting on – and the business is a hell of a luxury.'

'It's no longer a luxury for some of us.'

'Steady on! You're crossing your bridges before you come to them. Lloyd's may have the hiccups, but it's sure to cure itself before too long. You hang on in there, you keep the faith, and I bet you'll be okay. Leave things as they are – for the time being at any rate. That's my advice.'

Willo followed it: he let Anthony change the subject. Although he had received no guarantees, he was more reassured than he might have been. They spent an hour or so with bills and correspondence, and on proofs and plans.

At twelve-thirty Anthony yawned and called it a day.

[74]

Willo said: 'Where are you lunching?'

Anthony avoided his eyes.

'Where are you?'

Willo replied: 'Anywhere – we could have lunch together.'

'Oh – I can't, Will – I've got an engagement – I've just remembered. See you tomorrow – I'll look in if I can. I'm sorry you're being bothered by Desmond – tell him from me to pull himself together.'

These few words, and how they were spoken, hit Willo hard. He deduced from them that the days of Anthony Haden Limited were numbered: its proprietor would pack up and back out in order not to have to feel guilty in the company of his bankrupt partner. The office was becoming superfluous to Anthony's present requirements; and he was not the type to pay thousands of pounds in order to listen to anyone's hard-luck story. Therefore Willo's remuneration would not be forthcoming, and he was too proud to plead – more than likely in vain – for a golden handshake.

Family

O N the Wednesday of that first week of January, Willo received a telephone call in the Anthony Haden office from Desmond Simcox.

It was past noon. Willo had seen and heard nothing of or from Anthony since their comfortless talk on Monday. And Jenny had done her half-day's work and departed.

Desmond began: 'Are you alone? Can I speak freely?'

Willo with a sinking heart gave him the go-ahead.

Desmond voiced introductory apologies and Willo cut him short: 'I know all that – you can stop being sorry – I've had your second letter and expect the worst – just tell me what the damage is likely to be.'

The estimated figure was in the region of one and a quarter million pounds, not less, possibly more, Desmond said: in other words a sum considerably in excess of all Willo's assets.

He proceeded to redefine the meaning of accounts that could not be closed, to cite the forecasts of losses here, there and everywhere, to explain why figures were still approximate, to try to justify the conduct of underwriters and, in short, to tie his client in knots, for Willo never could follow or absorb complex calculations and statistics.

'What about you?' Willo asked at the end of it.

'Thank you for the kind thought, and thanks for your unselfishness. Well – I'll be wiped out – I'm inquiring right now into how one can bankrupt oneself before somebody else does it – and wondering how to keep body and soul together and feed my family. Of course I'm cut up to be losing my savings – but I'm acquainted with poverty – my parents were never rich, and I had nothing more than my gratuity from the army when I was given a job by Mr Alleyn. I owe everything to Lloyd's, including the decency not to grumble – I've had a great life and anyway refuse to repine – it's time to look ahead. That's my philosophy, Will – and I'd hazard a guess that yours is a damn sight better than mine. However, as you're good enough to ask, I will admit that having to tell my friends they're probably bust is something I won't ever be able to put behind me or get over. Don't sympathise – I'll pass out if you do!'

'Desmond – okay – no sympathy – shall we be practical? What's the next move?'

'I imagine that what I'm about to say won't interest you, but I ought to say it and I will nonetheless. Some Members are raising objections to their liabilities and potential bills – they're taking legal advice and thinking of issuing writs against their agents, their underwriters and the governing body of Lloyd's. They're banding together and refusing to honour their contract to pay on demand, though in previous years they were pleased as punch to be paid. The alternative course of action is to keep your word.'

'I'll stick to the alternative.'

'I guessed you would. But I couldn't blame anybody for fighting to hang on to a family fortune and home, and a respected position in society, and often in history too – my God, no! Don't worry, Will – I won't let myself get tearful again, even if the tragedies are multiplying and growing more tragic daily. You know you'll have to have your money ready by midsummer?'

'Yes – everything plus.'

'I hate to hear you say it.'

'I'm only repeating what you yourself said the other evening.'

'Did I? Sorry! The old adage is "Down to the last collar-stud" – and that does seem to be about the size of it. Judging by recent valuations, and taking into consideration your shortage of cash, there's going to be a difference between Lloyd's demand and your ability to supply.'

'So what happens?'

'Lloyd's won't pursue you for what you haven't got.'

'Well – small mercies are beginning to look like big ones. Tell me, the mite of cash in the bank, which I thought was mine, who does it really belong to?'

'If you follow my advice and my example, it won't belong to you for very much longer. I'm penniless at the moment – my wife and children will be paying bills with the capital I called my own for as long as it lasts.'

'Your people must be in the picture then?'

[77]

'Just about.'

'How did they react?'

'Wonderfully well. Have you spoken to your family, Will?'

'Not yet.'

'Are you expecting difficulties?'

'Maybe.'

'The sale of a house can take time.'

'Yes — but that means I'll have to warn everyone without delay.'

'Have you discussed your situation with any friendly outsider?'

'Not yet.'

'If I may ask, is there a sensible friend you could discuss it with?'

'Yes — yours as well as mine from our army days — Josh Kemball, who's been the parson of Tollworth for the last few years.'

'I'd forgotten — Josh would be a comfort, if you should need comforting. Give him my best, will you? Listen — I don't want to intrude or anything — but have you given thought to the future?'

'Not really.'

'Where do you stand in your publishing business?'

'It's not mine — it's Anthony Haden's show — and I have had a word with Anthony — and as a result can't see myself working here much longer.'

'Why's that?'

'Well — either because he understood that I won't be able to do what I have been doing for him, or for some other reason, I'm sure he decided as soon as I opened my mouth to give up and finish. He's probably right — he certainly couldn't manage on his own.'

'What other reason might he have had in mind, Will?'

'Anthony wouldn't like to feel he was financially responsible for me. The last thing he'd want in his office is to have a pauper staring him in the face.'

'I thought as much — poverty isn't popular — we live and learn, don't we? So I gather your future, like mine, lies in the lap of the deity?'

'Yes — and it's a bit late in the day for us to find ourselves on the bread-line. At least we won't be lonely there.'

'Nicely put, Willo. Thanks for making things seem better than they are, and for taking it all on the chin.'

Desmond added that he would be sending the relevant paperwork along in due course, and they expressed hopes of meeting again for a meal in some cut-price pub.

[78]

'About Anthony,' Willo rounded off their conversation; 'don't think I'm complaining or ungrateful. He's given me employment and paid me a hand⁄ some salary for years, and we've had a good time publishing bad books. He was bored with the business before I spoke to him, and what he may understand is that I'd hate to have to depend on him entirely.'

Willo then glanced at his wristwatch: the time would have allowed him to leave the office for lunch with a clear conscience.

But, instead, he paced the floor and stood by the window with his hands in his pockets, staring into Babel Yard.

A half⁄hour elapsed, and he sat down at his desk and drafted the following letter.

'Dear Anthony, I have just finished talking to D. Simcox, who has repeated and proved to me that to all intents and purposes I am now insolvent. My wealth, such as it was, my property and possessions – the whole bag of tricks and more besides – is owed to Lloyd's. The next move is for me to sell The Court in order to have the proceeds available when required in June or July. Clearly these intervening months are going to be filled with negotiations and with helping myself and my family to come to terms with our changed cir⁄ cumstances. Consequently I feel I would not be able to give my full attention to our business, or provide you with managerial value for money, and that I must tender my resignation.

'Sorry to be formal, but you'll read between the lines.

'In case you're interested, the chief effect of going broke, setting aside having no money, is that it's a sort of transformation, it transforms you and your dealings with everybody and everything, and I know I would soon be a use⁄ less partner to you, not worth my salary. Even if you were still paying me, I couldn't afford either to live in London, let alone live in it as I have up till now, or live in the country and travel to and from Babel Yard.

'I would like to clear my desk as soon as convenient – are you familiar with the modern euphemism for making oneself scarce?

'And I hope you will pardon me for closing the office now (1.30 p.m.) and for not coming in again until next Monday. You will appreciate that I need to contact house agents and auctioneers during the two remaining working days of this week.

'Finally, may I suggest you leave me a note here in answer? I would find it soon enough, and I am bound to be difficult to catch telephonically in the meanwhile.

[79]

'With my warm thanks for having been a kind friend and generous boss, and with regrets, Yours ever, Willo.'

He copied out the letter, sealed the fair copy in an envelope marked Urgent, and addressed it to Havinton Hall.

As he was leaving the office, hurrying to get out in case he should meet Anthony, he stopped. He had meant to communicate with Gloria Deane – he was shocked to remember he had forgotten Gloria.

He sat down again and wrote to her thus: 'Darling, A thousand and one dramas, not a chance to talk or meet, I'll explain all in a day or two. Missing you badly. Forgive me, your loving W.'

He took the letters with him to post.

He was dissatisfied by both. In the first he had not expressed his true and ardent wish, which was to continue to receive fifteen thousand pounds a year; he had just saved himself the humiliation of getting sacked and Anthony the task of sacking him. And the second was similar inasmuch as he had omitted to tell Gloria the truth, thereby postponing her response to his news.

His letter to Anthony could be called gentlemanly; but like his line to Gloria, for equally craven reasons, it amounted to false pretences.

The strangest fancy occurred to him: those letters were part of the skin he was shedding, snake-style. He locked the office door, descended the stairs, crossed Babel Yard, climbed the little hill of St James's and entered the Green Park tube station, paradoxically gratified to think how unlike himself he had already become.

Duty and reality between them smothered the obstinate flame of contrarily positive emotion that had flared within him.

Driving to Tollworth in the Mercedes, he had to revise opinions. He would have to sell his car for a start. He had imagined he could confine his explanations to Barbara, and take and choose his time to talk to Melanie and Prue, providing house-agents' intrusions into his home were kept to a discreet minimum. The closer he got to his destination the more gloomily he resigned himself to the fact that that schedule was wishful thinking. He could not tell Barbara today, Wednesday, without telling Prue on Friday or Saturday, and he could hardly tell Prue before he told Melanie. Besides, Barbara would no doubt warn Peggy Sparks, and Peggy ought not to know before Denis knew; and Barbara might well spill the beans to Byle the Vile, who might add gossiping to his other vices or virtues. And was it not a contradiction in terms, a discreet house-agent, professionally obliged to advertise his wares?

In short Willo realised he must not blunder about in the hornet's nest he was stepping into. He dreaded the pain and grief he was going to cause, and more than likely be caused by Melanie and by Mandy in particular. At the same time he braced himself not to cave in to his elder daughter and his sister, nor to purchase peace at the expense of Prue and others.

He arrived at The Court at teatime, entered the dark house through the front door, switched on lights and found his wife in the kitchen, seated at the kitchen table and eating a slice of wholemeal bread spread with her health-stores margarine and sugarless jam.

She did not get up. He kissed the top of her head. Tray barked at him and snapped at his trousers. She did not rebuke the dog.

She said: 'What on earth brings you down here in the middle of the week? I was so startled when you rang me that I never asked. And I forgot to mention plans I've got – for this evening, for instance.'

'Don't worry,' he replied, 'I won't be in your way.' And to divert attention from her curiosity to his curiosity, he inquired: 'What are you up to this evening?'

Her defiance was weakened by the suspicion of a blush: 'I promised to help Roger Byle with an essay he has to write. I'll be back in time for supper. Do you want me to make you fresh tea in the meantime? I'm leaving in a couple of minutes.'

'No,' he said, and shortly afterwards: 'Goodbye.'

Alone, having drunk his cup of lukewarm tea, he began to wander round the house, drawing curtains and reviving memories. His mother had always insisted on tea in the dining-room and the silver service of teapot and kettle: she resisted Mandy's hoydenish demands to move with the times and eat tea at the kitchen table. His mother had been a gracious lady: how she would have hated the indignity in store for her descendants!

The curtains in the sitting-room, now frayed at the foot, had been made by his mother and her sister, his widowed Aunt Annie, who would stay for a month or two every Christmas. He could still see them stitching away and chatting in intimate voices, the light with the green silk shade illuminating their bent heads, the skeins of coloured wool piled on a stool between them. His childhood in this house was really idyllic: his parents had not presumed to be his friends; he was too young to be troubled by the war, especially as Colonel Todd's age permitted him only to serve in the Home Guard; there had been no mysterious crises or discord, and when saying his prayers at school he associated heaven with The Court.

Here in the study was a framed picture by Mandy aged seven, representing with lurid approximation their home, their father pipe in mouth, and his yellow labrador Snipe. Although his sister was a mere year older than Willo, they had never been all that close. She was a loud-mouthed competitive child, jealously proud of being Daddy's girl. When she was seventeen, and notwithstanding her spots and puppy fat, she aroused the interest of a rustic oaf of twenty-two, the son of a smallholder over at Snathe, and reciprocated his feelings with enthusiasm. Colonel and Mrs Todd were against it for sensible as well as snobbish reasons; more to the point, since Mandy was too proud of her conquest to heed parental warnings, her boyfriend came to the same conclusion. Her disappointment was severe, and she by no means kept it to herself. For years the whole family suffered from her disquisitions on the subject of star-crossed love. At length, on the overdue rebound, she sandbagged Theo Wriggs and dragged him to the altar, and then prevailed upon his clerical middle-age and frail physique to sire a shoe-full of children.

Willo climbed the stairs and peeped into Barbara's bedroom, which was also, as it were, her refuge and her anti-matrimonial redoubt. A strictly single bed had replaced the old double; some bottles of pills on the bedside table reinforced the impression of loneliness. He wandered over to the dressing-table, one of the pieces of furniture Barbara had brought with her and managed to introduce into The Court. On the plate-glass top were a hairbrush, a comb, three hairpins and a small half-empty bottle of lavender water. The paucity of aids to beauty rather annoyed the husband who was obviously not to be given or to get the wrong idea. He noticed two snapshots under the glass, one of a dog, of Tray, the other of a man, not himself – no – a bespectacled youth – Roger Byle – Byle the Vile in person.

He left the room hurriedly. He was annoyed and, still more, embarrassed. He felt as if he had spied upon something disgusting and ridiculous, and that he was being ridiculed, at least in the eyes of his staff, of Peggy, who must have seen the photos and laughed at him.

He wished – he entertained another retrograde wish – that he had not entered the best bedroom in which, in a far-fetched manner of speaking, the worst had happened. He had loved his first wife there and lost her, and now had his suspicions publicly corroborated that he was supplanted in the affections of his second.

He went downstairs to the study and rang Sprocketts.

Melanie answered, that is to say she eventually lifted the receiver and, sound-ing harassed to the point of desperation, almost screamed into it: 'Yes?'

'It's me, Melanie.'

'Oh Dad!' Her voice conveyed anti-climax, exasperation, hostility. 'What do you want?'

But Willo was not in the mood to be snubbed by his daughter.

'Are you well?' he asked. 'You don't sound well.'

'Oh – sorry – but don't you start, Dad – I'm having such a damned awful time with William ill and everything.'

Willo took the hint, or rather the sharp reminder that he had not yet sup-plied Melanie's demand for money for the removal of his grandson's tonsils.

He said: 'Can you come over here in the next day or two? There's a matter I must talk about – and I could contribute to William's operation at the same time.'

'Is it important?' she queried, sighing.

'Yes.'

'Oh God! I am busy, you know. Well, I suppose I could get to you. Would the weekend do? Then Edgar could drive me and the boys over.'

'I'd rather you came alone. Could you have lunch Thursday or Friday? I'll meet you halfway if you like.'

'That's an idea. But Thursday's tomorrow – I can't just leave home at such short notice – I might be able to manage Friday. Where would we meet?'

'At that pub in Tockingham, for instance?'

'The Fox, it's called. It serves ploughman's lunches.'

Willo dug in his toes – he would not be blackmailed into buying her a meal he could not afford.

'The Fox at one o'clock – all right?'

She gave in gracelessly.

Willo looked at his mail. He tried in vain to concentrate, and soon resumed his pacing. Barbara returned at seven-thirty. She was somewhat flushed as if by marital guilt or adulterous satisfaction.

He would have liked to blurt out his secret. But she repaired to the kitchen without delay, perhaps to avoid him. He did not follow her – he could not tell her they were ruined while she prepared his supper.

In time they sat at the kitchen table eating cold chicken thighs and a salad of limp winter lettuce: cheese, biscuits and apples were to follow.

'How was Roger?' he inquired.

'Quite well, thank you,' she replied defensively.

'What was the essay about?'

She darted a glance at him, must have decided he was teasing her, and mumbled: 'You wouldn't be interested.'

'Why not? Please tell me.'

'Shakespeare's sexuality,' she admitted.

'Good Lord! By the way, Barbara, are you sleeping with Roger?'

'You would think that,' she accused hotly, not meeting his eyes. 'I'm helping someone to get a degree and qualification and with luck a job at the end of the day. Your low standards are not applicable.'

'I hope he makes you happy.'

She re-used his mildly satirical words with resentment: 'And I hope you're happy in London – but I don't pester you with stupid questions.'

They munched in silence.

He kicked himself for provoking her. She was right, his questions had been stupid, since he was more grateful to than jealous of Roger. Now it was hardly the moment to speak his piece: she would think he was exaggerating for punitive purposes.

They finished eating and adjourned to the chill sitting-room to watch the nine o'clock news. He switched on a bar of the old electric fire, and they sat apart, he slumped on the sofa, she on an upright chair. He was unmoved by, he could not take in, the hackneyed accounts of death and destruction.

At a quarter past nine he remarked: 'We're broke.'

'What?' she asked.

'I'm broke anyway.'

'Do turn off the telly.'

He did so.

'What did you say?'

'I'm completely broke – I've lost all my money.'

'Oh,' she commented without any particular inflection. 'Do you mean it?' she asked.

'Yes.'

'How much money?'

'I've told you – all, everything.'

'Is it to do with Lloyd's?'

'Yes.'

'I never liked the idea of Lloyd's.'

[84]

'Maybe not – you liked the Lloyd's income.'

'I personally took none of it ever. You know that, Willo. Your home, this house, was and is expensive, but that's not my fault. I spent my own money on myself.' She paused. 'Is my money intact?'

'I expect so.'

'Do you promise?'

'It's nothing to do with me, it was always your pigeon.'

'I'm sorry I asked.'

He shrugged his shoulders and said: 'The Court will have to go.'

'What?' she repeated.

'And the cottages.'

'Do they belong to Lloyd's?'

'Sort of.'

'Are you saying there's nothing left, nothing at all?'

'Exactly – every single thing will have to be sold.'

'Sold when?'

'Now – as soon as possible.'

'Who says so?'

'Desmond Simcox.'

'You don't mean you're going to sell your inheritance and the roof over our heads simply because Desmond tells you to?'

'It's not like that. He's shown me accounts. The bill I'm getting in the summer exceeds a million pounds. I have to raise all the money I can to pay it.'

'What happens afterwards?'

'I don't exactly know. Either I'm bankrupted or I bankrupt myself. I haven't bothered about the future, except to realise we'll be out of here and penniless.'

'How long have you known this?'

'Desmond wrote to me before Christmas, but I only found the letter on the day after Boxing Day. I didn't take it seriously at first. But I've seen Desmond since then.'

'Is that why you behaved so oddly on Sunday?'

'What happened on which Sunday? I'm afraid I've lost track of time.'

'You rushed away without eating the lunch I'd cooked.'

'Oh yes – and I'll say sorry now – but there's too damn much to go on being sorry for.'

'Yes,' she said. 'Willo, tell me again – I don't want to misunderstand this time – you're saying you're about to be destitute?'

'I am.'

'At least and at last you've surprised me. Well I never! Would you like a cup of tea by any chance?'

'I'll have whisky. You go ahead and make your tea.'

Ten minutes later they reassembled in the sitting room.

She observed: 'We haven't talked so much for ages — there never seemed to be an opportunity to talk about anything except bills and plans — and you were here so little.'

'I had work to do.'

'Oh yes, your work!' she exclaimed disrespectfully. She had always poured scorn on Anthony Haden Limited, calling it hopeless, second-rate, philistine. But now she checked herself and continued: 'Your work may be our bread and butter after all.'

'No,' he replied, shaking his head.

'Why not?'

'I've resigned.'

'Isn't that foolish?'

'I preferred to resign.'

'What did you prefer it to — Anthony wasn't going to get rid of you, was he?'

'My impression was, when I spoke to him, that he'd close the business.'

'Why — when you really need it — when you need it as never before?'

'Anthony's too rich to want to be involved with a poor colleague. And he's less and less interested in publishing — he doesn't have so many women as he did. I realised he'd squirm out somehow in case I asked him for money.'

'But he'll have to pay you off.'

'Not necessarily — or willingly — he's not extravagant, except to please himself. And I'm no good at begging. I was born better at buying than selling.'

'I don't like Anthony any more than I like Lloyd's.'

'No — he's not your type — but he did me a good turn.'

'Willo, where do you propose to live?'

'That's one question — propose to live on is another — I'll probably be on the dole, and your money won't go far. What a pity you wouldn't accept the odd gift of cash from me when I had it!'

'I never felt your money coming my way was a fair exchange.'

He assured her not very convincingly: 'We've rubbed along.'

'Along too long,' she commented. 'We shouldn't have married. I shouldn't have married you. I certainly shouldn't have been angry with you for making me feel I was wasting my life. Oh it's so difficult to say these things!'

'You could just say I've been an idiot and go to bed.'

'Oh don't keep on behaving better than me! I suppose you've had a nasty time. I should sympathise with you.'

'I don't deserve sympathy. I shouldn't have been so smug.'

'Who's to blame?'

'Desmond's above suspicion. Besides, he's in as deep a hole as we are. And he vouches for all the other people involved.'

'You'll have to get impartial advice.'

'I'll have to talk to Arnold.'

'Arnold was your father's accountant, for heaven's sake! I can't think why you continue to employ such a fuddy-duddy. You must get really expert advice.'

'What – pay lawyers – when I'm poor enough as it is or soon will be?'

'Oh – well – I won't be taking your money – I couldn't now.'

'That isn't what I meant.'

'No – but you don't understand – I feel more independent, and especially wouldn't want to count on you for money even if there was any left.'

'Are you tiptoeing round the subject of Roger?'

'Yes and no.'

'Is he in love with you?'

'Maybe he thinks so. I'm sorry – but it's nice for me – and he's not what you all say he is – he's not vile.'

'May I ask you what your intentions are?'

'You're forgetting how much younger he is than I am. I can't expect our friendship to last. But I don't see why I shouldn't enjoy it in the meanwhile. And he's introduced me to the pleasure of teaching – no, Willo, don't smirk, don't be smutty, I'm serious. If I was on my own – and you and I'd cut each other's throats if we were shut up together at close quarters – who knows? – I have wondered if I'm too old to try for a qualification.'

'As a schoolmistress?'

'You're so old-fashioned – nobody uses that word nowadays. Do we have to decide everything this evening? I've said too much already.'

He contradicted her. He asserted that he was glad one of them had a plan or half a plan for the future, and that news not absolutely negative was a relief.

Tray interrupted their conversation: the dog emerged from his basket, yawning and stretching.

Barbara availed herself of the opportunity to say: 'Tray's had enough at any rate, he wants to go out.'

Willo escorted Tray through the french window and on to the distorted rectangles of light falling on the lawn. He heard a car stopping in the village street and a girl's laughter – dogs barked and Tray responded snappily. He remembered how new the year was, and that in other years the first weeks of January had had the charm – however misleading – of hope refreshed. He studied and succeeded in reading his wristwatch in the dark: twelve thirty-five – it was tomorrow. He was suddenly too tired to care: hope and despair were alike beyond him.

He locked up the house and switched off lights. Tray had mounted the stairs to join Barbara who had apparently retired to her bedroom. With help from the banister rail he reached the first floor landing, and called out: 'Good night!'

After a slight pause Barbara called back in clipped repressive accents: 'Good night!'

Willo's sleep was short: he was awake again before four o'clock. Worry was getting the better of his former sleeping pattern: he was hectically wakeful earlier every morning. He tiptoed down to his study at seven and laid breakfast in the kitchen and was eating it when Barbara and Tray appeared at eight.

She was evasive and unforthcoming. He wished they had not been so confidential yesterday evening, and, almost, that she was still boldly hostile. Reconciliation in any full sense was out of the question; and he divined that the inhibiting factor for each of them was fearing the other might be thinking along different lines.

He escaped to his study, where there was no escape from his predicament.

He rang Josh Kemball.

'When can I come to see you?' he asked.

'Is it private?'

'Yes.'

'And important?'

'Yes.'

'I can manage five-thirty, unless you'd like me to cancel appointments.'

'Five-thirty's fine. Thanks, Josh. Are you all right?'

'Very well.'

They said goodbye.

He took a deep breath and rang his sister.

Mandy began badly.

'Heavens, Willo, is it really you? I thought you were still snoring your head off at this hour of the morning. Or perhaps you're phoning from London – what it is not to have to count the pennies!'

'I'm at The Court, Mandy.'

'Are you on holiday then?'

'No. No – how's Desirée? Are you still in quarantine?'

'Desirée's mending – and about time. Theo's not too grand – but we're hoping it isn't mumps. We may be in quarantine – I don't bother any more – and who's to object? Why ask? Nothing's wrong, is it?'

'Can we meet?'

'What? Yes, I've no objections. You sound like the Secret Service. What's going on?'

'How are you placed now?'

'I can't manage that! I've an invalid and a family to look after. And I've shopping to do in Tetbury. You're forgetting how the other half lives.'

'Mandy, call in here at twelve, will you? I want to tell you something that I don't want you to hear from anyone else.'

'Oh all right – but it's going to be a frightful rush for me – and I hope it's not a wild goose chase, Willo.'

'That'll be for you to judge. Goodbye.'

When Willo had recovered from this typical exchange with Mandy, which would have justified his daughters' comparison of a conversation with their aunt to Grievous Bodily Harm, he left the house and walked round the garden searching for Denis.

The weather was raw. Billowing grey cloud scudded across the sky in front of a northerly wind. Apart from snowdrops shivering under trees and hedges, the garden was flowerless and seemed to be planted with nothing but short brown sticks.

'Morning, Mr Todd.' Denis hailed him. He had been hoeing a flower-bed, and now stopped, holding and leaning against the long-handled hoe, and said in his jovial voice: 'At this time of year you can't tell what's under the ground and what'll stay there.'

Willo asked: 'Have you got a moment, Denis?'

'I have.'

They moved together into the lee of some shrubbery. Denis wore his tweed hat, short waterproof coat, tweed trousers and gumboots, and Willo was sorry not to be wearing warmer clothes.

'I've had bad news,' he began. 'To cut a long story short, I've lost a lot of money and can't go on living here.'

Denis commented in his slow humorous way, putting equal emphasis on each word: 'Oh dear!' He then laughed as if refusing to take the information too seriously.

'I'll have to sell up, I'm afraid.'

'I expect you will,' Denis agreed.

'I'll pay your wages while I can, of course.'

'That's good of you.'

'About your cottage,' Willo continued, shivering.

'I was wondering about my cottage.'

'It'll have to go in with the sale of The Court. I'm hoping somebody will buy the house and the cottages. Whoever does buy the place is going to need a gardener. But I can't give any guarantees at this stage – I would if I could – the situation's out of my hands – nothing belongs to me any more. I'm sorry, Denis.'

'I'm sorry too, I'm sure. Who does your house belong to, may I ask?'

'Lloyd's of London, the insurance people – I was involved in the insurance market, which is now in bad shape – it's difficult to explain.'

'I see,' Denis said, probably meaning that he saw nothing.

Willo resumed in conclusive accents: 'I'll keep you informed of developments, and please believe that I'll do all I can to safeguard your future. Think over what I've told you and come back to me with any questions. I'll have to leave you – I'm so damn cold, and I've such a lot to see to. We'll talk on other days. Goodbye for the present.'

'Bye-bye, Mr Todd.'

Willo retreated into the house via the back door. It had not been as bad as he expected; but what did those noncommittal comments signify? Was Denis sizzling inwardly with radical resentment, or filled with compassion, or simply stunned? Willo's conscience smote him from a different angle: why had he aired such misleading sentiments at the end? He could do nothing for Denis, that was the truth, taking into consideration the prior claims of family and the shortage of resources. A fib that might have raised hopes would now have to be retracted.

Sounds emanating from the kitchen replaced one worry with another. He looked in: Peggy Sparks was seated at the kitchen table in an attitude of distress, while Barbara stood by her, administering comfort by means of an occasional squeamish pat on the back.

'What on earth's the matter?' he asked.

Peggy raised her head and blubbered at him reproachfully: 'Oh sir!' Her purple face with red hair sticking out in all directions seemed literally to be a mop of tears. She cried as violently as she conversed.

Willo took the point and confirmed it by saying to Barbara: 'You've spilled the beans, I suppose?'

Peggy wailed again: 'Oh what will become of us?'

He said to her: 'I'm hoping we'll be all right, but I can't guarantee anything.'

Peggy was far from satisfied with this accurate statement.

'All right for some it may be – but I'm thinking of the years I've worked hard for Mrs Todd – only to be thrown out of my home and denied my livelihood – oh it is cruel – I never would have expected it of you, sir!'

Willo controlled his impulse to correct the errors in the above: that he rather than his wife paid Peggy's wage, that she had never worked hard, that she had other money coming in, not least by diddling the Social Security system, and that she had always appeared to expect him to behave cruelly.

'Steady on, Peg!' he ordered her. 'It's premature – you're crying before you've been hit – nothing's settled yet!'

And he trotted out the possibility that she would be employed by the new owners of The Court.

'Oh yes – they'll be after my cottage if I won't work for them,' Peggy prophesied. 'It'll be the death of me – it will, sir – so there!'

Barbara intervened, addressing Willo on the subject of Peggy's inclination to blame him: 'I've explained that none of it's your fault.'

'Obviously,' he retorted with loud sarcasm.

Peggy uttered a little extra shriek, as if to warn that he was about to batter either his wife or herself.

'Oh for God's sake!' he exclaimed, he shouted, and strode off and along the passage to his study.

For the next half an hour he tried first to justify his loss of temper, then by means of deep breathing to regulate the thumping of his heart and soothe his sense of being badly treated by everyone, after which he began to regret his outburst and finally braced himself to go and apologise to Peggy. He found her snivelling in the airing cupboard upstairs and sought to persuade her that he was not opting to become a pauper specifically to do her down.

She ended by saying she was sorry too, but no doubt meaning sorry for herself and that he had proved conclusively he was a typical man, untrustworthy and selfish.

He retreated to his study and forced himself to make two more telephone calls.

The first cut both ways. He was relieved to find that Arnold Waters had been fully informed by Desmond Simcox, therefore Willo did not have to recapitulate the whole sad Lloyd's story. On the other hand Arnold had also been convinced that Desmond was right and Willo, in a financial sense, was done for.

For another reason this conversation was unsatisfactory from Willo's point of view, since he had to spend nearly all of it consoling his accountant, assuring him he was in no way at fault, promising not to sue him for negligence, and begging him not to worry.

Eventually he was able to ring Harold Beever, his childhood friend, who now ran an estate agency in Tetbury.

Harold came on the line, saying: 'Willo – how are you – what can I do for you?'

'I want you to sell The Court, Harold.'

'Good grief! Why's that? Are you in trouble, or shouldn't I ask?'

'It's Lloyd's.'

'Oh my dear man, say no more. My heart bleeds for you, although you probably wouldn't believe it if you knew how much extra business has landed on my desk courtesy of Lloyd's. How badly are you hit?'

'It couldn't be worse.'

'Poor chap! You know I'll do my very best for you. What's the time scale?'

'I need the money by June.'

'That's tight. Let's hope and pray we're not heading for a forced sale. We'd better get a move on. When shall we start the ball rolling?'

Willo asked him over on the day after tomorrow, on the Saturday morning, and Harold said he would bring with him someone to measure and someone else to take photographs.

He then prepared for the interview with Mandy.

She was late, flustered, had forgotten to lock the doors of her veteran Volvo Estate which was full of shopping bags, had to return to the roadway to secure

[92]

her property, failed to make the key turn in the rusty rear door of the car, complained to and of her brother when he opined that it did not matter, eventually and unwillingly took his advice, re-entered the house and allowed herself to be propelled into the study.

She immediately spotted her own childish portrait of their father with Snipe.

'I'm glad you haven't chucked it out,' she remarked, peering at it. 'I wouldn't mind having it at Shoe House – it's a nice reminder of Daddy, though I say so myself – and there's Snipe, who I just loved to death; but I like to keep this room as it was in the old days – with nothing altered – it brings back memories!'

'Sit down, Mandy.'

'What is this silly mystery? You know I've only got half a minute – I've hungry mouths to feed.'

'Please sit down.'

'Oh all right.'

'I can't think of a good way to say what I have to say.'

'Are you deliberately trying to make me nervous, Willo?'

'Of course not! I'm trying to tell you my money's gone west.'

'I don't believe you.'

'Yes!'

'You've lost it?'

'Yes.'

'That'll teach you to scold me for losing mine.'

'I've never scolded you, and I didn't entrust my money to a crook.'

'How then – not gambling?'

'Investing.'

'It comes to the same thing.'

'It does not. I invested in the same business that Father invested in. I invested for safety.'

'In Lloyd's?'

'Yes.'

'How much have you lost?'

'There'll be nothing left.'

'No! How are you going to live?'

'Ask me another.'

'You can't live at The Court on nothing.'

'Exactly.'

'What?'

'I can't live here.'

'What do you mean? Where are you going to live?'

'I've no idea.'

'Stop it, Willo – you're so dashed calm you're confusing me – is it possible in this day and age to be rolling in money at one moment and stony broke the next?'

'I wasn't ever rolling in money, Mandy.'

'You seemed to be. How much money did you inherit?'

'That's beside the point.'

'It may be for you, but I never agreed with you having the lion's share.'

'Oh Mandy, please!'

'You must have had getting on for a million.'

'Don't be funny! We've been through all this before – and it's not relevant now. You've no reason to be jealous any longer.'

'Jealous? I'm not jealous. I'm talking about justice – if only poetic justice in the circumstances.'

'Okay! I inherited enough money from Grandpapa and Grandma to become a Name at Lloyd's – I followed in Father's footsteps and was doing his bidding – and when he and Mama died I got a bit more and added it to my Lloyd's funds. I bet you inherited as much or damn nearly.'

'Out of which I had to buy a roof over our heads. And my husband was penniless, whereas you've had at least one wife with independent means. And I've three times as many children as your two. No, Willo, it's no joking matter.'

'You could say that again about my situation. But I will not take the blame for your children.'

'No – sorry – I am sorry if you're really on your uppers – but my consolation always has been that you were keeping up family traditions at The Court, running it in the style we were accustomed to and setting an example to my kids and everybody – and now you seem to have squandered the family fortune – and it's one more trouble, it's the straw that breaks the camel's back, it is – and I'm as sick as hell!'

'Mandy – you're the second person I've reduced to tears this morning – which is odd, considering I think I'm the one who has the reason to cry.'

'Give me your handkerchief. Who was the first person?'

'Peggy Sparks. She took the view that I was going bust on purpose to spite her.'

'Have you given her the sack? And what are you doing about Denis?'

'I haven't sacked either of them. But I can't afford to pay their wages. I can't afford to breathe, so far as I can see. With luck, the new owner of The Court will employ them.'

'I hate to hear you say that!'

'The Court's bricks and mortar, nothing more – don't rub my nose in its sentimental value – I'm not seeing Harold Beever on Saturday morning for fun.'

'Have you spoken to Barbara?'

'Yes.'

'How has she reacted?'

'Better than you.'

'Oh you're tough, Willo – you can be so tough!'

'And you can be unfair.'

'What about Melanie and Prue? The Court's their inheritance – I shouldn't wonder if Melanie's been counting her chickens – she won't be best pleased to hear they're never going to hatch.'

'I'm seeing Melanie tomorrow, and Prue at the weekend. Mandy, promise me you won't talk to my girls before I have!'

'Of course I won't.'

'Of course you would if you had half a chance.'

'Thanks! All right, I promise. So what's your position exactly?'

'My debt to Lloyd's amounts to more than my resources. I have to pay over the money – or everything I'm worth – by next June. All that does not belong to Lloyd's is a few thousand pounds in my bank at present, and a handful of trinkets.'

'How many thousands of pounds are a few?'

'I can't help you with cash, Mandy, if that's what you're thinking – I've too many obligations, and almost legal ones – and I must hang on to the wherewithal to enable us to eat.'

'Oh come on, Willo – you haven't mentioned your earnings or your flat in London – it won't wash, your pleading poverty to me of all people!'

'I'm going up to London next week to try to sell the tail-end of the lease of my flat. Whatever money that brings in belongs to Lloyd's. And my job doesn't exist any more – I'm unemployed from now on.'

'Has Anthony Haden kicked you while you're down? I wouldn't put it past him.'

[95]

'No one's to blame. I've told you the whole truth and nothing but. I am, or shortly will be, poorer than you are.'

'You'll get another job in publishing.'

'At my age? Besides, my sort of publishing would be regarded by other publishers as a hobby – and they wouldn't be far wrong.'

'Well – you've Barbara's money.'

'That's a contradiction in terms.'

'Won't Barbara come to the rescue?'

'The short answer's no.'

'She hasn't offered to?'

'I haven't asked, and I'd refuse if she did offer.'

'Can nothing be done?'

'No.'

Mandy blew her nose comprehensively on her brother's handkerchief.

'Hell's bells and God alive!' she exclaimed in language surely not spoken by most parsons' wives, and justified herself irreverently: 'Well – He's done precious little for His servant Theo and the inmates of Shoe House, and now He seems to have picked on you. I am sorry, brother, but can't help feeling cross with you for losing our parents' money and our home.'

'I haven't lost the money you inherited – you lost that without any help from me. Anyway, not much has changed between us – you've been cross with me for years for not losing my inheritance.'

'Don't, Willo – my life's such a mess – don't make it worse than you already have.'

Mandy cried again, mopped up, and said she had to go, otherwise she would be in hot water for not getting lunch on the table by one o'clock.

'What are these trinkets you mentioned?' she inquired.

'The picture you painted of Daddy and Snipe, for instance – they're things not included in the valuation of the contents.'

'I'll take that picture – may I?'

'Go ahead, Mandy.'

She picked it off the wall, revealing a discoloured rectangle, and carried on: 'Will you list these trinkets so that we can share them out between us?'

'If you insist.'

'I do – I do think my children are entitled to souvenirs of their forefathers and the beautiful place we all lived in, just as your children are. Souvenirs are all they're getting, isn't that right?'

'Quite right.'

They moved into the hall and towards the front door.

'Where's Barbara?'

'I expect in the kitchen.'

'Poor woman, I pity her.'

'Goodbye, Mandy.'

'Goodbye, Will. Hard lines! I wonder what's the matter with us – why are we cursed?'

'Speak for yourself,' he laughed with difficulty.

She handed him his wet handkerchief, and landed an equally wet kiss on his cheek.

In the doorway, under the porch, she said: 'Oh – I forgot – I've probably given you mumps.'

Barbara merited Willo's gratitude not only for cooking luncheon on that Thursday, but also for not adding to his trials and tribulations.

Her single question and his answer perhaps disposed her to be tactful.

She asked: 'What was it like with Mandy?'

He replied: 'Awful – GBH with a vengeance, plus tears and pinching a picture and threatening to take a whole lot more and a final kiss with mumps thrown in for good measure.'

They ate almost in silence.

At some stage she tried to explain and excuse Peggy's hysterical behaviour. Then he told her he was calling on Josh Kemball and would be out to tea.

When the meal was finished she hurried upstairs to view an Open University programme, and he returned to his study and fell asleep in his desk chair without meaning to.

He woke from a bad dream with a start and a crick in his neck; decided he could not settle down to paperwork; nor could he again face Denis Willett, or be bothered with Tray; and at four o'clock he tiptoed from the house via the front door and, skirting the village by Stink Alley and Beech Coppice, walked through the deepening dusk the two miles to the hamlet of Measham and the vicarage there.

A light was on in the porch of the Edwardian house with driveway and garden alongside the Tetbury road. Willo rang the bell and opened the unlocked door. Josh emerged from the sitting-room and the two friends shook hands in the passage serving as a front hall.

Josh wore his uniform of grey flannels, tweed jacket and dog-collar. He and Willo were the same age and height, also had their service in the army in common, not to mention respect for each other. Their friendship had been revived by the coincidence of one becoming the other's parish priest.

Josh's sitting-room was a good example of making the best of a bad job, at least in Willo's opinion. An awkwardly shaped space with regrettable decorative features had been rendered cosy and amusing at the lowest possible cost. Unframed posters covered a multitude of sins committed with fancy plaster-work on some of the walls, while ranged against others were full bookshelves made of planks balanced on bricks. A lurid carpet was largely hidden by an assortment of chairs hard and soft, their faults redeemed by cushions and pieces of material thrown over them, also by tea-chests beautified by tablecloths. The modern tiled fireplace had had a coat of white emulsion, and the light fitting in the ceiling was used as a plug for the table lamps.

There were no curtains – Josh said he liked to see into the night and be seen. But on this particular January evening the golden glow of shaded electric light was welcoming, and the coal fire in the grate, and teapot and mugs and plate of buttered toast on a tray, lent extra force to the comfortable impression.

Josh poured out the tea and offered the toast, and they sat facing the fire, mugs in hand and munching, the host burly and heavy-headed, exuding receptivity, and his guest more slightly built and tenser.

Willo broached the subject of his finances.

Josh said how shattering, how difficult for everyone concerned, and how sorry he was, and wanted to know all the details.

When Willo had supplied them he thanked Josh for his sympathy, adding: 'Especially as I know you chose to give away your own money.'

'Oh but I don't expect anybody else to do what I did, or feel the same,' Josh replied. 'Besides, you're almost the only person in the world who knows what happened to my money, and you're meant to have forgotten.'

Willo laughed, apologised for remembering, and asked: 'What is your attitude to having money, accumulating it, and inherited wealth so-called, like mine is or was? The Bible, and religion in general, seem to disapprove.'

'I think not – and I personally don't disapprove in the slightest. Wanting to do better usually means wanting to make money and then to help your children, and that's human nature, which God's responsible for. Taking a strong line against self-improvement, success, money, wealth, capitalism if you like, strikes me as rebellion against our Maker and therefore heretical. Anyway it's doomed to failure – look at the record of socialism. Sorry for the sermon – I found it hard to preach to begin with, and now I've acquired the taste for it and can't stop.'

'Funnily enough,' Willo said, 'you preached about change on Christmas Day, and everything had already changed for me without my knowing it. I only got the letter telling me I was ruined when I returned to London.'

'How attached were you to your life as it was?'

'Mandy came to see me this morning – I had to put her in the picture. She didn't like it, she ranted and raged, and ended by saying that she and I were cursed. I didn't agree with her – considering my various advantages past and even present how could I? All the same, my life between leaving the army and up until last Christmas – my private life, that is – was a washout.'

'You didn't have the Christmas spirit, I recall.'

'What I'd accumulated mainly was a sense of pointlessness and futility.'

'Perhaps you'd contracted the disease of the man who has everything. It's called acedia, and monks catch it too, because their lives are repetitive and secure, or meant to be. Your life's taken a new turn with a vengeance – how are you bearing up?'

'Well – you can't feel futile while you're wondering how you're going to survive – the suicide rate in concentration camps is exceptionally low, isn't it? What's a bit extraordinary is that I would be excited if no one else was involved – I am quite excited, terror and guilt permitting.'

'The Bible would give you full marks for not loving your money and not hating to lose it. The Bible bangs on about the root of all evil being the love of money.'

'But I do hate to lose it, I hate having to tell people I've gone and lost it, I hate to disappoint and hurt them, and be blamed and blame myself, and I can't keep cool or my temper.'

'That's different.'

'And I'm scared stiff at moments. The change in store reminds me of being someone at school and becoming no one in the army.'

'You did well in the army, Willo.'

'This change is more sweeping than that one was, and I'm much older and more set in my ways.'

[99]

'Can I help? If I may ask such a hackneyed question, to what do I owe the pleasure of your company?'

'I'm not sure – to the pleasure of yours, and your toast and tea. No! I wanted to prepare you for the day when you'll probably find me crouching and cringing on your doorstep.'

'My home's always available.'

'Thanks – but I don't want to be like that loathsome prodigal son. Listen, can I have another shot at answering your last question? You know me of old – I've skated along on the surface, haven't I? Now I'm thrashing about in deep water. I could do with assistance. And although I never was religious, I keep on wondering if the Almighty might be interested. Sorry if I've said the wrong thing – but I'm not used to talking about your business – and you'll get my drift.'

'Have you asked Him?'

'What?'

'The Almighty isn't called the Almighty for nothing. You'll do better with His assistance than with mine. You should ask for it.'

'I'm embarrassed to – I can't abide foul weather friends, who only get in touch when they're in trouble and want you to do something for them.'

'Yes, but – but God may not share your opinion – He wouldn't be God if you could forecast and understand His reactions.'

'That's a thought.'

'Have the last piece of toast, Willo.'

Willo's refusal was the more grateful because Josh had brought the conversation down to earth. Although he was the grandson of a man of the cloth, God had become merely a mild expletive in his social circle; and to speak seriously of the deity in his experience was not done. He had not intended to bare his soul to Josh; he had bared it to no one else in all his born days; and he was relieved when the discretion of his friend allowed it to scuttle back into its hiding place.

'Incidentally,' he said, 'our old chum Desmond's in the same boat.'

They spoke of Desmond and revived a memory or two of their active military service during the Suez crisis of 1956.

The doorbell rang and somebody entered the house.

Josh left the room and Willo overheard the following exchange.

'Hullo, John, hullo Ellen – that's right, come along in, let me have your coats – how nice to see you – how are you both?'

A young man's voice with a Gloucestershire accent returned: 'Fine, thanks, Mr Kemball – yourself?'

'Fine, too. Would you mind waiting half a mo in here?'

Josh must have ushered the people into his dining-room. Then a door closed and he rejoined Willo, who had stood up preparatory to leaving.

'Don't go,' he said.

'I won't take any more of your time,' Willo countered.

'Time's my stock-in-trade, and if I've got it for John and Ellen – a young couple with a baby on the way making belated tracks to the altar – I've got very much more for you and always will have. Besides, there's something I've been meaning to say for weeks. You told me your Melanie, my god-daughter, was tired of marriage and possibly on the move. Are there any developments? Are you seeing her soon?'

'I'm seeing her tomorrow – and she's bound to give me an earful on every subject. Why?'

'I don't believe she'd be any happier in a second marriage, or in a third or fourth for that matter.'

'You're probably right.'

'Will you tell her from me that the devil she knows may be preferable?'

'I'll tell her you recommend the devil.'

They moved into the passage and towards the front door, laughing.

'How many more people's lives, marriages and deaths are you sorting out this evening?' Willo asked.

'I only listen and look.'

'Well, I feel the benefit of being listened to – thanks again, Josh – and I hope you feel the benefit of looking at me. Sorry if we all bore you to death.'

Josh conceded: 'You're more fun than the telly.'

That evening at The Court, relevant words were exchanged by Barbara and Willo Todd in the study round about seven-thirty.

She took an unwonted liberty by walking in and saying she had questions that needed answering.

'I'm probably interrupting, I know you've got a lot on your mind, but it makes life even more difficult if you lock yourself away,' she began force-fully.

Willo resisted the temptation to retort that she had locked herself away for most of their married life, whence its difficulties, and pacifically offered her a chair and a drink.

She refused both, and, standing in the doorway while he remained in his desk chair, brandished a handful of papers and demanded: 'What am I meant to do about these – invitations from the Ellerys to lunch at Waddington on Sunday week, and to drinks with the Murrays, and dinner on another day with the Stevensons?'

'I can't go anywhere now – I'd feel a fraud – what about you?'

'You know I hate stuffy social occasions. The last thing I've ever wanted is to become a paid-up member of the county set. I never had enough money not to feel a fraud with your friends.'

'Oh Barbara!' he exclaimed, pleading with her not to muddy the waters with her radical opinions.

'It's true,' she insisted.

'No,' he returned with loud exasperation and authority; 'it's the old old story of you wanting to have your cake and eat it – live like a lady and disapprove of ladies and gents at the same time. I'm having to resign my membership of what you call the county set, so you might as well resign yours of what I'd call the chippy brigade. Can't we say pax? Can't you? Yesterday evening I thought we had. Anyway, will you deal with the invitations or shall I?'

'Will you, please?'

She extended her hand holding the pieces of paper, which he took from her.

He had been surprised by her disinclination to argue the point, and her relatively meek request. He was more surprised by her saying in an unhappy tone of voice: 'I called in at the Building Society today.'

He looked up at her face, which was oddly contorted.

'I've got nineteen thousand pounds left,' she confessed.

He could not help smiling: her bad mood and her grimace were no doubt due to the tension of having discovered that she had at once too much money to suit her egalitarian notions and too little to support her life-style.

'Bad luck,' he said satirically. 'I sympathise with you for having more than me. For a moment you had me worried – I thought something serious was wrong.'

'What will nineteen thousand buy today?' she asked.

'We can discuss all that at a later stage. Meanwhile I'd love to know what's become of the rest of your capital – you had forty thousand after you sold the Studio and moved in with me – although it's no business of mine.'

'I've told you – I used my money instead of having to hold out my hand for yours.'

'Well – that was unselfish – and you probably imagined you were asserting your independence – but if you'll forgive me for calling a spade a bloody shovel you've missed the gravy train.'

'Oh don't talk like that! I loathe and detest money – and discussing it.'

'I'm sorry to have to tell you that we're similar in that respect, Barbara. We didn't respect money, and now it's getting its own back.'

'What a ridiculous idea! But I'm obviously boring you, Willo – there's not much similarity between us considering I tried to sympathise with you for being hard up and you laugh at me for finding out how badly off I am. Besides, I've dinner to cook for you.'

'Oh God,' he groaned as she departed huffily. And he called after her: 'I'll help you as soon and as much as I can. And I'll come and get myself a sandwich later on.'

Notwithstanding his last offer or peace offering, she cooked him a cutlet and vegetables with martyred obduracy, and added a bad flavour to his meal by making hers of a morsel of cheese and a lettuce leaf. Their talk consisted of polite nothings, they avoided each other's eyes, and parted for the night immediately after eating, she to watch the news upstairs, he to refuse invitations in his study.

The next morning he rewrote one formal refusal thus: 'Dear Mrs Ellery, Thank you very much for asking us to lunch. Unfortunately my circumstances are about to undergo a dramatic change owing to my Membership of Lloyd's. As a result I regret to say I am unable to accept, and must also tell you that we are leaving Tollworth and probably this neighbourhood. It has been such a pleasure to visit you at Waddington. I have known the house ever since I was a boy and always thought it was one of the nicest possible places. So glad it's in good hands again, and I do hope you'll be happy there. Yours sincerely, Willoughby Todd.'

When he had copied out this missive, and fretted and paced floors for an hour or two, he prepared to leave for his lunch with Melanie.

Barbara relented to the extent of wishing him luck.

He replied that he was sure he would need it.

He arrived at The Fox at Tockingham before his daughter. The various bars of the original coaching inn, at least the saloon, public and snug bars remembered by Willo, had been unified into a rambling classless open-plan space on

[103]

different levels. Dark corners abounded, and light music droned. A small number of customers, obviously well-heeled and probably regular, huddled together on bar stools, while two paunchy artisans downed pints of bitter and ate something with chips at a distant table.

Melanie swept in at ten past one, tossing back her pretty dark hair and brandishing car keys. In due course Willo ordered for her scampi and a vodka and tonic, and for himself a cheddar ploughman's with a half of mild and bitter, and they sat at a table as far away from everybody else as possible.

She immediately wanted to know what was up. He had to tell her before the food had arrived.

The result was predictable. She burst into tears, she was soon crying all over her scampi, and she blubbered the following confession, which partially accounted for her grief: 'I always banked on living at The Court.'

He tried to minimise her loss and disappointment: 'If you had inherited the house, your sister would have inherited every available penny I used to possess. Doling out fair shares to you and to Prue would have meant, more than likely, that you wouldn't have been able to afford it.'

Melanie did not fail to raise objections to her father's reasoning: 'But I'm your elder child – I don't see why Prue should ever have the same as me. And how do you know I wouldn't have been better off when the time came?'

To stop her weaving comfortless fantasies based upon his death, he said: 'I thought of contributing two hundred and fifty pounds to the cost of the operation on William's tonsils.'

'It'll cost far more than that,' she sobbed.

'I'm sorry.'

'It's no good, Dad.'

'We're being stared at,' he said repressively.

'What the hell!' But she did ask for his handkerchief, and then observed with a trace of her teasing humour: 'They'll think you're being cruel to me, and they'd have a point.'

But he could not laugh, he rebelled against being in the wrong, and said, keeping his voice as quiet as he could: 'Are you accepting the money for William or aren't you? If that's all you care about, let's clinch the deal and call it a day.'

Her bluff was called, she was duly taken aback, apologised, wiped her eyes and began to talk more reasonably. She thanked him for the hand-out and regretted the fact that it was probably the last.

[104]

He replied: 'I'm not hanging on to any money for myself. Honestly! There's too little to make much difference to me, or to anyone else for that matter, because lots of people have rights and claims.'

'Where will you live, Dad?'

'Ask me another! Both the cottages are for sale.'

'Beggar's Roost isn't.'

'No – but Mrs Twill's in residence.'

'The Grayvener trustees would chuck out the Twills if you asked them to. Who are the trustees now?'

'Arnold Waters and a partner in his firm called Byburn. But I'm not chucking anyone out of anywhere, least of all a family retainer of ninety and her nitwit of a daughter – the ghost of Mr Grayvener would probably haunt me, always supposing I was able to dislodge Mrs Twill.'

'You're too soft, Dad.'

'Your aunt Mandy says I'm too tough. Actually I'm neither as soft nor as tough as you two seem to think – Beggar's Roost has no indoors sanitation and one bedroom.'

'You mean you wouldn't want to share it with Barbara?'

'Or vice versa.'

'So what will you do?'

'We'll see.'

'Poor you!'

'You've said it.'

'Is Prue in the know?'

'Not yet.'

'She'll rush to the rescue.'

'Maybe.'

'Oh Dad, I couldn't stand it if Prue had you all to herself.'

'Don't worry – I'm not asking to be rescued – but you could spare me your jealousy of your sister.'

'I hate her being so good – it makes me look bad.'

'You have everything compared with what she has, and the more you have the more jealous you are of Prue. It was always silly, and becomes sillier with every day that passes – and that's my final word on the subject.'

'I don't want a lot of what I've got.'

'Well – Prue wouldn't mind being married to the man she loves and having two healthy children. What you look to me is not bad, just spoilt.'

Melanie's mouth turned down at the corners.

'Now you are being cruel,' she accused.

'Not at all,' he corrected her; 'but I no longer have the money to buy time and waste it by beating about the bush. I can see why poor folk are more outspoken and blunt than rich ones. What are you crying for – why are you crying when I'm not?'

She tried to justify herself: 'My dream was that I'd live in the Court one day, it'd be mine, and I'd hand it on to my boys, or at any rate to William.'

'Did Edgar feature in your dream?'

'No.'

'You'll have to begin to count your present blessings – I mean the roof of Sprocketts over your head and a nice husband and breadwinner under it.'

'My life's such a struggle.'

'Join the human race! Whose isn't? And remember, from now on, I have every excuse not to listen to your grousing any more. I'll write you your cheque.'

While he was doing so she volunteered in a small voice: 'Are you sure you can, Dad?'

'Thanks for that kind thought – it was worth waiting for. Yes, darling, I can and I have.'

She kissed him for it, and asked: 'What about Barbara?'

'What indeed!'

'Has she been nasty to you?'

'Not particularly – no, it's the other way round, I'm afraid – we're working on our future.'

'Is Byle the Vile pressing his suit?'

'Time will tell – I don't know – and it can't be helped. I must contact your mother and give her my glad tidings. Oh – and I had tea with your godfather yesterday – he sent you his love and best regards to Edgar.'

She made a dismissive gesture.

He added: 'Please tell Edgar from me that his wife can't continue to believe the grass is greener at Tollworth, I've accidentally disinherited her, and she's going to have to make do with his worldly goods.'

'Oh Dad,' she scolded him indulgently.

They sat on in The Fox until three o'clock. He was quite pleased with his daughter in the end, he somehow converted plaintiveness into her fugitive

charm and vaguely anguished high spirits, although he was as usual embarrassed by the closeness of her embrace in the car park.

He waved her away, climbed into the Merc, and was overcome by a power-
ful unwillingness to go home. Rather than subject his nervous system to more
matrimonial discord and the dilemmas awaiting him in his study, he drove to
Tollworth by a widely circuitous route. The light faded in the lanes strewn with
cowpats, along which as a boy he had ridden on his grey pony Moonshine
beside his father on Man-of-war. He passed through villages where lights were
being switched on and curtains drawn: in this one had lived the first girl he
loved, Caroline Lord, who was then a precocious fourteen-year-old and two
years younger than he was; that one boasted the tennis court where Caroline in
her seductive short white skirt had played with him and their friends through
the sunshine and laughter of summer afternoons. Could he altogether turn his
back on the territory and the hopes and illusions of his past?

He arrived at The Court at six and found a note on the floor outside his study.
It ran: 'I have an invitation to dine out. Trust you won't mind. I've left cold ham
and salad in the fridge. Don't wait up for me. B.' Barbara must have been as loath
to spend another evening with him as he was with her, he deduced.

But he was more relieved than offended. The paradox crossed his mind that
they were being drawn closer by their reciprocal desires to avoid each other. He
obediently ate his ham while trying in vain to find something worth watching
on the telly, and took refuge upstairs in his dressing-room early.

He did not hear his wife come in: a sort of exhaustion had the effect of an
anaesthetic, at least until about four in the morning. He postponed getting up
until seven, and was down in the kitchen half an hour later.

Barbara was already preparing breakfast. Her unexpected presence, her
unwonted smiles immediately aroused suspicion. But he was ashamed of it; he
should and he would not repulse any conciliatory move; he must not dread the
explanation of her altered demeanour; nor let novelty have an inhibiting effect.

He ate the breakfast she laid before him.

'I've been thinking,' she said hesitantly as she opened and shut drawers and
wiped down surfaces: 'We shan't be at The Court much longer — I'd like to
make the most of it. I am fond of the house, setting aside the difficulties we've
had here, forgetting all that, and I don't want to spoil our last few months,
regretting things that have happened and haven't happened, and worrying.
Willo — sorry — I won't add to your problems — that's a promise or at least my
intention.'

[107]

He returned, laughing off their embarrassment: 'It's mutual – I'll do my best too – but can't we start by putting a ban on being sorry?'

She agreed, and he excused himself in order to prepare for the visit of the estate agent Harold Beever.

In his study, while he fished out title-deeds and Land Register plans, he pondered Barbara's sentiments. It could be that she was coming to half-hearted terms with her husband because she counted on going to her lover full-time in the near future. What had she meant by 'our last few months'? But he preferred not to be sceptical and cynical. He resolved with gratitude to believe in her sincerity.

He was interrupted by a heavy knock on his door.

It was Denis Willett, saying in stentorian tones: 'Mr Todd, ought I to be looking for work elsewhere?'

Willo had to spend half an hour persuading Denis that he had sufficient funds to pay a horticultural wage in the meanwhile, that he had not given his gardener a cowardly push by pleading poverty, that he greatly valued Denis' services over the years and respected his craftsmanship, the first and last lesson of which surely was to continue to cultivate flowers and vegetables and await developments.

Denis withdrew, bawling a happier 'Bye-bye', and Harold Beever arrived with a likely lad to assist with the measuring.

Then Prue's Mini parked by the garden gate.

Willo escaped from the house and joined her out in the village street as she began to unload plastic bags.

They hugged each other, and he said: 'Walk with me for five minutes, will you, darling?'

'What is it, Dad?'

'I'll tell you.'

'I've brought shopping for Barbara.'

'It can wait.'

'All right – I'll lock the car.'

She realised it was a crisis – he never could keep secrets from her – and concern caused her countenance to blush a darker red. She gazed up at him anxiously through her spectacles and linked her arm in his to console and encourage.

He guided her towards Stink Alley.

Her responses to his news were to keep on saying 'Oh Daddy!' in assorted tones of distress and sympathy, and to squeeze his arm ever tighter.

He had to break it to her so abruptly, he explained, because of the estate agent already in the house.

'When did you know?' she asked.

'Only a few days ago definitely – so much has happened that I can't quite remember – Wednesday, I think it was. The money has to be ready by June, that's why I had to start selling the house in a hurry.'

'How are you?'

Her voice trembled tearfully.

'I'm not too bad – but how are you going to be?' he returned, looking sideways at her but not seeing more than her downcast profile.

'Oh me! You helped me to buy my flat and I earn my living and I've never needed much or anything.'

As they turned for home he said: 'I've done so badly, I've let everyone down, and disappointed them – perhaps not you, darling, but Melanie and the people who work for us – and others. I suppose that losing all my money is fair enough, because I was like you, not keen on it, not interested – and I should have been interested, and thought about money as seriously as the people did who once earned it by the sweat of their brows. One lives and learns – somebody said it to me the other day – but there ought to be a couple more words tacked on to that phrase – the words "too late". One lives and learns too late.'

'Don't, Daddy,' Prue urged.

'Oh I'm all right,' he quickly reassured her. 'And I will be all right somehow. You're so kind and tolerant you bring out the worst in me. I don't pity myself much – strange to relate, my symptoms include a peculiar sort of relief – but it's indescribable and certainly unreasonable. Sorry, sweetheart – I haven't even asked what's been happening to you.'

'Nothing,' she replied with a little choking laugh; 'Nothing, as usual. Daddy, I must have time to think it over and get used to our new situation.'

'Of course, darling.'

'I want to help as much as I can.'

'You can't help – but I knew you'd want to.'

'What a shock – I mean for you most of all.'

'Yes, but – it didn't ought to be – isn't there a Chinese proverb, which says that wisdom consists in not believing one's investments are secure?'

They both laughed ruefully.

She gave his arm a long last squeeze, and they reached The Court, where Harold Beever was waiting to claim the attention of Willo.

An hour and a half later Willo joined Barbara and Prue in the kitchen. His wife's glance was apprehensive, his daughter's smile tentative: they must have expected him to be in a bad temper, or to have succumbed to despair.

He said: 'Things could be worse – we're still alive – and there's a nice lunch coming up – I can smell roast chicken. I'll fetch a drop of wine – we can drown our sorrows.'

They all laughed. He walked along to the dining-room and was taking a bottle of white wine out of the old mahogany wine-cooler when the telephone rang. He let Barbara answer it and set about uncorking the bottle.

'Willo!'

Barbara was calling him.

'I'm coming!'

'It's a woman from London.'

For a moment he wondered if it could be – and hoped it was – Mary Cole.

Barbara called along the passage: 'Who is she? Why did she ask me if you were all right?'

Oh no, he thought.

He called back: 'I'll speak in my study.'

It was Gloria, who exclaimed as he lifted the receiver: 'Darling!'

He shouted at her: 'Don't talk yet!' – and then even louder through the half-open door: 'Hang up, please!' He heard the overdue click of the kitchen telephone being replaced.

Gloria was saying she had had an awful letter from him – she had heard nothing for days, he had disappeared – and then she got this awful letter, which made her think he might be going to commit suicide or something – and she could not, and could not be expected to, stop herself ringing up to see if he was alive or dead.

He calmed her down as best he could, trotted out apologies, ran though the rigmarole of his financial crisis, fixed a meeting with her in forty-eight hours time, on the following Monday, and hastily bade her goodbye.

He hurried to the kitchen, sweating and anticipating trouble.

Barbara was gone, retired hurt, he guessed, hurt and angry as only the pot can be with the kettle, and Prue sat at the table, bowed over with her head resting on her arms, shaking with sobs.

'Prue, my darling, don't upset yourself – what's wrong? That call wasn't and isn't important – truly! Please don't cry!'

'It's nothing, take no notice, it's not your fault, Daddy,' she sobbed. 'But having no home makes nonsense of everything for me.'

Friends

THE rest of that day, that weekend, the next weeks – all were varying shades of black for Willo Todd.

Reality caught up with him in the shape of his vulnerable Prue. Her sobbing sentence in the kitchen of The Court seemed to pierce his heart: she meant that her life, her adulterous love affair with that rotter John Seward, her work with others' children, her so-called independence and her solitariness, had only been rendered bearable by her visits to The Court, by getting away from all her difficulties, escaping into an older safer world and seeking the solace of the affection of her father, who was now, as it were, casting her off and locking the door of her home against her.

She said, she promised him, that she did not mean it, she was not accusing him of anything – far from it – how could she?

But he took the point that he was no longer protecting her spinsterhood, her thirty years of age, or, to put it another way, had inadvertently breached her defences and exposed her to panic and defeat, while burdening himself with another load of guilt.

The practical consequence was difficulty of communication. He could not tell her that her tears had made him more miserable than anything else; she could not tell him that he had provided the element of security missing from her adulterous attachment, that he and The Court between them had rendered her love of John Seward possible and prolonged even though he was against it, and that she would probably have to renounce her lover, lose John, and be left with nothing except a cruel consciousness of having wasted her youth. They understood each other – that was the problem – and shyness exacerbated it.

[111]

On successive Friday evenings, Saturdays and Sundays they both tried to touch hands, metaphysically speaking, across the abyss that had opened between them.

He invited her into his study or suggested a walk, and she would agree with a contradictory hesitant eagerness.

Their exchanges were sadly abbreviated.

He would ask: 'How are you, darling?'

'Very well, Daddy, thanks. But how are you?'

He even broached the subject of John.

'Is he being good to you?'

'He does his best – it's not easy for him, you know.'

'Will you and he ever get together on a stable basis?'

'I don't know.'

'Would you like to bring him here? You never have – and perhaps you'd like to show him The Court before we leave?'

'No, Daddy, thanks.' And her eyes sparkled suspiciously behind her specs, and she changed the subject: 'Is Mr Beever beavering away? Has he found a buyer yet?'

Once he said: 'I'm afraid you most of all are going to miss The Court.'

'Yes,' she replied with a catch in her voice.

Then they chorused their over-worked apologies and disclaimers: he had not intended to sadden her, she had not intended to bother him with her sentimentality.

On another occasion on a walk he inquired: 'How are you getting on with your kindergarten children?'

'Not badly – they're adorable,' she replied, adding after a pause the observation, inconsequential although perhaps connected, and a trifle hostile: 'You never approved of John, did you, Daddy?'

He denied it – he had not met the man – and she was free to choose her friends – and so on.

'But how could you approve?' she insisted. 'Mother says she hates him and she hasn't met him either. She says he's exactly the opposite of what Mrs Bennet in *Pride and Prejudice* was looking for.'

He laughed – he did not dare continue this dangerous conversation – which ended with her declaring that not he, but she herself, had let everyone down, since she had no husband and no offspring of her own.

She refused to be comforted. Words of comfort were shaken off like water from a duck's back. She put on a show of imperviousness.

One weekend she volunteered what passed for an explanation of her distressful state of mind: 'I'm not seeing so much of John.'

His response was a cautious 'Oh?'

'I'm not seeing anyone else,' she continued hastily; 'no chance of that!'

Willo might have concluded that the brighter side or side-effect of his failure was the potential success of rescuing Prue from a relationship which was wrecking her life. Instead, just as he had worried lest her monogamous temperament would bind her to John Seward for ever and a day, so he began to be afraid she would finish with John and never be able to start with another man. What he saw was that he could be transferring her from John's frying-pan into a fire of his own fatherly making. Her 'No chance of that' was a gentle threat inasmuch as it hinted at permanent celibacy.

They might have done better if he had had fewer other worries and more time to spare; if she had not established a connection between his catastrophe and hers; if he had been the type to disregard restraints and demand to be let in on her secrets; above all, if they had not been father and daughter.

As it was, a month after he had found her crying with her head on the kitchen table she broke with the tradition and the habit of her weekends at The Court: she was too busy to come over, even for a meal. Seven days later, and seven days after that, it was the same story.

His heart grew heavier – what was she doing? What had he done to her? But the rest of him entertained involuntary and scarcely admissible feelings of relief.

He did not telephone. They never had telephoned much – they had met and talked at weekends. He heard nothing from her, and was secretly pleased to feel he was following her lead.

He had excusatory preoccupations and obligations.

Reverting to the telephone call that came through all too clearly on that critical morning at The Court, he needed to cope with Barbara. While his daughter sobbed inconsolably, he had to find his wife, if only for the sake of their Sunday lunch.

Barbara was in her bedroom, through the locked door of which they spoke as follows.

'Why are you in there, what's the matter?' he asked superfluously, knowing the answers.

'Go away!' she replied.

It was like a second-rate melodrama or a farce.

'Do stop it! Come downstairs at once!'

'No – I'm not talking to you – you've lied to me.'

'Please, Barbara – we're too old – and Prue's upset – I can't muck about – please come down – lunch will be ruined at this rate!'

Eventually she emerged, calling him a hypocrite; then over-cooked chicken was consumed in an indigestible atmosphere of tension; and Prue departed earlier than usual for Cirencester, saying she had always intended to and giving her father all sorts of apologetic assurances.

For the rest of the day Barbara rehearsed her grievances against Willo.

She challenged him to swear that the woman who called herself Gloria, omitting her surname like a common prostitute, was not his mistress. The conventional outrage of a wife discovering she has been deceived by her husband was reinforced by the possibility of getting her own back. For too long she had put up with being or being made to feel she was guilty, with Willo's careless complaisance, with covert mockery, and lack of evidence with which to rebut the subliminal charge of her selfishness. But the telephone rang. Her suspicions were confirmed: he was at least as selfish as she was, he was worse, more dishonest, and she would not forget or forgive him, she would repay with interest the unfair insults that had preceded the injuries now inflicted on her by the loss of his money.

She interrogated him thus: 'I'd like to have a word with Gloria – what's her surname? Do you pay her? How much? Is that where most of your money's gone? I was saving you expense and you were lashing out on Gloria, is that it? Did you laugh at me for half-believing you watched telly in the evenings in London? Did you and she laugh at me for trying to trust you? Were you together in Edgware Mansions? Does Mary Cole know? Does everybody know except me?'

It dragged on intermittently. He argued a point, or was dismissive, when he had the chance; but she paid no attention. He retreated into his study, he had a bath before supper; but she resumed where she had left off.

'Are you going to London tomorrow?'

'I must.'

'Why – for slap and tickle?'

'No – I must organise the sale of Edgware Mansions and so on.'

'So on's a nice euphemism. Why don't you stay in London with Gloria? I'm sure you'd prefer to be with her. Go on doing exactly as you please – and as you always have!'

'I'll be coming home in a day or two – with luck I'll have to show people round this house.'

'Why not leave that to me? I'll tell the people what an unhappy place it's been, and there's probably a curse on it.'

Under such pressure he referred more aggressively than defensively to Roger Byle: 'I thought Roger made you happy.'

But she would not have it that in an adulterous sense they were two of a kind.

'My private life's private, unlike yours,' she said. 'Roger's never bothered you, and I don't see why I should give you details of his friendship with me. You don't deny that Gloria's your mistress. I do deny that I shall satisfy your curiosity.'

In the context of adultery she remarked: 'Prue's obviously a chip off the old block – it's John Seward's wife that I'm sorry for.'

Willo finally rebelled and expostulated that he did not know what the fuss was about – what had she expected him to do for love? – talk about the dog in a manger! – and she was more than welcome to a divorce.

Her reaction was to snap and sneer at him: 'Divorce won't do me much good now.'

The revelation of the strength of her accumulated animosity was depressing. The idea that he seemed to have damaged everyone emotionally as well as financially kept him quieter than he might have been. He hated quarrels anyway, he was not a fighter. He pined for peace, armistice, sanctuary, a bolt-hole, to be somewhere and even someone else. He retired to bed in his dressing-room as soon as he was allowed to, and wished he was sleeping or failing to sleep there for the very last time. But how could he leave Barbara in her present frame of mind in sole charge of selling The Court? He also felt that for Prue's sake he could not desert his paternal post: which was ironical, or became so, in the light of her desertion.

On the Monday morning he left Tollworth before anybody was about, drove to London, reached his flat after he judged Mary would have left it, and returned Gloria's telephone call of the previous Sunday.

Her greeting was tempered with wariness.

'Hullo! Fancy hearing from you! Hold on a moment, will you, while I shut the door?'

He suspected she was just gaining time, but although annoyed he dredged up a flirtatious question when she returned to the telephone: 'Who's with you, may I ask?'

'Mr Nobody,' she replied, forcing a laugh. 'I promise. But I'm longing to know what's been happening to you, sweetie. Are you in one piece? Was it terrible of me to track you to your lair? I'm sorry – was it your Barbara I spoke to? She sounded a real acid-drop.'

'What did Barbara say? I'll give you my news in a minute.'

'She asked me where I was speaking from and what I wanted – you never told me she was such a jealous cat.'

'What did you say to her?'

'Nothing – I can't remember. I wasn't born yesterday, more's the pity. I may have said I was in London – no harm in that, was there? Did she make something of it?'

'Yes – she twigged – not that it matters.'

'Clever old her! She must be brighter than I imagined she was. Are you sure my fame hasn't spread to Tollworth?'

'Maybe – but I guess she jumped to the correct conclusion. She can think whatever she likes.'

'She won't do anything silly, will she?'

'Commit suicide, you mean? Never! Barbara has a nice young man to live for – a young man anyway.'

'No – actually I didn't mean suicide – I meant cite me in a divorce case – I wouldn't want to be cited, sweetie.'

'Don't worry – divorce is not on the cards for reasons I'll be giving you – not yet, that is. Listen, I'm hoping to see you this evening.'

Gloria hesitated.

'This evening, Willo?'

'I thought we fixed up to see each other this evening – on the telephone yesterday – have you forgotten?'

'No – but you were in such a hurry – I didn't take you seriously – can I peep in my diary? What did you have in mind?'

'I was expecting you to dine with me. Aren't you interested in the next chapter of the history of the house of Todd? But let's call it off – we'll meet some other time.'

'No, no – don't be cross – I'll be free from eight onwards. The fact of the matter is that I'm not sure how you stand – I was nervous of running you into a lot of expense. That's all. And I'm dying to hear how things are with you – of course I am – I said so to start with – and I rang you in the country because of your naughty worrying note – I've been really concerned.'

'Well, you needn't be any longer. Shall I call for you at eight?'

'I would offer you dinner in my place . . . '

He interrupted her – she always wriggled out of cooking for him: 'It's okay – eight o'clock!'

He had intended to look in at the office and to treat himself to lunch at the Bachelors Club. But his conversation with Gloria caused him to change his plans. She had been half-hearted, to say the least, and he had been touchy. And her quibbling had sapped a little more of his confidence: he cringed inwardly before the prospect of Anthony Haden's response to his letter of resignation, and then having to answer the awkward questions of friends and strangers. He mourned the withdrawal of the privilege of never being the economic under-dog. He had taken it for granted: he now seemed to have lost not only money but a skin or two, and to be too sensitive to expose himself to the outside world, or at any rate to the world he had previously considered his oyster. He was not sure that he had any real desire to be with Gloria again, doubtless preparatory to being without her, and he certainly should not be frittering still more money on another bad investment. He could definitely not face the duties he had meant to attend to, relative to selling his lease of the flat.

Later in the morning he sneaked or felt he was sneaking out of Edgware Mansions, bought a newspaper and some iron rations, returned, made a scratch meal, and fell asleep over his paper for most of the afternoon: he must have been tireder than he knew.

He then went for a long walk northwards in the twilight and soon in the dark, through Maida Vale and the poorer streets of Kilburn, an area where he had never set foot: he belonged there after all, and it preserved his anonymity.

At seven forty-five he drove south to fetch Gloria.

'Darling!' she said.

He explained that he had come by car because he was taking her to eat in Kensington, and they must hurry before it was towed away.

'Kensington,' she said without enthusiasm; 'how exciting!'

She fetched her bag and her coat. Her capped teeth reflected the electric light unnaturally, he noted. He had often wished she would use less lipstick and scent.

He checked himself: he was being unfair to her. It was as if he were insuring himself against the withdrawal of her favours by devaluing them.

In due course he parked the car in Queen's Gate, not far from the canopied entrance to a hotel called The Sandringham.

'Here we are,' he said.

'Goodness!' she exclaimed in accents of surprise and derision.

'The food's eatable and we can talk quietly,' he insisted.

They joined a small number of guests sitting at tables far apart in the spacious and ill-lit dining-room of the Sandringham Residential Hotel. An elderly waitress took their order, and a younger talkative one offered them a basketful of bread rolls.

'How on earth did you know about this place?' Gloria inquired, assuming a congratulatory tone.

Willo's reply was irrelevant. 'I'm sorry — the fact is I'm completely broke — I can't afford anything better — and I was determined to steer clear of people who might know us.'

'I'm not objecting, sweetie.'

'It's not what you're accustomed to, or I was in my palmy days. But I've been feeling so damned low — and I imagined it would suit the circumstances.'

'You're going too fast for me, Willo. How much trouble are you in? You've kept me in the dark, remember?'

He told her the tale, answering her questions with a brusqueness that derived partly from being sick of the subject, partly from awareness that she was more accustomed to pleading poverty than to being friends with anyone who pleaded it.

That she introduced touches of frivolity into his gloomy rigmarole, saying at one moment that she would kiss him better, and at another that he was probably bound for the Foreign Legion, annoyed him. And her routine expressions of sympathy, while her eyes roved around the room, were also unhelpful.

During their main course he broke off in mid-recital to demand: 'Can't we talk about something else?'

She looked momentarily startled, but was too used to dealing with men to argue the point.

'Shall I bring you up to date on the Jane and Dick saga?' she cajoled him, meaning the dramatically savage carnal relationship of her sister and brother-in-law.

He indicated assent. She regaled him with scandalous details. He was not so amused as he would have been in the old days, and was suddenly put off by her smuttiness and her practised manner of dealing with a bad male mood. He was not jealous; loving her only occasionally, as he did or he had, he never expected or claimed fidelity; rather, he was repelled by the latest proof of the width of her experience and by being treated like some lowest common denominator.

To add to his mounting discomfiture, he was nagged by the sense of his injustice, since he was now turning against the very character of their association for reasons connected with his own conduct, not necessarily with hers.

He pulled himself together and strove to be more agreeable. They left The Sandringham at ten o'clockish. Walking to the car, Gloria held his hand and said she was sorry he was so cut up.

'I'll be all right,' he replied.

'Of course you will, I know you will,' she humoured him as if he were a child.

Outside Avebury Flats he stopped the car without switching off the engine.

He stared through the windscreen and admitted: 'I'm afraid it hasn't been much fun – I'm not fit for human consumption for the time being.'

She now challenged him forcefully, although still with laughter in her voice: 'Are you saying goodbye, lovey?'

He turned the ignition key. Silence fell.

'I'm no good to man or beast at the moment,' he said. 'I've ruined our evening – I didn't think I would or mean to, but I have – I was pretty calm until a few days ago, but suddenly the truth's come down on me like a ton of bricks – I can't be good to you or for you for the foreseeable future – I won't even be able to get to London – no! And I realised ages ago that you wouldn't want me any more – when I first mentioned this Lloyd's business.'

After a pause for thought she excused and perhaps accused herself: 'I'm not so mad on money as you think.'

'Well – you probably appreciated before I did that I was going to have to drop out and become a different person. You've been lovely to me. But I'm no longer the man you were prepared to be lovely to.'

'Come in with me, sweetie.'

'No, don't tempt – and I'm too strained to be good to you in any way.'

'We could see about that.'

'No, Gloria.'

'There is such a thing as one for the road.'

[119]

'Not if you're driving.'

She laughed and he joined in a little more freely.

'I may feel better some day – but I can't promise,' he said.

'What about my feelings?'

'I'm trying not to involve you in my muddle. Be realistic – this evening should have proved that I've lost the knack of making you happy – I've lost that too – don't let me drag you down to my present and future level!'

'It's a blow,' she commented, not quite able to hit the tragic note. 'Will you get rid of your flat?'

'As soon as possible.'

'Can I reach you there in the next few days, or should I ring the office? I may know someone who'd buy your lease.'

'That's better, that's more like you,' he observed.

'Don't be nasty to me,' she countered with a hint of sauce.

He kissed her on the cheek, and sanctioned a gentle kiss on the lips, and said thank you for everything, and asked her to contact him without fail not only about the flat or if she heard of a decent job going begging, but also if she ever needed help he was capable of providing.

She laughed at him then, saying: 'I always need help – so watch out! No, don't worry, sweetie, I won't be bothering you. There – night-night – you're a good fellow – and they don't grow on trees – listen, it was nice while it lasted – remember that, and take care!'

He watched her walk across to the entrance of Avebury Flats, turn, wave and disappear through the door.

His regrets were erased by the reflection that he seemed to have tidied up one of the loose ends of his life.

His night's sleep was interrupted by looking forward or not looking forward to tidying up another.

But at eight in the morning Mary Cole failed to knock and enter his bedroom.

She was not in the flat, and her absence was so unusual as to be a new cause of anxiety. He had not told her, he never did tell her, he was coming to London; he understood that she looked in on pretty well every morning of the year; she must be ill, or involved in an accident. The thought did cross his mind that fate might be sparing him the ordeal of having to give her the sack; but he banished it.

He could do nothing for the moment: Mary and Biddy were not on the telephone. He shaved, washed and dressed, resolving to drive to Cricklewood and
investigate after breakfast if Mary had not clocked in by then. In the kitchen
he found a loaf of fairly fresh bread, indicating that she had put it there yesterday – Monday – morning: whatever had happened to her had happened in the
last twenty-four hours. He cut a slice and brewed himself a mug of tea – he was
too concerned to look for butter or milk – and was heading for the sitting-room
when he heard a key in the lock of the front door of the flat.

It was Mary.

'Where were you – how are you?' he asked.

'Morning, Capting – not a very bright one,' she replied with composure,
removing her gloves and her hat.

'I've been worried,' he said.

'Yes – you would have been, Capting – I was always strong on punctuality.'

'What was it, what kept you?'

Her answer was two mysterious syllables, spoken as if he should understand
them: 'Madam!' – and she divested herself of her overcoat. 'That's never your
breakfast, Capting?' she continued, directing her magnified gaze at the slice of
bread and the mug. 'You sit down and read your paper – here it is – and I'll
bring you your usual in a jiffy.'

'Madam who?' he said.

'Madam, our cat.'

'Oh that Madam!'

'She was taken poorly in the night.'

'I'm sorry.'

'So am I, Capting. Then Biddy went the same way, nurse though she used
to be.'

'Which way was that?'

'She was taken poorly too – she's that devoted to Madam – and I'm no
better than my sister.'

'Do you mean you're poorly as well?'

'No, Capting.' Mary laughed for some reason, possibly the idea that she
could be ill or would be deterred by illness. 'I'm as silly about Madam as Biddy
is. You go in there and I'll see to your breakfast now.'

'What's wrong with the cat, Mary?'

'She was trying to tell us in the night – she speaks with her eyes, you know

[121]

'– but we couldn't be sure what she said. This morning I was delayed by dropping Madam at the vet's and Biddy at the doctor's.'

'How bad is your sister?'

'It's her legs. I'll be five minutes, Capting.'

Willo obeyed orders and, while he glanced at the newspaper in the sitting-room, hardened his heart to the extent of deciding that he must reveal his troubles to Mary, although they would greatly add to hers.

She entered with his breakfast tray.

'Mary,' he began, 'I've fallen on hard times, my money's all gone west, and this flat's going in the same direction.'

'How's that, Capting?'

'It's difficult to explain. I shall be very hard up shortly, I'm having to sell The Court and the flat and literally everything I own – and I'm so sorry, I can't pay you any more, that's the long and short of it. I'm sorrier than I can say, especially when you're worried and seem to have had a sleepless night.'

She regarded him with huge brown eyes: perhaps, like Madam, she was trying in vain to speak with them.

'It's getting on for twenty-three years I've worked for you, Capting,' she said.

'Is it that long? I knew we were old friends. I'll do the best I can for you with the little money I'm left with, but I have many demands to meet, as I'm sure you realise.'

'I would never have expected to get my notice after twenty-three years. My sister Biddy – she won't believe it. We'll both be feeling the pinch.'

She appeared not to be flustered. Yet she had reason to show emotion, and her words were comparable to salt rubbed into his wounds. He wondered how many more of her reflections he could bear to listen to. Meanwhile his untasted scrambled egg congealed on the plate.

'It's not like giving you notice, Mary,' he protested. 'I've been impoverished by forces beyond my control – as a result I'm poor and can't pay anybody a wage – in fact I really don't know where my next meal's coming from – my London job's finished, and I've got no money coming in from anywhere until I take the dole or find other work.'

'Oh well, don't let your breakfast go to waste, Capting. It's a sad day for both of us – but could be for the best.'

'What do you mean?'

'I'll be having Madam to look after, and Biddy too, I shouldn't be surprised.'

'You mean you'll swap me for your cat?'

She did not see his joke.

'It wasn't only Madam and Biddy who kept me up last night,' she explained solemnly. 'I was thinking how could I fit in Edgware Mansions with visits to the vet and the doctor. I'd be late for you – I was this morning, wasn't I?'

'If you wanted to pack it in here, you'd make things much easier for me.'

'Yes – well – I'll have to be where I'm needed most – blood's thicker than water.'

Willo failed to repress a smile: was she bracketing her blood with the cat's?

'I've told you I can't pay you, Mary,' he said: 'almost every penny is ear-marked for my wife or my daughters or my sister – but I intended to offer you two hundred and fifty pounds, and I hope you'll accept it as a not very golden handshake.'

'Thank you, Capting – I'll accept with pleasure – that money will pay for our holiday in Bournemouth, health permitting. Shall we call this my last day then?'

'If it suits you.'

'Yes, Capting – and I'll just be doing your bedroom.'

He ate some of his breakfast and studied his Daily Telegraph; but he could not concentrate on stories less surprising than his own.

Half an hour later he presented her with the cheque, and they exchanged more thanks, then good wishes and a handshake – he was afraid that a kiss on her virginal cheek might be going too far. She gazed at him dry-eyed: he realised that he had been replaced by Madam in the kindly forefront of her mind.

In her outdoor clothes she popped her head round the sitting-room door to say 'Goodbye, Capting,' as she always had and as if she were coming in tomorrow.

'Goodbye, dear Mary,' he replied.

The telephone rang.

It was Desmond Simcox, who said: 'Have I caught you with your trousers down?'

Willo answered no, not exactly, gathering his wits as best he could after Mary's brisk yet convenient exit from his life, and asked for news with the rider 'especially if good'.

'No such luck,' Desmond replied. 'I've got an awkward query for you.'

'One more awkward query makes no difference – what is it?'

'I've been approached by your sister Amanda.'

'I can guess what about. But does she know you — do you know her? She's never been able to mind her own business.'

'She reminded me that we met years ago at Tollworth — it was before she married Wriggs — and I do have a vague recollection of a girl built on a grand scale.'

'Correct — grander now — she's the mother of six. What was she on about in particular?'

'Lloyd's — and your reluctance to stand up for your rights and fight your corner.'

'What did you say?'

'That you and I were going to honour our contractual liability, even though we'll both be ruined. She then advanced two arguments: she referred to the groupings of Names who are contemplating legal action against the Lloyd's establishment. I told her that you and I had neither the money to sue anyone, nor the inclination to drag through the courts people we had previously instructed to manage our affairs for better or worse.'

'What was her other argument? She has no right or reasonable claim to family money — my finances are nothing whatsoever to do with her, you realise that, don't you?'

'She said she was speaking up for your daughter Melanie.'

'Oh?'

'She said Melanie had asked her to speak.'

'Oh.'

'That's the awkward part.'

'Melanie counts her chickens before they're hatched. She's always imagined The Court as good as belonged to her. When she comes to visit us I get the idea that she's mentally re-hanging the pictures. I won't get it any longer — and she won't get my pictures or my home. But you haven't asked your question yet, Desmond.'

'Oh yes — Lloyd's may be organising a hardship fund — you and I could be eligible for a handout — though I don't see how the market can have much money to dispense, or that it can start dispensing it in time to help us. Would you be interested in details, if any exist?'

'Are you thinking of applying?'

'I haven't decided.'

'Well — confidentially — and you're never to breathe a word to Melanie or Mandy of what I'm going to say — I've somehow got beyond the point of rescue

– my life up to now seems to be over and done with – my present's the past, if you catch my meaning – and I don't think I could adjust to going back to where I used to be or anywhere near it. Am I mad? Don't answer, Desmond! Some people would be shocked by my not screaming for help or – in plain English – for someone else's money to correct my mistakes. You'll understand – you warned me it would be hell, doling out disappointment, cutting everyone off with a shilling, feeling a dunce and being made to feel a brute – it's been such a wrench to do the very things I was brought up and have spent the last half-century trying my best not to do that I couldn't bring myself to revive hopes and risk having to dash them yet again. I'm probably wrong, I seem to have done nothing right, but I made my bed and deserve and am damn well going to lie on it. Sorry to be long-winded.'

'The apologies are owing the other way round,' Desmond replied. He then voiced respect for Willo's position as stated, while Willo issued further assurances that Desmond had nothing to be ashamed of.

He was proceeding to ask Desmond about their comparative progress along the road to ruin when the doorbell rang.

He rang off and went to see who could possibly be calling at nine-thirty in the morning: he hardly ever received a visitor at Edgware Mansions.

The smart lady who embraced him warmly was his first wife Minnie, Mrs Christopher Miller-Boyd.

They had not seen each other for how long? Ten years, they decided. She was pleased to be told she looked good. He was less pleased to be called a poor old boy and asked how on earth he had managed to bankrupt his family. What was she doing on the wrong side of the Park, and how had she found him? The answer to the last question was Melanie. He invited Melanie's mother into the flat, although he guessed she had been sent to browbeat him by their daughter.

Minnie had kept time at bay by the proven method of deportment: she carried herself well – back straight, shoulders down, head held high – and doubtless by the unextinguished twinkle in her eye. She said she had been staying somewhere up north – and the reminiscent shadows under her eyes suggested she had had fun there – and was motoring along Edgware Road on the way to her mews house in Belgravia when she remembered his London address and thought of surprising him with a tiny friendly visit. The retention of her verve was not conducive to the dignity of nearly an old age pensioner.

[125]

'How's the bookworm?' she asked, using her nickname for Barbara, and rattled on before he could remonstrate or reply. 'But you must be sick at heart, darling – The Court was your first and last love. I couldn't believe it when Melanie told me – she was in floods, I was too – can nothing be done to stop the rot?'

'Nothing,' he said. 'Please tell Melanie. You're the second person this morning she's set on me. All she's lost are her assumptions, and without them she may settle down. If you're so concerned for our girls, why don't you come forward with the material remedy?'

'Goodness – you have changed, Willo – spare me the fire and brimstone, do!'

'It's all over bar the shouting, Minnie. That part of my life, being a moneyed man and a country gent and having two homes and daughters with expecta, tions and the rest of it – there's nothing even to talk about on the subject.'

'I only asked a civil question. Anyway – if darling old Willo's finished, where do you go from here?'

'I don't know – wait and see.'

'You're not planning anything stupid?'

'I've given you a civil answer.'

'How are you really, Will? I'd be wretched in your shoes. I'd be wretched if I was still married to you. And I'd like to cheer you up – or are we too old for that sort of thing? What do you think?'

'I think it's early in the morning.'

'That's true.'

'Too early and too late, Minnie.'

'Too true as well,' she chipped in.

They laughed, and she said: 'No, but it is cruel, being left penniless through no fault of your own.'

'I don't agree – it isn't like that – but I'm tired and won't argue. Tell me how you are, Minnie?'

'I could be a lot worse.'

'Happy?'

'I have a nice time.'

'With Christopher Miller,Boyd?'

She giggled at their former joke about the length of her husband's name. 'And without,' she said.

'You haven't changed much at any rate,' he complimented her.

'What's it been like, marriage to the bookworm?'

'A mistake.'

'Perhaps we both made a mistake to part – I was silly when I was young – I've probably loved you best – and I must have made you unhappy.'

'Yes.'

'Oh dear! Has your life been unhappy, Willo?'

'I didn't think so until the other day. But now – well – dull might be the word, although it had its purple patches. You were one, and some of my service in the army was another.'

'Perhaps it was a bad idea, tracking you to your lair.'

'Raising me from the dead might be nearer the mark. I hope I haven't given you a fright.'

'Don't be gloomy, darling.'

'Shall I let you into a secret? Gloom for me is caused by other people's reactions to my situation.'

'Oh – I suppose I stand corrected – I'd better be on my way – you've become a bit of a mystery and not surprisingly a bear with a sore head. What are you going to do about our little ones?'

'My best – especially for Prue, who's still stuck with John Seward. My best isn't good enough for Melanie because it has no cash value. I'll leave Melanie to your tender mercy.'

'Thanks! I've no money to spare for anybody, not even myself. And I can't ask Christopher to fork out for your children.'

'You don't look as if you're starving, Minnie. What's become of your Todd marriage settlement, let alone the Miller-Boyd millions?'

'Oh God, Willo, this is like being married to you all over again. I'm off. Goodbye, my Will.'

They laughed and they hugged, but with more restraint than a quarter of an hour before, and he saw her to the door, where they exchanged good wishes that did and would cost nothing.

He returned to his sitting-room and slumped into the armchair. One day this new life of his might be all very well: in practice in the meanwhile he was not sure how much more of it he could stand.

But he failed to make himself unavailable before another telephone call came through.

He was preparing to leave the flat, and lifted the receiver against his principles and his will.

'Willo, it's Anthony Haden.'

'Oh Anthony! I was thinking of you a moment ago and wondering what had become of you.'

'We flew over to France for the weekend, and I only found your letter waiting for me at Havinton on our return.'

Willo tried to remember when he had posted his letter and when it might have arrived. His suspicions extended to thinking that as a rule a weekend visit ended before midday on the subsequent Tuesday.

Anthony continued: 'I am so sorry, Willo — your problems have been haunting me — you've put the wind up me in no uncertain fashion. I must say I do thank the good God for not letting me hand over any of my money to Lloyd's.'

'To be perfectly honest,' Willo returned, 'my personal preference is not to believe God took it on Himself to bankrupt this Lloyd's Member.'

Anthony laughed uneasily and seized his opportunity to turn the talk from God to Mammon: 'Is bankruptcy actually on the cards?'

'I don't know — I can't imagine people would bother to bankrupt me in the expensive legal sense if I had no money — what would anybody do it for? But the fact is I'm already as good as broke.'

'It's too bad,' Anthony said, and hurried on: 'Listen — I hope you understand that I accept your resignation from our business with bags of regret, gratitude and that sort of thing.'

'Thank you, Anthony — I wrote to you regretfully too — but I don't want to complicate all the issues.'

'No — we must both take care not to do that — which reminds me — I suppose you've pondered the point that strictly speaking you've done yourself out of severance pay? I don't know much about the laws of the land, but I do happen to know that one. Of course, between you and me, the legal stuff doesn't come into the picture.'

Willo repeated absent-mindedly: 'Of course.' He was deducing that his former employer had been waiting to make the telephone call in progress until he had spoken to his solicitor and received assurances in respect of his financial liability.

'But I ought to show appreciation of all you've done for A. Haden Limited,' Anthony said too tentatively by half.

'Don't worry,' Willo returned.

'No — honestly.'

'Forget it,' Willo said.

'Come and have lunch with me at least — come to the office tomorrow — you'd see Jenny.'

'Sorry — tomorrow I can't — I have to be back at The Court to show prospective purchasers round.'

'How hellish! Well — another day. Willo, I'm closing down — the business has traded at a loss for too long — if I tried to soldier on and incurred more debt, there might be embarrassment all round, and I'd be in Queer Street with you. What's in the kitty at present is a minus quantity — that's why I can't offer you money — with the best will in the world I can't give you what doesn't exist — as I'm sure you'll appreciate.'

'I do — and I expected you to shut up shop — and we've already thanked each other — so we could leave it at that.'

'But we have things to talk about — the Plewes book, for instance — won't you have lunch? Who's going to put the Plewes book to bed? What am I to say to Lord Plewes?'

'Everything's in order, Anthony. Jenny can cope with *Nip and Tuck*. I'll have to go now.'

'Hang on! You're not fed up with me for any reason?'

'No — why should I be? I'm grateful — thanks again. Good luck and goodbye!'

He attended to his duties. He resigned his memberships of White's and the Bachelors; contacted the managing agents of Edgware Mansions; kept appointments with Arnold Waters; saw solicitors in town and then in the country. He traded his Mercedes for a secondhand Mini. At The Court he turned out the contents of sheds with assistance from Denis: they had to have a skip in which to dispose of tins of paint dating back to the year dot, anti-quated machinery of no value, spoilt saddlery, worm-eaten timber, broken glass, rotting sacks and the corpses of mice and sparrows. Inside the house he made a start on attics and the cellar, both of which were crammed with furni-ture, trunks, dilapidated toys, black tin boxes full of letters, and so on. He sum-moned and talked business with auctioneers and removal men.

And time passed. Time acclimatised if it did not heal. Spring arrived at last even for Willo Todd.

There was no reconciliation with Barbara. On the other hand they again

[129]

made a virtue of that necessity of matrimony known as rubbing along. When he returned home on the Wednesday following the jealous exception she had taken to Gloria Deane, she cooked food for him, watched the news with him, and they discussed the weather. He volunteered the information that he might never have to go back to London, in return for which she steered clear of the subject of adultery. He was busy and otherwise tired; she seemed to be bicy-cling elsewhere when she was not in her bedroom.

To Mandy he administered the carrot and stick treatment. He gave her bits and pieces out of the house and scolded her for interfering in his affairs.

Documents from Alleyn and Simcox and Waters and Byburn arrived almost daily. He was so alarmed, bewildered and ultimately bored by them that, in one area, he decided to do as he pleased without bothering about Lloyd's rules and regulations. He divided, and would distribute later on, his less valuable household effects between his wife, daughters, sister, nephews and nieces.

Barbara reminded him with sour exaggeration that it was a little too soon to bequeath all his possessions. Even Melanie, acquisitive as she was, made the point that he might need some of the things he said he intended to hand over; whereupon he seized his opportunity to tell her that the pictures and furniture coming her way represented the least and probably the most he could do for her. And he explained to his wife that he did not like the idea of spending the rest of his life with evidence of the home he had loved and lost.

He worried nonetheless. Barbara was right, although she was too sulky to say so: how were they to furnish their future quarters? And where would they live? And on what? He worried about everything. Would he have the nerve or the patience to communicate the news that he was broke and dropping out socially to yet another friendly neighbour or acquaintance? When could he tear up invitations and have his telephone disconnected? When would he sell The Court, and how much longer could he afford to pay for its upkeep? What, in short, lay ahead?

Underlying every other worry was Prue – how she was, and where, and whether or not to try to talk to her or see her. That he heard nothing from her for a fortnight, for a month – not a word of support or encouragement in his crisis, let alone an offer of help – did not exactly hurt his feelings, or offend against his code of good behaviour: it was too untypical. His heart simply ached, he blamed himself, he hoped and even prayed she was not having too bad a time, and waited indecisively.

He also put a brave public face on her absence or absenteeism, announcing that it was prearranged as she had a whole lot of extra work to do, in order not to tempt any busybody to ring her up and reproach her; and he defied Melanie's greedy objections and set aside some familiar things for his younger child.

Activity and exhaustion were his chief allies. He either had no time in which to get too emotional, or was apt to be asleep. He was certainly not happy; but his temperament, to which a variety of epithets were applied by friends and enemies, equable and indomitable, for instance, or rash and careless, did begin to assert itself.

One morning at Tollworth he was sitting in his study, drowsing at the desk, when he heard a car loudly approaching – the noise was such that he thought it was a tractor or a tank on the move – and saw through the window and the arch in the hedge a big battered antique Armstrong-Siddeley saloon parking by his garden gate.

Three people emerged from it, a white-haired man with a countrified complexion who might be a retired farmer or gardener, a plump woman of about the same age shaped like a cottage loaf and wearing a hat, and another female, elderly, stringy, also hatted, but with one of those shapeless white cotton hats generally used to protect heads from the sun, which was not shining on this grey drizzle of a day.

The plump visitor marched up the garden path, followed by the man firmly holding the arm of the third member of the party, by whose eccentric apparel and audible laughter Willo now with a start recognised Florrie Twill, the simple-minded daughter of the redoubtable Mrs Twill of Beggar's Roost.

The doorbell rang. When he opened the door the lady who was not simple introduced herself as Mrs Barnett and first cousin of Florrie, and asked with a mysteriously meaningful glance if she might have a word.

He was then introduced to Mr Barnett, who seemed to be taken aback by the hand Willo extended, and to Florrie, who was reduced to a fit of giggles by his handshake.

He led the way into the sitting-room. Once they were seated he asked after the health of old Mrs Twill. Mrs Barnett thereupon assumed a mournful expression, Mr Barnett looked out of the window complacently, and Florrie emitted a shriek of laughter.

Mrs Barnett's explanation did not altogether account for the trio's contradictory reactions to his question: 'My aunt's been took bad.'

[131]

Willo expressed sympathy and interest.

'She's been carried off,' Mrs Barnett continued.

'I'm so sorry – poor Mrs Twill – but she was a great age, wasn't she?'

'She's not dead,' Mrs Barnett corrected him sharply. 'That's why we're here.' And she directed a glance at Florrie with more than a hint of martyr-dom about it. 'No – my aunt was taken peculiar, and they had to carry her off to hospital.'

'Oh I see – forgive me. What happened, Mrs Barnett?'

'Well – she would get dressed for rainy weather.'

'Is that all? It has been very wet these last weeks.'

'She'd put on her wellies and the mackintosh and hood and open her umbrella and get into bed.'

'Oh dear!'

'She'd been doing it for weeks before we found out. We drove over to Beggar's Roost for tea on Auntie's birthday – it was her ninety-sixth – and there she was in all her wet weather clothes in bed with the umbrella up. Isn't that right, Henry?' Her husband responded to this appeal by staring through the window and quietly whistling. 'It was such a shock,' Mrs Barnett resumed. 'I've never come across anything like it. I'd rather not think of the state she was in. And what made it worse was Florrie sleeping in the same bed all those nights.' Florrie herself was tickled by the memory of the nights in question. 'Well, we rang the doctor, and he arrived with the ambulance, and Auntie was injected to stop her fighting with the medical people, and we cleaned the place as best we could, then we had to take my cousin home.' Mrs Barnett raised her eyes heavenwards in a long-suffering manner.

'How's Mrs Twill now?'

'They have a job keeping her in her nightie – she's always on about her umbrella – otherwise she's wonderful, though she's not talking sense any more. She's in the special hospital in Wimbury.'

'Oh, that one, is she? Poor soul! I'm sorry for all of you.'

'It's not how we expected to spend our retirement.' Mrs Barnett glanced accusingly at Florrie. 'But we couldn't turn her loose, could we, Henry?'

Mr Barnett paid no attention.

'Mrs Barnett, am I to understand that Beggar's Roost is empty now?'

'We've come to tell you it is, Mr Todd. Give Mr Todd the key of Beggar's Roost, Flo.'

Florrie fumbled in her bag, giggling at Willo and showing the awful gaps between her teeth, and produced the cast-iron eight-inch key.

He thanked her, and offered the company sherry or other refreshments, which were refused by means of an explanatory aside from Mrs Barnett: 'It's the mess she makes.'

Aloud Mrs Barnett announced: 'We're on our way to Tetbury to buy my cousin a pretty dress to wear. Auntie had a useful bit in the Post Office, and she's signed it over, which is some consolation for our grief. Florrie's never handled money, you know, so we're looking after that side, aren't we, Henry? And she's always worn her clothes well – stand up, Flo, and show Mr Todd.'

Florrie was too amused to obey.

'Oh the stubborn thing!' Mrs Barnett sighed, rising to her own feet. She thanked Willo for his goodness to her relatives, made threatening signs to her husband and cousin and led them towards the front door.

Willo, having realised Mr Barnett was deaf, shouted at him as they followed the ladies: 'You have a fine old car.'

Mr Barnett spoke at last: 'That's right.'

'Is your exhaust pipe wonky?'

'Yes – it's going well,' Mr Barnett replied.

'Your exhaust pipe must be rusted through,' Willo insisted.

'It's thirty year old and still going strong,' Mr Barnett boasted, smiling proudly.

'You'll be arrested if you don't get it seen to,' Willo warned.

Mr Barnett's considered answer was: 'I'm pleased to hear you say so.'

Goodbyes were exchanged, and Mrs Barnett bundled Florrie into the back seat of the Armstrong-Siddeley and climbed in beside her. Mr Barnett started the car, which backfired, sounding like heavy artillery, roared, and in a cloud of smoke rattled and drummed along the Tetbury Road.

Willo immediately sought out Barbara, who had taken evasive action and was in the kitchen.

He described the visitors and the visit, and said: 'Here's the key of Beggar's Roost' – laying it on the table.

'What am I to do with it? Why are you giving it to me?'

'The cottage is yours, subject to the approval of the Grayvener trustees, and if you'd like it.'

'What?'

He repeated himself.

[133]

'Our future home, do you mean?'

'I think it should be yours alone.'

She sat down on one of the kitchen chairs, but recovered herself sufficiently to ask: 'Will you be living with your London woman?'

He tried to allay her suspicions, and convince her that his offer was disinterested and his intention was to start again from scratch, that is without ties or possessions.

She did not believe him. Her questions struck him as more prosaic than she would have liked to think he found them, as well as patronizing. Did he aspire to be a tramp; who would cook him square meals; where would he keep his pricey clothes; what sort of work would he stoop to; who had put these preposterous ideas into his head, she asked at intervals.

But his answers were tempered by appreciation of the dilemma in which he had placed her. Beggar's Roost without the beggar who owned it and she was married to, a sweet cottage to herself, where she could dally with Byle the Vile and study school texts to her heart's content, would solve most of her existential problems. But to accept it was to eat a large slice of humble pie. She would have to acknowledge that she had got Willo wrong: he was not after all a typical representative of a nasty grasping class, nor was he crushed by the prospect of the bitter end of his luxurious fifty-six years of life.

She could not instantly break the habit of her ideological reflexes: Willo's altruism and her own materialism contradicted too many of her opinions. However, she allowed herself to be persuaded not to look a gift horse in the mouth, nor to cut off her nose to spite her face, as urged by her spouse. She grudgingly agreed to bicycle over to Beggar's Roost, which name, she then suggested, might be changed back to Honeysuckle Cottage.

Three days after he gave her the key of the place she admitted that it would suit her very well, although she could not possibly move in there when he had nowhere to move to. He restated his position; told her the Grayvener trustees had raised no objections to her tenancy; overcame her face-saving objections and obtained her agreement to their separation; whereupon with suspect promptitude she produced builders' estimates for installing a bathroom and patching the roof. He insisted on contributing something to her costs, she said no meaning yes, and the deal was done.

The only not very happy effect of it for Willo was another set-to with Peggy Sparks.

On the morning after he and his wife had settled their differences he was walking through the kitchen and had the following abusive sentence hurled at him from the direction of the sink: 'I'm not working here without madam!'

Peggy, washing up, had spoken without turning round.

He had anticipated some such outburst and replied: 'Shall we talk it over?'

'It's past the talking stage now you're getting rid of madam, poor thing,' Peggy said, but did begin to dry her hands.

'You're miles away from the truth of the matter.'

She interrupted him scornfully, nodding her red head: 'I know men!'

'What do you propose to do, Peggy?' he asked in a voice as repressive as he could muster.

'Work for madam and see she's all right, whether or not she has money to pay me.'

'That's a nice idea, and you're welcome to suit yourself. But you know I'm trying to sell your house together with this one – and Denis' house into the bargain? What I'm hoping is that the buyer will employ you and therefore let you stay on in your houses either rent-free, as at present, or for a peppercorn rent.'

'Oh Mr Todd, what are you saying to me?'

He was surprised by her shocked and accusatory tone, but explained further: 'I'm advising you to continue to work here at least until a buyer materialises. If you're working exclusively at Honeysuckle Cottage, the new owner of your house will either charge you a market rent or evict you.'

Her face crumpled as she looked at him, tears spurted out of her eyes, she fumbled for a handkerchief in the sleeve of her jumper, and bawled: 'You want to get me alone – you do, Mr Todd, don't you?'

He had to laugh.

'My dear Peggy . . .'

'I'm not your dear, nor won't be!'

'Well, at the risk of offending you, I must say that you couldn't be wider of the mark. You have nothing whatsoever to fear in that line, I assure you. You can stop crying. Have I made myself clear?'

She turned off the tears as if by a tap, sniffed and said: 'Time will tell.'

'Quite right,' he agreed, adding to emphasise the purity of his intentions: 'If you should decide not to work for me, I wouldn't have to pay your wages, which I really can't afford – in other words you'd be doing me a favour.'

Peggy sniffed again, signalling that she would rather suffer rapine and pillage than help him in any way, and normal business was resumed.

[135]

Barbara, meanwhile, combined long days of decorating Honeysuckle Cottage with a sort of rearguard action at The Court.

One evening she inquired: 'Are these arrangements fair?'

'Better not speak about fairness,' he answered: 'you married a rich husband who's becoming a poor one.'

'Please don't run away with the notion that I'm leaving you because you're poor, or indeed that I'm leaving you of my own volition.'

'But I was apologising, not reproaching you – and you want to go – let's not split hairs – what's the argument?'

'You don't leave a lot to the imagination,' she countered sarcastically. 'Your reluctance to see the last of me is touching.'

'Oh Barbara, for heaven's sake!'

On another evening she asked: 'Have you talked to Josh lately?'

'No,' he replied. 'Josh has rung me a couple of times, but I've always been busy, and then I haven't liked to bother him.'

'He'd love to be bothered by you, I'm sure – and you'd profit from some counselling.'

'Why – do you think I'm mad?'

'Not at all – everybody can benefit from a session with a trained counsellor.'

'Speak for yourself!'

'That's an ignorant thing to say, Willo.'

'Sorry!'

Again and again, no doubt because she hated to feel more beholden to him than ever, she would qualify her expressions of gratitude with punitive references to Prue.

'Don't you think Prue would come and look after you when I've gone and just until the house is sold? . . . Why not ring her – shall I ring her and find out what's happening – may I ring her to say goodbye – why on earth is she not to be rung? . . . It's quite extraordinary that Prue should have abandoned you completely at this juncture, I was led to believe she was so fond of you . . . What does Prue think she's doing? . . . Don't you care?'

Willo bore most of it for the sake of peace. When too many people were snapping at his heels, he might turn on the nearest – namely Barbara – and quell her with a sign of exasperation or an angry word. But he would remind himself that he was on the last lap of his marriage and would soon be relieved of that particular pressure. He mollified her with vague undertakings to inspect the changes she was making at Honeysuckle Cottage if he had the chance, and not to lose touch with her in future. Once or twice, when he forced himself to look at and concentrate on her grey hair severely cut and her pasty countenance unsullied by cosmetics, he could only recall with a little shock of difficulty that she was or had been his wife.

Their parting resembled a summary of their relationship.

He was having his breakfast in the kitchen when she came to say goodbye: she had told him she could cope perfectly well with the men removing her bedroom furniture, bicycle, luggage and so on. She stood awkwardly in the doorway, wearing her anorak and shapeless corduroys, and with Tray on his lead at her feet.

He said: 'How quick you've been! I didn't think you'd be leaving already.'

'Why drag it out?' she asked rhetorically.

He rose to see her off.

'Don't bother!' she advised. 'Don't let your breakfast get cold – I'll just be at the other end of the village – it's ridiculous – you always were too polite.'

'Oh well – goodbye!'

He crossed the floor and kissed the cheek she turned in his direction.

'Thank you, Willo – and I hope all goes better for you.'

'That's nice – thank you.'

'You can camp at Honeysuckle Cottage if the worst comes to the worst.'

'Thanks – but I won't.' He bent down to pat Tray. The dog drew back, snarling and showing his front teeth. 'Tray still loves me,' he laughed.

'Sorry,' Barbara said with an unexpected trace of emotion.

'Don't be – nothing to be sorry for – well done!'

'No – not well done – and why do you say such silly things?' she retorted and marched along the passage.

It was almost a case of out of sight out of mind. He finished his breakfast, listened for the front door to close and the removal van to drive away. Then he rang Prue's number.

'Hullo?' she said.

'Prue!'

'Dad!'

She burst into tears.

In time he managed to say: 'I shouldn't be badgering you with a telephone call.'

'Thank heavens you have!' she returned. 'I've been in such a bad way – I couldn't have been any use, but I ought not to have deserted you – it was so wrong. But I was afraid – and didn't want to hear horrid news – forgive me, Dad.'

He did so, and tried to persuade her that not all his news was horrid, and promised he was not in the depths of despair. At length he ventured to ask how she was.

'Okay – no, not okay, not very bright – but I suppose my nose is above water. Dad, I'm running out of time, can we talk again?'

'Yes, whenever you like.'

'Will you ring me, please – tomorrow – no later! Please, Dad?'

He agreed.

The following morning they spoke at roughly the same time.

He said: 'I've told you more than you've told me. I don't even know if you're still teaching at the kindergarten.'

'For the moment yes,' she replied. 'But I'm not settled any more – I don't know what's going to happen or what I'll do – I'm sorry to be so uncertain and unsatisfactory, Dad – I hope you understand what it's all about – I can't bear to discuss things in detail yet.'

He blamed himself for having unsettled her: 'If I hadn't lost The Court, if I hadn't put all my money into Lloyd's, neither of us would be in the middle of a crisis.'

'No, no,' she contradicted; 'it wasn't your fault that our home always meant so much to me. The Court made up for the parts of my life that weren't your fault either – Tollworth was my rock or my anchor – when you told me we would all be cast adrift, I had to face up to the central issue. My happiness or unhappiness couldn't be regulated by a house that wasn't mine, or a particular village, or for that matter by you, poor Dad – it was too babyish – and I realised I wouldn't be able to sort out my life and simultaneously say goodbye to my childhood and security and everything easy and sensible – that's why I had to stay away.'

'And that's more or less what I've been thinking,' he chipped in.

'But my absence wasn't ever to do with judging you, Dad, let alone blaming you – please don't think it! I hated myself for leaving you in the lurch – and when my difficulties dragged on, I kept on putting off the telephone call I really longed to make. I've been weak, although I was trying to be strong.'

He sympathised and said: 'One thing you never could be in my eyes is unsatisfactory.'

[138]

Perhaps she sobbed, and perhaps that was the reason she cut this second conversation short.

But the next day she took the initiative and rang him in the evening.

She confessed: 'It's such a relief not to be afraid of getting through to Barbara. Do you mind my saying so, Dad?'

She went on: 'I want to thank you specially for being patient and leaving me to my own devices. I left home, I ran away, partly because I could never answer your questions, even the questions in your eyes – I wasn't able to talk to you then, so the simplest thing seemed to be not to see you – but now it's different, at least you and I have talked, and you still don't probe.'

He said something about respecting people's privacy.

'Darling Dad!' She laughed wryly, indulgently, as if to suggest she loved him for his old-fashioned principles and his innocence. 'Of course you're right – nobody's needed to have her privacy respected more than me – and you've been wonderful about respecting it. But I will let you into one little secret. What I pine for, what I've envied, is to be able to live my life in the open, without confusion, or shame or shyness.' She caught her breath – or could it again have been a smothered sob that interrupted her? She resumed hurriedly to cover the pause: 'Dad, it's Friday – I'm meant to be seeing John quite soon – even possibly for the rest of the weekend – can we have our next chat on Monday? I'll ring you – and let you know immediately if there's any change of plan.'

He said yes, and dared to add: 'How is John?'

'Worse than me – in a worse state, I mean – he's being torn in two. He's not just selfish, Dad – I know it's looked like that, but he's not selfish enough, I could argue and have argued. I can't say more – I feel so bad and sorry for John and his family and myself – I'll tell you everything as soon as possible.'

They rang off.

Willo's reaction to these exchanges verged – figuratively – on schizophrenia. Many of his fears were confirmed, he was more than ever anxious and sad, he cudgelled his brain for a method of alleviating the lot of his daughter, who deserved better than to feel tortured for loving somebody more deeply than he himself had loved anyone. On the other hand he was excited and happy to believe that the barrier between them was somehow overcome, had been removed, might cease to obstruct communication, at any rate judging by her uninhibited and confidential manner on the telephone.

Admittedly she had not, or thought she had not, told him much of her story

[139]

as yet. But his imagination filled in most of the gaps, he had long ago imagined what she was going and would have to go through, and one of her phrases
reinterpreted the past and consequently the future. She had spoken of her
'shame and shyness' and her desire to have done with them; she had not only
shared out the burden of blame for the constraint that had dogged Willo's adult
relations with her, and attributed her own 'shyness' to the 'shame' of loving
another woman's man, but also implied that waiting within her was a more
out-going and easy-going self, which she ardently desired to release.

Willo might have applied himself even harder to the unwonted task of
analysing the feelings of everyone involved in Prue's crisis of love, and the whys
and wherefores, if he had not been rung up by Harold Beever five minutes after
he had finished speaking to her on that Friday evening.

Harold wanted to bring over a couple of people interested in The Court.

It was already six-thirty, getting dark, and the house could have been tidier.
'Now?' Willo asked.

'Yes, please,' Harold replied. 'The gentleman's with me at present, and he's
extremely keen. We can leave at once and should be at Tollworth in ten
minutes.'

In due course a large car, a new red Jaguar Sovereign, stopped beyond the
yew hedge and garden gate, and Willo somewhat breathlessly, having rushed
to clear the kitchen table and put away the clothes discarded in his dressing-
room, greeted Harold and was introduced to a Mr Wall and a Miss Pearsall,
who preferred to be called Sammy and Marilyn.

He was not pleased. He had expected a recognisable type of householder,
gilt-edged individuals sufficiently forceful to persuade Harold to show them a
house after office hours and in the dark. Instead Sammy was a youth with
shoulder-length hair and some regional accent, and Marilyn a pretty blonde
slip of a teenager. And their unisex apparel was discouraging: they both wore
sky-blue anoraks, white polo neck sweaters, white jeans and white trainers,
and crested black baseball caps with beak-like brims.

He showed them round the house as quickly as politeness allowed. They
seemed awestruck, and smiled at him without comment, if disarmingly.

But at the end of the tour Sammy surprised Willo by addressing him thus:
'Thanks very much, Mr Todd — we like it — the deal we're looking for is a
manor round here with all the trimmings — we'll pay cash for the right place
and vacant possession within fourteen days — if you're interested, can we come
back tomorrow? We're staying across in Tetbury.'

Willo's next surprise was that Marilyn drove the Jaguar: she said it was hers.

Half an hour later Harold rang again to tell Willo that Sammy Wall was a computer expert who had recently floated his own public company, and Marilyn Pearsall a pop singer and possibly equally rich; that they were from Birmingham and engaged to be married; that their liking for Todd property could extend to his flat in London; and that they would be with him at nine sharp the following Saturday morning.

That Saturday exhausted Willo. He spent four hours inside the house answering questions, another hour in the garages, sheds and gardens of The Court, more hours at the two Tollworth cottages lived in by Sparks and Willetts, where Peggy and Denis were soon on Christian name terms with Sammy and Marilyn and enthusiastically agreed in principle to work for them, and a prolonged session of negotiations to end up with.

Sunday was also hectic. Sammy and Marilyn again rang Willo's doorbell at nine, had a last look round the house, then wanted to see the sights of the locality. At least they had a proper lunch together in Bath, whereas the previous day it had been nothing but sandwiches. In the afternoon they drove up to London in their respective cars and at six o'clock met at 25D Edgware Mansions, the extremely discreet appeal of which to the interested parties turned out to be that it was furnished; ready to walk into; the tail-end of its lease was cheap; and it would enable them to look for something better at their leisure. By seven all was arranged: Willo had sold the three Tollworth houses and the lease of his flat, and would stay overnight in London in order to expedite legal matters in the morning.

He tried to telephone Prue. She had said she would ring him at The Court on the Monday, but now he was not going to be there and was impatient to tell her why. But he got no answer from her Cirencester number. In the morning she was still not at home. And he had to keep the first of several appointments without speaking to her.

A whole range of pessimistic hypotheses had by now ousted any optimism resulting from the double-edged success of divesting himself of his inheritance. Concern for his daughter was uppermost in his mind; he was dogged by sleeping and waking nightmares. How could he have taken his final conversation with her so calmly? She had said she would be with John and they were both desperate — what might they, what might she, not have done?

To help him to resist the temptation to fear the worst, and to see him through his day, he confined his imagination within the limits of a single outcome of her weekend with her lover. It was bad enough: he guessed that she, or John, or they together would decide or had already decided to burn their boats.

He was not against divorce: how could he be? He was not in favour of matrimonial misery. He had no wish to sacrifice true love on the altar of duty. But he had intermittently dreaded for years that Prue would settle for John and vice versa, although he had obliquely implored her not to and she had obliquely assured him she would not. That the object of her affections was so much older than she was, a noted philanderer, had a popular wife and four under-age children, including one child born during his affair with Prue, and treated his faithful mistress in the most cavalier fashion, as it suited him and as it often made her very unhappy – these facts did not recommend him to Willo for the role of his daughter's consort or his own son-in-law. The one consoling notion was that John was not very likely to ditch his family at great expense in order to marry a woman with nothing new to offer him and no longer any monetary expectations.

In London, all day, he would have liked to think he was exaggerating. He tried to persuade himself that to lose – in any sense – the person he loved best in the world as well as his money, home, job, position in society and the rest of it, was not on the cards. But experience whispered in his ear that fate stopped at nothing; and he recollected with alarming clarity Prue's agitated hint that these days when he would not be able to reach her telephonically were crucial.

As soon as he had finished his business he hurried back to Edgware Mansions, again rang her number in vain, collected his car – the Mini, which he wished was as fast as the Mercedes – and drove to Tollworth.

Amongst the letters delivered to The Court and lying on the floor of the hall was one in Prue's writing. It was not stamped: how had it got there? He tore the envelope open shakily and read the following message.

'Darling Dad, will you meet me for lunch at The Fox at Tockingham next Tuesday? It's a bit difficult to talk till then. Leave a message at the pub if you can't make it. A girlfriend has promised to take this to The Court. Hope you're well. Much love, Prue.'

At first he was relieved: she was alive, or had been whenever she wrote the letter, which was not dated. The time was seven o'clock in the evening, and he could concentrate on a long call to Harold Beever, thanking for the introduction to Sammy and Marilyn and discussing the schedule of the multiple sale. But second thoughts reasserted that Prue at The Fox would break the news that she and John intended to make some sort of match of it, and even that she was going to bring John along to the rendezvous.

He did not sleep well. On the Tuesday morning he gritted his teeth and spoke to Mandy and Melanie. Having more or less weathered the storm of their objections to the upstarts who had bought their old home, and to himself for being so money-grubbing as to sell it to them, he motored into Tetbury to buy food and things, then on to The Fox.

He waited for Prue from about twelve-fifteen to twelve-forty-five. He sat in his car, looked for her in the pub, checked and rechecked in a beer garden, gazed along the road to and from Cirencester. At last she arrived from the opposite direction, and startled him by calling out across the car park.

She was alone. She looked quite well. They embraced.

'Where have you sprung from?' he asked.

'That's part of what I want to tell you,' she replied.

'I was expecting you to come the other way – not that it matters – I'm so glad you're here.'

'Have you been worried, Dad?'

'No,' he fibbed not very convincingly.

'But you got my note?'

'Yes – it's all right – I'm just pleased to see you after however long it is.'

'You do understand why it had to be so long?'

'Yes,' he said. 'Everything's all right.'

And he was not fibbing. Strangely, his worries had subsided or dispersed for the time being. They were being replaced by an irrational light-heartedness.

'Are you terribly hungry and thirsty, Dad?'

'No. Are you?'

'No. Can we sit out of doors for a little while? It's such lovely weather.'

He now noticed the dazzling spring sunshine, the cerulean sky, the crisp air, the echoing coo of pigeons.

They sat at one of the tables in the beer garden, a grassy area beside a stream or ditch fringed by willows already bursting into silvery leaf.

Prue was thinner and paler than when Willo had last seen her over eight weeks ago. But her soft blue eyes behind her spectacles were receptive, not shy or shrinking.

'I've got something to tell you, too,' he began.

A slight movement of her eyelids, her smiling lips, was not far from a flinch.

'I'd say it was good news,' he added.

'Thanks, Dad.'

She smiled gratitude at him for the reassurance.

'The Court and my flat are sold in a single deal.'

'Oh!' She repeated the syllable in a less dismayed and more interrogative tone: 'Oh?'

'They're only bricks and mortar,' he said.

'Yes and no.'

'And selling them is a weight off my mind.'

'I'm glad for you, Dad. Who's the buyer?'

'There are two of them – young people getting married – Sammy Wall and Marilyn Pearsall by name.'

'Marilyn – isn't that Marilyn the pop singer?'

'Yes – do you know about her?'

'Everybody does, except you.' They laughed. 'What's she like? And who's the man?'

'He's called Sammy Wall, a computer whizzkid. They're both like charming children with money to burn.'

'Will they love The Court?'

'I think so – they say they do already. Your Aunt Mandy and your sister have given me socks for selling it to people who are not like us. But Sammy and Marilyn are very nice, down to earth, and dress beautifully in the modern style as if they were twins. The only drawback is we have to complete within fourteen days – or thirteen from today.'

'Does that mean they take possession in thirteen days?'

'I had to agree to their condition.'

'But where will you live?'

'Don't worry!'

She mocked him fondly: 'No – I won't – you're the last person I'll worry about – you can sleep under the stars for all I care. No – if you've no other arrangements in mind you'll have to come with me.'

'Come with you to Cirencester?' he asked, and before she could answer said that such a solution was out of the question, he was not quite ready to become a burden, he had not had a chance to arrange anything but would do so as soon as possible.

She said with her face averted and the hint of a break in her voice: 'Not Cirencester – I'm going to live miles and miles away – that's what I had to tell you.'

[144]

Willo thought: I know – I guessed – don't do it – please!

Aloud he said: 'Where are you going?'

'Cornwall – Penzance – I drove here from Penzance this morning, not from Cirencester, as you expected – I've got a new job and I've rented a flat in Penzance – I'll still be teaching children.'

He hesitated, braced himself, and asked: 'Are you going alone?'

'Yes.'

'Without John?'

'Yes – we said goodbye last Saturday – and on Sunday I drove south and fixed up the job and the flat yesterday.'

'I see.'

'You see why I've been elusive, Dad?'

'Yes.' They exchanged a glance. She was dry-eyed, but he felt like crying for her. 'How painful!' he commented.

'Yes,' she agreed.

'I wish I could have helped you.'

'No one could help.'

'How long have you known John?'

'I could count the exact number of days – too long – but I don't like to think of how long.'

'It can't be a waste of time to love someone.'

'I wonder.'

'You're brave, Prue.' She shook her head, and he insisted. 'You are – you've survived – you'll spin pearls around the experience.'

'I won't let it kill me – I won't – you haven't let being broke kill you, Dad – and you won't, will you?'

'No. But our situations aren't comparable – yours is much more serious, more worthwhile, than mine – whence my conviction that you haven't wasted your time. Being broke could be a lucky break for me – I'm so sorry it isn't yours or Melanie's or anyone else's. I don't underestimate the pleasures and advantages of having means, the comfort of cash in the bank and so on. But – without generalising – for me, in my own case, and pretty painlessly considering, not having money and even the uncertainty of my future – well, forgive the corniness of what I'm saying – it's opened up new avenues. It may end by doing the exact opposite of killing me. Who would have thought it? One never knows. One never knows a single damn thing. The exception is Penzance: I can't and I won't accept your invitation, darling, thank you all the same.'

[145]

'At least promise me not to forget my offer! I haven't taken care of you while you've been battling through on your own. I haven't behaved dutifully or nicely for ten-plus years, whatever you may say, Dad. I can admit now that John's conduct wasn't perfect. But I'm not proud of mine. I was selfish to get into my muddle and I've been selfish to get out of it. That's the story of adultery. Thanks, Dad, for not turning against me – and thanks again for not asking how John is – no doubt he'll be a lot better than I used to think he would be if I made myself scarce. About Penzance though: you could help me to settle down there.'

'No, darling – I'm too fond of you to do it – and neither of us would be starting again if we were still clinging to each other.'

'Oh well – we won't lose touch, will we?'

'Never – you're my tonic – I feel much better for seeing you even if I haven't done the same for you. I was expecting a sadder tale.'

'I'm happy that someone's pleased. Dad, could I have a drink? No – wait a mo – could we order some food? I haven't eaten much lately, but I fancy a little nourishment – in fact I'm ravenous. And we could eat out in the sunshine, couldn't we?'

'Let's,' he said.

For all that

MELANIE and her boys, Mandy and her available children, and to
some extent Peggy Sparks and Denis Willett, helped Willo to clear
The Court of its contents in the ensuing thirteen days and even the
nights.

The valuable stuff was sent up to Sotheby's; Willo was keeping nothing for
himself except two or three souvenirs and some clothes; he was in a better frame
of mind thanks to Prue, who was now back in Penzance and had telephoned
to say she liked it; he presided indulgently over the fairest possible distribution
of the residue of his possessions, including a few pictures removed from the flat
in London.

Solicitors had been browbeaten into moving with unwonted rapidity, signa-
tures were appended at the appointed time, keys were swapped for cheques, and
the last of many Todds of Tollworth drove away from The Court in his Mini.

He knew where he was going. He had rejected not only the offer of
accommodation urged by Prue at The Fox at Tockingham. Melanie also had
views to air on the subject.

When he rang to ask Melanie over to bag a share of the spoils of The Court,
she sounded different, not as grumpy as usual. She explained that Edgar had
landed a new and better-paid job in his insurance company, and she was pregnant again. He congratulated her encouragingly, and then in the context of his
imminent homelessness she expressed cautious interest in his plans.

He told her he had decided not to move – or squeeze – into Honeysuckle
Cottage.

She brushed aside his separation from Barbara, said it was predictable,
agreed that Honeysuckle Cottage was out of the question, and resumed: 'But

[147]

you can't afford a hotel or even a lodging-house, Dad — somebody will have to take you in — you should have spoken to me before agreeing to be rushed and bullied. Where's Prue? It's high time she began to pull her weight. What does Prue suggest?'

He gave her an edited account of his recent meeting with her sister.

She expressed pleasure in passing that Prue had finally shown John Seward the door, and continued: 'Listen — if Prue's in Penzance the obvious place for you to stay is in her empty flat in Cirencester.'

He ruled it out: he had advised Prue to let her Cirencester flat in the meanwhile to help her pay for the flat she was renting in Penzance.

At last Melanie volunteered: 'Oh well — you could come here — not for ever — especially not with the new baby on the way — but for a week or a month. William and James would love it anyway.'

Willo's sister's invitation was even less appealing.

Mandy's reaction to his homelessness was combative. 'Barbara's behaving so badly, grabbing Honeysuckle Cottage and locking the door in your face. You could evict her, you know.'

'You've got the wrong end of the stick, Mandy. Barbara's complied with my wishes. The cottage is hers for as long as she wants it — ask the Grayvener trustees — and there's no room in it for me.'

Mandy attacked from another quarter: 'It's your daughters' duty to look after you.'

'They've both tried to do so,' he explained, 'but the very last thing I want is to be looked after by anybody, let alone either of them.'

'You can't sleep rough, Willo.'

'Why not?'

She ignored his question and pursued: 'We'll put you up at The Shoe House if we have to, provided you don't mind sleeping on a sofa or the floor. Desirée's mumps are ancient history and whatever's wrong with Theo has still not been identified — I don't think we're infectious.'

He concluded this conversation firmly, that is loudly, with his voice raised in fraternal exasperation.

His attitude to his future was not reckless: he had received assurances from the landlord of The Fox that a bed and breakfast would be available whenever required. He still had money in the bank, just about three thousand pounds after paying off household expenses and giving goodbye presents to Peggy and Denis.

He got round to ringing Josh two days before he was due to leave The Court.

It was five o'clock, and he eventually heard Josh at the other end of the line.

'This must be a bad moment to talk to you,' Willo began. 'Were you in the garden? Have you been out?' He quickly followed up: 'You don't sound right, Josh – what's the matter?'

'I've got flu.'

'Since when?'

'Yesterday.'

'Do you feel rotten?'

'Yes.'

'Can you go to bed?'

'Not really. Where are the curates of yesteryear? I hear you've sold The Court?'

'Not only sold, I'm almost out of it.' And Willo explained the terms of the sale.

'So what becomes of you?' Josh asked hoarsely.

'I'll have to let you know.'

'You're not at a loose end by any chance? You wouldn't like to do me a very good turn?'

'What do you mean?'

'A lot of my work can't be called religious. Why not stay here and do it for me until I feel more human? You could have my spare room.'

'Seriously?'

'I wish you would.'

'All right – thanks.'

The consequence was that Willo left The Court for ever to drive to the vicarage at Measham.

Josh was still on his feet, but obviously feverish, alternately sweating and shivering and shaking. Willo packed him off to bed and brought him cups of Bovril and dry toast. Twenty-four hours later Josh was much worse, purple in the face, breathing stertorously, and Willo summoned his own private family doctor, Dr Ward, who diagnosed pneumonia and prescribed medicine and gave instructions and returned to check the patient's progress. Josh was not completely out of danger for a week, and then had to recuperate for a month or so.

Willo, in the first phase of his friend's illness, was pleased to be kept busy.

[149]

He had to supply remedial drinks and in due course tasty food, change sheets and wash pyjamas, answer the telephone and reply to well-wishers, keep concerned and largely female parishioners at bay, persuade the parsons of other parishes to conduct services, deal with the vergers, churchwardens, sextons, bellringers, flower-arrangers and cleaners of the churches of Measham, Snathe and Tollworth, on one occasion make an address from a pulpit, also teach children at Sunday School and chair the meeting of a Parish Council.

The following snatch of conversation proved that Josh was on the mend. Willo aimed to reassure with the remark: 'Your show's still on the road.'

Josh replied: 'You shouldn't have bothered – I didn't mean you to bother.'

'You'd have been in trouble if I hadn't.'

'That depends. I'd be dead. I might be in paradise. But I'd better not boast. Thanks for all you've done.'

Josh's impatience to resume his duties was counter-productive. He agreed to christen a baby without Willo's knowledge, sneaked out of the vicarage, had a relapse in church, and spent two more days in bed. He then resigned himself to taking it easy, and his convalescence happened to coincide with a spell of exceptionally beautiful May weather.

Old wickerwork chairs were carried on to the terrace, and Josh sat in one for most of every day, reading and sleeping, writing and observing the rustic scene, and talking with Willo when the latter had attended to chores, shopped, cooked and organised everything. The two friends' diet was austere: they ate a lot of bread and baked potatoes, a little meat, bacon, an occasional chop, eggs, vegetables and apples. They drank tea and indulged in post-prandial sweets. They would carry their plates out of doors, and in the evenings stay put until night fell and the moon swung up into a sky made of velvet and diamonds.

The view from the back of the vicarage was of rough lawn flanked by ancient sycamore trees and leading to a decrepit iron fence, beyond which was meadow grazed by a herd of cows, a middle distance of burgeoning hedgerows and a hilly blue horizon. Swifts, swallows and house-martins had already appeared on the scene, and shrieked and swooped through lengthening days in the high empyrean; and blackbirds and thrushes piped their defiant arias at dusk. The squeaking of playful fox cubs in the dark distance was apt to cause a chain reaction of barking village dogs. Sometimes the chunky shape of a barn-owl passed in ominous silence across the face of the moon.

One night Willo observed: 'My life's been nothing but surprises in the last five months.'

Out of the darkness came the query: 'All bad ones?'

'By no means.'

'I could say "How surprising"! You've certainly surprised me, Willo – you might have collapsed – I was half-expecting to have to pick up the pieces – instead of which you've performed that service for me.'

'My services cut both ways – your illness has done me a power of good. Incidentally, your doctor's my treat – I'm paying Dr Ward as usual – no argument – I owe it to you – regard it as rent if you like.'

'Can you afford it?'

'No – I bet I have more money than you, as we used to say at school – but what I've got is next to nothing, at least by Lloyd's standards – so it might as well be spent.'

'Aren't you worried about the future, security etcetera and old age?'

'Aren't you, Josh?'

'I believe the Lord will provide.'

'Try again – you're a man of the world, not a theology student.'

'All right,' Josh laughed: 'I'm not afraid of dying – and you can't get more secure than that. Now you'll have to answer my question.'

'The Mr Micawber in me has come out – I keep on expecting something to turn up.'

'You have faith in other words.'

Willo laughed in his turn and said: 'You'll never make a religious man of me.'

'Well – you've done half my job in the last few days – you've preached a sermon about the road to Damascus – I was thinking you might take holy orders.'

'It was an address – I only harked back to a sermon of yours, the one you gave on Christmas Day, telling us to be ready to adapt to change, do you remember? Far from being a sermon, I'm afraid it was on the blasphemous side, since I compared St Paul with Names at Lloyd's, who were rich and are poor. But you know my religious views – which haven't changed as a matter of fact – I'm what my grandfather used to call a Laodicean, who blows neither hot nor cold – by no means an atheist, not so arrogant, nor a pagan, because one really can't be sensual in our climate – rather a bad Christian of the Christmas and Easter type.'

A pause ensued, a cow mooed in the meadow, an unidentified bird fluttered and twittered in one of the sycamore trees.

Willo asked quietly: 'Are you asleep?'
'No – thinking of Trooper Biggins,' Josh replied.

To Josh and to Willo, and to no one else in the whole wide world, that remark was relevant.

It referred to an episode in their army days. They had been conscripted for National Service in 1955, joined the old cavalry regiment known as The Duke of Clarence's, otherwise the 10th Lancers, in consideration of family connec-tions, met and trained together and won their commissions, and thus became part of the Suez Expedition.

The regiment was motorized, equipped with Daimler armoured cars, and by the time it disembarked in Egypt Willo and Josh were each in charge of a troop of three cars and their crews. Their squadron was commanded by Major Hugh Porter, known to some as Potty Porter, and their Colonel was a first-rate and experienced regular soldier, David Hughes D.S.O.

Willo's life as a subaltern had been considerably complicated by one member of his crew, his driver, Trooper Biggins by name. Billy Biggins was nearly twenty years older than his troop leader, an old soldier in every sense, a professional who had fought through the 1939–45 war. He looked young for his age, and was handsome with best quality black hair forming a marked widow's peak, a broad brow, small firm features and a charming smile and manner. His bright blue eyes were misleadingly innocent, and his skill at the wheel of an armoured car was legendary. The telltale crack in the golden bowl of his appearance and his capabilities was his rank: he wore no stripes. After all his years in the army he should have been at least a sergeant. In fact he had become a corporal half a dozen times in the distant past, but was always and soon demoted, indeed was lucky not to have been flung out of the regiment, and for three quarters of his military career had not even had a foot on the hier-archical ladder.

The reason was his character, or maybe in another sense his lack of it. He could resist no temptation: he drank too much if possible, seduced women by the score, or, as he said, was seduced by them, pinched things, conned people, owed and borrowed money, broke rules, in short had neither a moral nor an inhibition to bless himself with. His saving graces were threefold, his smile, his skill and his quick wit. He could talk himself out of the trouble he usually deserved to be in, and argue with some success that black was white. He was not only a barrack-room lawyer, he would argue if he was given the chance on civilian subjects – politics, religion – with his officers.

Predictably he was a republican and an atheist: restraints of any sort were against his principles. He mocked God in all the immemorial ways: he challenged the Almighty if He existed to strike Billy Biggins with a thunderbolt, he knew the Bible well enough to make fun of the parables in the New Testament and Jesus' sexual inclinations and ascension into heaven. He was never more subversive than in these contexts, and he subtly managed to ridicule military as well as regal and divine authority.

He addressed teasing questions to Lieutenant Kemball in particular, knowing Josh had religious leanings. During smokebreaks he would ask, for instance, smiling with his neat head on one side and in his lightly accented Londoner's voice: 'Can I speak off the record, sir? Do you believe God's on the side of the British Army?'

He also made provocative statements: 'We never should have fought the Germans, because God chose them to punish the Jews for crucifying His son . . . When you know all the bad things that go on in this world, you can't forgive God for creating it.'

Trooper Biggins' atheism had its own sort of field day with the Suez Expedition: 'So God's fixed it for us to knock spots off the followers of His rival – He isn't half jealous, God is.'

He had a disruptive, not to say destructive, effect on the morale of the troops with his anarchic attitudes, and he unsettled even Josh, who once complained to Willo prophetically that his driver deserved to be shot.

In October 1956 the 10th Lancers, after disembarking at Port Said, joined an enormous convoy of British and French vehicles cruising southwards on metalled roads beside the Suez Canal. Whatever had happened to the opposition, they met none; and the regiment turned west as night fell and camped near a village called Bir Ben. That is to say, the squadron was split up on the orders of Colonel Hughes, the strategy being more or less to surround and lay potential siege to Bir Ben, although the place was only an agricultural hamlet and its inhabitants seemed friendly or at any rate neutral.

The so-called harbour assigned to the troops of Willo and Josh was a dilapidated open-sided barn in the middle of some empty-looking enclosures, possibly rice fields. Drills were followed: the six cars were camouflaged, latrines and slit-trenches dug, sentries posted, and a detachment of armed men commanded by Josh's sergeant was sent to recce the village and see if water was available. Half an hour later, during which no firing of guns near or far was audible, the detachment returned with full jerrycans, also with four dead chickens and garden vegetables – Trooper Biggins had been a member of the party.

The two young officers read the riot act about looting. But the peaceful day and the eastern night with stars like tiny searchlights had induced a mood of general euphoria, some of the men were already plucking the chickens, and soon two bonfires were lit, a fine meal was cooked in tin cans, and in time the soldiery slept on their groundsheets.

At first light a vehicle approached. It was the Jeep used by Colonel Hughes, Colonel David to Willo and Josh, who welcomed him and led him into their own HQ, a space cleared and enclosed by walls of bales of hay in the middle of the barn.

They had just sat down when raised voices reached them and Willo went to investigate.

At a glance the situation was bad from a military point of view, and, too quickly to be remedied, it got much worse. The only sentry on duty must have challenged a group of male and female rustics standing fifty-odd yards away in front of the nearest village buildings or sheds. The sentry, a youth called Roberts, was shouting and pointing his rifle at these people, who were not only shouting back and shaking fists angrily but were now joined by two men in crumpled uniforms with guns slung from their shoulders. Although the armed men were probably Egyptian soldiers, and for that matter enemies, their British opposite numbers began to laugh at them, just stood there laughing and either making rude gestures or with hands in pockets as if at some comical peacetime show. And before Willo could issue any orders or summon his non-commissioned officers from wherever they were or remind the men of their basic duties, the following events occurred almost simultaneously: Trooper Biggins ran towards the rustics strewing chicken feathers into the air in his customary challenging style, one rustic knelt down and revealed another behind him aiming a blunderbuss or fowling piece at the chicken thief, there was a loud explosion, Biggins was shot, and the whole scene was enveloped in smoke.

All was confusion. The smoke was thick and virtually blinding, and the crackle of flames at close quarters could be heard. It took Willo a moment to realise that while some villagers had attracted the attention of the invading force others had crept up from the rear and set fire to the tinder-dry hay and straw in the barn. He cursed himself for his military failure, was concerned for that idiot Biggins, wondered what had become of Josh, thought of Colonel David; and through the smoke he was suddenly able to see with stinging eyes that the exit from the spot where he had left his Colonel was a wall of flame. He plunged through it, heard and felt hair and eyebrows singe, stumbled across the prostrate and half-asphyxiated form of the commanding officer, and bending double to avoid the hottest heat dragged him by the legs to relative safety, open space, where Josh and another smokey figure took over. Guns were going off, men were shouting, somebody was hitting Willo on the back to extinguish smouldering areas of his battle-dress, and someone else was pulling and pushing him out of the smoke and towards the parked armoured cars. He breathed again and saw more clearly: his men in the slit trenches and the – now invisible – Egyptian soldiers in the village were taking pot shots at one another, and a burst of machine-gun fire rattled from Josh's car, and Trooper Biggins was still alive, writhing about and kicking his legs unattended and in an unprotected position. Willo ran forward to haul the poor fool out of harm's way at least, bellowing the order to stop shooting and being bellowed at and called back by Josh. Almost together the two friends reached Biggins, who was terribly wounded and obviously dying, but conscious and voluble. A shot ricocheted and whirred away, the report of the gun followed, and they lay flat on their bellies as Biggins spoke his last.

He said: 'Oh God, forgive me – I was wrong, but you be kind to me, God – please God, forgive me – oh my God, please . . .'

When Willo and Josh were sure he was dead, they left him where he was and crawled to rejoin their party. Soon Potty Porter with two more troops of the Squadron hove into view, and not long afterwards all the Duke of Clarence's men were reunited. No further resistance was offered by the village. The corpse of Biggins was removed into one of the transports. Neither Colonel David nor Willo was irreparably burned, and they succeeded in getting the smoke out of their lungs. The regiment resumed its progress alongside the Suez Canal, then turned and returned to its point of departure when the politicians changed their minds.

For their gallant actions at the barn near Bir Ben, or, as they put it privately, for making a proper mess of things, Josh received his Mention in Despatches and Willo his Military Cross.

*

On the terrace of the rectory at Measham in Gloucestershire, Josh's enunciation of the name of Biggins warned Willo that he too, when he least expected it, might cease to be a 'bad Christian': the two friends had often discussed what could be called Biggins' conversion.

For some reason they did not pursue the subject; but a night or two later, back on the terrace in the moonlight, Willo reverted to it.

'Biggins didn't have much effect on you – religiously, I mean – not at the time or not to notice,' he said.

'Perhaps that's true,' Josh replied. 'But watching him die was awful – neither of us have ever forgotten – and it was probably influential in my case at any rate.'

'Nevertheless Biggins was a sham, pretending to be an atheist. He must have been a choirboy or something, and realised he could create an impression by having a go at God. And what changed his tune was fear, not conviction, because he was about to meet his maker.'

Josh commented: 'Atheism's a deep old subject. Biggins was a version of the man who believed in no God, and worshipped Him. Believing and not believing in God are nextdoor neighbours, only separated by three letters of the alphabet. Agnostics, don't-knows, are harder nuts to crack than atheists – they're like people without principles, who can't be brainwashed. As for believers suffering from doubts, there's a special prayer for them: Lord, if we are deceived, it has to be by Thee. Sorry, I'm losing the thread – you were saying Biggins was afraid, not converted – actually that's normal enough.'

'I bet you didn't become a parson because you were frightened, Josh.'

'Maybe I did, maybe I was.'

'Well, in the army a white feather never came your way, and you were brave throughout Clare's illness, and not a coward in middle age to go and study for the priesthood. I can't see where fear fits in. Would you rather not talk about what happened to you after Clare's death?'

'I don't mind now, after so long, and to you. The point for me – and I can't speak for anyone else – is that religion's an expression of love – it's love or nothing. If exclusive sex is the beginning of the most important human activity, religion may well be the end. I was lucky to meet Clare, and of course I fell in love with her, and longed to marry her for one inclusive overriding reason: because I dreaded losing her. She sweetly said ditto ditto, and we were duly spliced. I've no idea why her health failed – to the best of my knowledge we were wonderfully happy – her illness and her death were cruel – the mercy was that nothing she was capable of doing could be altogether bad so far as I'm concerned. Afterwards, by staying beside me in spirit she kept me approximately sane, and by not staying in the flesh she released me from a commitment. And – and I don't want to get mystical, or make your toes curl with embarrassment – yet the fact is I saw or recognised or met God – and another sort of love took over and from then on governed my actions. Worldly and religious love are, have to be, should be different – all the same they share one authenticating condition in my experience – I was so afraid of losing God that I made every possible effort to commit myself to Him and thus vice versa – I became His servant. I know they say that love casts out fear, and I know what they mean. But personally I believe that love isn't up to much which isn't fearful, and which doesn't try to bind the beloved to it by every available means.'

After one of those friendly pauses for thought Willo observed: 'The love you talk about sounds like a power struggle.'

'Well – of a sort,' Josh agreed.

'But even after struggling for power over the beloved, she or he or it can still escape, witness Clare,' Willo said.

'Oh yes,' Josh answered. 'All we can do is our best, the rest is not our business.'

'Do you ever lose God?'

'Certainly. Isn't there some theory about the intermittence of the heart? I keep on losing Him, but I believe He doesn't lose me.'

'Here's a last awkward question: would you like a cup of tea?'

'Very much – please and thank you.'

For the next couple of days Josh's friends and parishioners called at the vicarage in the evenings and shared the balmy joys of the terrace.

When the friends were by themselves once more, seated side by side and facing the nocturnal landscape, Willo began: 'I've envied you.'

'Why's that?'

'Your life's so much more serious and successful than mine.'

'Where did you hear that story? Have I been boasting again?'

'Yes,' Willo quipped, and continued: 'You loved your wife more than I've loved either of mine, for instance.'

'As a result I've had to confess the sin of inordinate affection. No, that's not serious – forget it – and remember your biblical span is three score years and ten, and your life's far from over.'

[157]

'The same applies to you, Josh.'

'Yes.'

'Would you, could you, love another woman?'

'I hope so. I'm learning the lesson that the dead must bury the dead. Would you, Willo?'

'I don't know — and my situation doesn't merit comparison with yours — there's really no connection.'

'The connection is that you've been released from some of your commitments — to family traditions and social conventions, to wealth and work, and your wife and your home.'

'But I haven't come across God. And I can't be proud of frittering away my existence, and letting other people fritter away my family fortune. Frankly, my story's a fiasco.'

'Nonsense — false modesty — your steadiness under the fire of these last months has been admirable — I can't imagine how you've kept so cool — and with or without the assistance of the divinity you've turned the whole bad business to your advantage.'

'Thanks, Josh — I'm almost penniless, I'm sponging on you, I've no prospects — nothing — and pretty well no one to call my own. I can't say that I feel my position's particularly advantageous.'

'Well — nearly every religion would regard it as an ideal state, seldom attained, the precondition of a new true life and the beginning of wisdom.'

Willo laughed at this optimistic description of his misfortunes, but Josh, having joined in, persisted: 'Whatever you may be feeling you give yourself away. We talked last Christmas, I must remind you, after Matins and before I came to lunch at The Court. You're no longer the person you were then — I mean you may be more worried and sadder, you're not discontented — you've dismantled barriers. No, listen, Willo — you can blush in the dark — accept my tributes with humility! You've done two terribly difficult things, you've regained an open-mindedness, that rare quality, lost for ever by most people at about the age of ten, and secondly you've cooperated with life in its less agreeable manifestations instead of panicking, opposing, fighting and being defeated by it. God knows what the future holds for you or me. But I know you're like a younger person than you were six months ago, and there are possibilities ahead of you.'

Willo replied: 'You're a good friend, Josh, even if you do get me wrong.'

Another few days passed, Josh was recuperating visibly, his big face looked less bony and the countrified colour edged back into his complexion, and the number of his visitors increased, so that he and Willo had no opportunity for further extended intimate conversation.

But late one evening, after a pair of pious local ladies had come in, cooked and shared dinner with the two gents, cleaned up and gone home, Willo delayed Josh's retirement to bed in order to say: 'It isn't strictly true that I have no one to call my own. I've told you that Prue's moving down to Penzance without John Seward. I haven't told you more for fear of tempting providence. She offered me asylum – she wanted us to begin again together. The most difficult thing I've done this year may have been to say no. I can't pretend to you that she isn't my favourite daughter. I was always fond of her, as you know – but while the rest of my life was disappearing down the drain I've grown fonder – and when I saw her the other day I got the feeling that we were closer to each other than ever before. I suppose I do have a special sort of commitment to Prue, I try to measure up to my idea of her values and standards, and I'd rather not be disapproved of by her. And I suppose I am afraid of losing her, losing her to the wrong man, losing her emotionally. But I ask nothing much – really just that she should continue to exist in my world, and ideally to be free and well. To that extent she is my own, my own to love if not to be loved by, and now like my consolation prize, like winning or having won it – which can't ever be completely taken away from me.'

Josh's response was: 'Aren't you lucky?'

When Josh was fully restored to health and strength, Willo attempted to say goodbye.

'What on earth are you talking about?' Josh asked.

Willo explained: 'I don't want to overstay my welcome. I'm superfluous here since you're yourself again.'

'Where do you think you're going?'

'I'll find lodgings, maybe at The Fox at Tockingham, and as soon as possible a job.'

'Meanwhile you might like to take my views into consideration,' Josh advised. 'They are that you could never overstay my welcome. You'd help me a lot by continuing to relieve me of household chores – I'd have another three or four hours a day for my work. And you could look for your job from this address, which sounds respectable and would perhaps help you to find it. But of course you must do as you please.'

The consequence was that Willo remained at the vicarage. He was more than pleased to do so, and, after observing Josh's daily round of nonstop activity, convinced that he was useful. He kept house and cooked food. He shopped in towns far enough afield from the haunts of his former friends and acquaintances: personally he was no longer inhibited by his changed social status, and he met many known and unknown people through the agency of Josh, yet was well aware that financial embarrassment could embarrass.

He still had his Mini, and he chugged to remote markets and supermarkets, also to see what was on offer at the Jobcentres of various localities.

It was depressing. Now he began to concentrate on employment, his common sense did not spare him the catalogue of his lack of qualifications. He was too old for most jobs, had no particular skill or expertise, could not claim to be good with figures, and realised his toff-like appearance, accent, clothes and attitude would be inclined to count against him. He had to ask for an explanation of the letters CV, and then was mortified by the insubstantial story of his 'work experience'. One day he succeeded in pinning down Anthony Haden telephonically and asking with some force for a reference, which he eventually received: but he kicked himself for bothering – it was lukewarm and not worth the half-sheet of personal writing paper it was scrawled on.

He had rung Havinton Hall from call-boxes. Although Josh urged him to use the telephone of the vicarage, Willo refrained in order to avoid difficulties with bills, contributions to which the subscriber – altogether too generous for the good of his stipend – was unlikely to accept. Willo also cut short the conversations that he had with the few people – Mandy in particular – to whom he had given the vicarage telephone number: he was nervous of monopolising the instrument and getting in the way of either Josh or Josh's parishioners.

He rang Prue to make sure she was all right and to say that he was, then had to remind himself of his paternal duty to keep his distance. When he wanted to talk to her he remembered that he would have felt hemmed in by any excess of parental attention. He was determined not to impose upon her too much responsibility for his emotional well-being, but sometimes wondered if she was suffering from similar inhibitions. She wrote rather a lot of postcards sending much love underlined, saying that she looked forward to seeing him again, and wishing him masses of luck in his hunt for a job.

One morning on the way back to Measham from shopping in Tetbury he kept his promise to call on his wife.

Barbara was at home. She admitted with uncharacteristic enthusiasm that she was quite pleased with Honeysuckle Cottage. She even went so far as to own up to being glad she was living there: which was a relief to Willo notwithstanding the implied aspersion it cast on their cohabitation at The Court. She offered him tea and a digestive biscuit, and a tour of the premises which took about two minutes.

The little sitting-room, cosy in the days of the Twills with worn Windsor chairs and a collection of polished horse-brasses, now resembled an office: the walls were strictly white, the chairs stainless steel and leather, and a Japanese typewriter with screen attachment stood on the table by the window. The bathroom had been installed in Mrs Twill's larder beyond the kitchen, and the bedroom up the steep staircase, in which mother and daughter Twill had slept together, was almost entirely filled by Barbara's single bed.

How was Roger Byle, he ventured to inquire.

She looked at him askance to check she was not in danger of being teased, and replied that he was well and about to sit his exams.

Willo had no idea which exams were referred to — Roger seemed to have been sitting exams for ever and a day — but congratulated Barbara vaguely and asked how far she had got with her plan to become a professional teacher.

'I may go into counselling instead,' she replied.

'Counselling? Isn't that what you think I need?' He added, laughing: 'Not marriage counselling?'

'Possibly,' she retorted. 'What's so funny?'

'Nothing — sorry!' He straightened his face. 'But we'd better not get divorced if you're wanting to tell couples how to live happily ever after.'

'Don't be stupid, Willo!' she snapped. 'Marriage counselling is a job you have to train and qualify for — the work's completely objective — personalities are not involved — and as a matter of fact several counsellors I know have been through a divorce and they're all the more experienced and therefore supportive of others.'

He made peaceable noises and said: 'You can have a divorce whenever you wish, Barbara, but money's a different story.'

'It's not a question of money,' she huffed, eyes averted.

'You mean it is a question of divorce?'

[161]

'Well – if only for the sake of tidiness.'

'Oh yes – tidiness – that's important – I mean it – and I agree.' He proceeded in order not to get involved in questions of remarriage: 'Two favours – will you arrange everything – and keep it as cheap as possible?'

'I gather it won't cost either of us much. But I'm in no hurry – are you?'

'No,' he said.

Shortly afterwards, as he was leaving, she put a tentative question to him: 'How long can you stay with Josh?'

He shrugged his shoulders.

'Have you somewhere else to go to?' she pursued.

'Not at the moment.'

'By rights you ought to come here.'

'Don't worry – I'll never do that.'

They stood in the open doorway, not knowing how to bid each other what might be farewell.

He said: 'This cottage is yours for your life, you understand? Don't thank me, don't! I like to know you're settled comfortably.'

She looked up at him more directly than for years. He bent over and kissed her on the cheek. She raised her arms as if to embrace him, but changed her mind and lowered them again. He called out, 'Goodbye,' and she responded inconsequently and drily, 'You deserve better, Willo.' He strode down the garden path and through the gate and climbed into his car and drove away.

A few days later he went across to Sprocketts to see Melanie and his grandsons. For most of his brief visit he was commandeered by William, minus tonsils and adenoids and clearly stronger without them, and by James. They showed him their treasures, cross-questioned him, clambered all over him, and objected vociferously when he had to leave. His daughter's goodbye was the opposite of his wife's: Melanie's embrace was again too close for comfort, and the more so because of her pregnancy.

Pressing against him and leaning back she asked her own version of Barbara's query: 'Is Josh likely to chuck you out?'

He replied: 'I don't think so, but I can't stay there much longer.'

Her pretty face assumed an apologetic expression.

'Edgar and I have kissed and made up, Dad – and he's working so hard in his new job – and the boys and the baby and everything . . .'

He interrupted her: 'I wouldn't inflict myself on you if you begged me.'

She was grateful; he pleased her by saying how well she looked; she sent love to her godfather and he entrusted her with good wishes for her husband; and they parted.

In the car a funny old paradox struck him: to wit, that they had been united by disowning each other.

He not only shed no crocodile tears over the distance between them which seemed to be increased by her attempts to close the gap physically; he was sorry that his sister Mandy would not take a leaf out of Melanie's book and leave him to fend for himself.

Mandy's invitations to The Shoe House were becoming more pressing and less enticing. Her offer of a mattress on the floor of the room he could share with his two nephews had been relatively attractive. Her next suggestion was a coal-shed, where he would have more privacy: it only needed a watertight roof and a lick of paint to make it habitable. Recently she had told him that, since her grown-up sons Jim and Peter were at last leaving Tollworth to find remunerative work, and their father and her husband Theo was growing older and weaker, it was the plain duty of a brother without a home of his own or other responsibilities to come and lend his sister a hand.

Although Josh transformed Mandy's tactlessness into a laughing matter, Willo refused even to cross her threshold and was nervous that she would cross his and rout him out of the vicarage.

Instead of visiting her, one evening he walked across the fields to Tollworth for what proved to be an influential chat with Denis Willett.

Denis was cultivating the garden of his antiquated thatched cottage, bearing the euphemistic address New House, which Willo had sold to Sammy and Marilyn, and still went with the job of gardener at The Court.

He greeted his former employer with expressions of pleasure, and they passed the time of day across his picket fence.

Yes, Denis boomed, he was doing nicely and had no complaints about the 'youngsters' who were seldom in residence and paid him 'silly' money.

In time, via meteorology and local gossip, he arrived at a diffident inquiry as to how Mr Todd might be getting on.

Willo explained that he was looking for a job.

'What sort of a job would that be?'

'Nothing fancy – I can't afford to be fussy – any job plus a roof over my head, if possible – I'm a player rather than a gentleman nowadays – and I seem to be hale and hearty, even if long in the tooth.'

Denis eyed him speculatively and remarked: 'I was thinking of you not long since.'

'Have you got a job for me, Denis?'

'That'll be the day,' the other scoffed with a loud laugh. 'No – I did hear there was jobs going at Waddington.'

'At the big house, where the Ellerys live, you mean?'

'They were wanting an under-gardener, I do know.'

'But I don't know gardening, Denis. Jobs, you said – what other jobs were going? And where did you hear about them?'

'Mr Ellery was engaging extra staff through the Estate Office. The man who told me saw a clipping in a newspaper.'

Willo failed to get any more information out of Denis. He would have liked to work at Waddington Hall; but he imagined the jobs were either beyond or beneath him; and anyway his acquaintanceship with the Ellerys would create difficulties – their former guest becoming their servant would or could be awkward.

He scrapped the idea.

Coincidentally, that same evening as he re-entered the vicarage, the telephone rang.

It was Desmond Simcox, apologising both late in the day and belatedly for his response to Willo's bits of news.

'I've been exceptionally busy,' he said. 'And to tell the truth I haven't known whether to congratulate you for selling The Court or to sympathise. But thanks for your note and for letting me know. I'm glad you're with Josh, and I just hope you're beginning to feel better, as I am at last.'

Why Desmond was feeling better, and had been so busy, was that he too had sold property, his house in Lincolnshire, Shilley Grange, and his flat at Pimlico Gate, although not with immediate vacant possession, and was at present engaged in negotiations with a potential buyer of his Lloyd's agency.

'Whatever happens to Alleyn and Simcox won't make any difference to you, Willo,' he reassured. 'I promise to see you through.'

He was additionally bucked to have found alternative employment for his gardener in the country and his maid in town.

Willo inquired: 'What about alternative employment for yourself? And where will you lay your head?'

Desmond and his wife Sarah would live in a tiny flat in Cowes, Isle of Wight – it belonged to Sarah and was where members of his family had previously spent holidays – and he had the offer of a job, believe it or not, in a betting shop in the area, and had accepted it provisionally.

'I seem to have fallen on my feet,' he concluded. 'What's extraordinary is that without a penny of my former resources, but with my pay from the betting shop, I should have quite enough money. I can't stop thanking the heavenly powers-that-be – I never do and never will forget how merciful they've been to me. My worst worry now is the predicament of my clients, not to mention sympathy for everyone in our sort of trouble. Dare I ask if the Fates are treating you any better?'

Willo said how pleased he was for Desmond, and Desmond rephrased and repeated his question.

Willo had to admit that with great regret he had just ruled out the possibility of a job – the first he had heard of, and the first he fancied – in a house or on an estate he loved.

Desmond requested details.

Willo supplied them, and expatiated upon the negative social aspects.

Desmond said: 'My future boss in the betting shop used to call me sir when he took my bets. These days we must all be adaptable – the brave new world belongs to adaptability. We're at the sharp end of another revolution, Willo, or is it the beginning? This Lloyd's business has knocked out half the gentlemen of England – I quote from Shakespeare – and not only gents and ladies in the sense of very wealthy folk, as you and I know from experience. The map of our world is being redrawn, Willo. You've sold your home to today's clever money – you say your Sammy and Marilyn have behaved admirably, and you've become friends – you never were standoffish – I'd call you the least snobbish of men – so why be backward and hang back now? Apply for the job if you want it – the Ellerys ought to be impressed by your willingness to buckle down and earn your daily bread – and if not, that's their misfortune and mistake.'

The upshot of this conversation was that Willo mentioned the matter to Josh, who also advised him to take it a stage further. The next morning he therefore nerved himself to obtain the telephone number of the Estate Office at Waddington, and after some hesitation to ring it.

The voice of a girl asked politely how she could help him.

He began: 'Would you be kind enough to tell me if there are still any vacancies for staff at Waddington?'

'The only vacancy now is for a butler,' she replied.

'Thank you,' he said. 'Goodbye.'

He was surprised as well as disappointed: he had imagined butlers were an extinct species, except for Anthony Haden's Perry. And although he claimed to be ready to do any job, and was too poor to be fussy, he never contemplated domestic service. Besides, butlering was not for amateurs: he remembered a butler employed during his boyhood at The Court, Mr May, who had blinded Willo with the science of his trade, the art of folding napkins, for instance, and how to bone polish into shoes. He lacked the expertise, and continued to shrink from the unavoidable personal involvement with the Ellerys. He had hoped, without exactly formulating his ideas, for outdoor work, driving maybe, being in charge of transport, or something in the forestry or game-keeping lines.

He applied himself to his routine at the vicarage. Gradually his second thoughts were reduced to the heartening question: why not? He had experi-ence of gracious living after all, if only from the other side of the green baize door: he knew how butler's work should be seen to be done. And he had learned how to look after – in a word, valet – his clothes in the army. Moreover he was already a 'domestic', according to the jargon of bygone days – he served Josh – and might be equally happy to serve an employer showing respect and goodwill.

At this point in the internal discussion Willo sat down with pen and paper. He wrote draft after draft and eventually a fair copy of the following letter, which he read aloud to Josh that evening.

'Dear Mr and Mrs Ellery, I would very much like to be considered for the post of your butler. Please forgive me for addressing you directly – it seems the simplest way of applying for the job. As you may know I was a Member of Lloyd's, and have now lost virtually every penny I possessed. My home, The Court at Tollworth, is sold, and I am lodging at present with my old friend and your acquaintance the Reverend Joshua Kemball. I have been a soldier (10th Lancers) and a publisher (Anthony Haden Ltd), yet believe myself capable of discharging all the duties of a butler and valet. Although I lack practical experience of the work, I assure you that no employee of yours could be more grateful than me or keener to give satisfaction. I am fifty-six years of age; have no health problems at present; and would need accommodation. As for possible difficulties of a social nature, my aim is to forget the past and start again from scratch, presuming nothing. Yours sincerely.'

Josh not only approved the letter, he immediately sealed and stamped it and marched out of the house with Willo in pursuit and along to the Measham Post Office, where he popped it into the letter-box.

Willo in the next three days wished his friend did not know him so well: he would have torn up the letter if he had been able to.

But on the fourth day, a Saturday, the vicarage telephone rang at eight-thirty in the morning, and when he answered it a soft yet firm male voice said: 'Is that Willoughby Todd? My name's Max Ellery.'

'Oh hullo,' Willo replied, blushing with shame and bracing himself to apologise for his impertinence.

'Could you come and see me in two hours, at ten-thirty?'

'Yes, of course.'

'Good – ring the front door bell – until then!'

Willo prepared for his interview by donning a white shirt, quiet tie, dark grey suit and black shoes, and arriving half an hour early in the environs of Waddington and having to wait apprehensively in a lay-by.

At ten twenty-five, driving towards the pillared and porticoed side of the great house, his nervousness was replaced by an exclusive resolve, an unusual and uncharacteristic determination, to work and live within its golden ambi-ence at all costs if he could.

Max Ellery opened the door, wearing smart casual clothes, and led him across the marble outer hall to his business room, which in its farther wall had a french window into the orangery. Willo remembered the room from days gone by: it still had a glass-fronted bookcase on one side of the fireplace and a gun cupboard on the other. He was gestured towards a wing chair covered with new green leather, and sat facing his potential employer, seated in a modern revolving chair by a desk bearing various coloured telephones and some electronic equipment.

The first question related to names.

'What shall I call you?'

'You could use the abbreviation of my Christian name, Willo, or my surname.'

'Willo will do fine. Thanks for your letter. I admire you for writing it. May I extend sympathy for your changed circumstances and congratulations for trying to make the best of them? Should you decide to work for us you'd have to call me Mr Ellery or sir and my wife Mrs Ellery or madam. We're not formal people – but you'd be mucking in with other members of our staff – and special relationships wouldn't be popular.'

[167]

'I agree.'

'Do you want to be our butler and nothing but our butler?'

'No. I applied for the only vacancy that I understood was on offer. I'd be pleased to help in any way I could.'

'What makes you think you'd be happy here?'

'Part of my answer has to be personal. When I met you and Mrs Ellery last Christmas I liked you both. And my opinion has been that you'd judge my application on its merit and without reference to the conventions. And I've always loved this house.'

'There are two empty rooms in the basement or semi-basement here. If one was equipped as a kitchen and the other as a bed-sitting-room, would they suit you?'

'Yes – very well.'

'I understand that you're separated from your wife?'

'Yes.'

'Permanently?'

'Yes.'

'You could stay in a spare room until the conversion of your own quarters was complete.'

'Thank you very much.'

'Did you work for a salary at Anthony Haden?'

'Yes.'

'May I ask how much?'

'Fifteen thousand a year.'

'I could pay you the same. I know nothing about butlers' wages, but I'd pay you fifteen K gross on certain conditions.'

'That's generous.'

Max Ellery smiled. His hair was greying, thick and neatly cut, parted and brushed. He was younger than Willo, perhaps in his mid-forties, but authoritative. He exuded confidence and controlled tension: he was more dynamic than restless. His eyes were dark brown, and his regard at once disturbingly straight. He had well-shaped hands with long mobile fingers. His smile was quick and charming.

'The conditions of work may change your mind,' he said. 'I'm extremely and probably excessively busy – and the same applies to my wife – we're both more active than we should be, I expect – but we mean to keep going for the foreseeable future, and therefore require absolutely reliable service. As our butler so-called, you would be in charge of the smooth running of this house, the senior member of staff, and responsible for security. Problems of any description would be referred to my personal assistant in my London office, not to me or my wife. When we're in residence you'd be worked almost off your feet – weekend parties, late nights – and it would be up to you to engage extra help and to cope. When we're away, you'd have to look after our interests and amuse yourself. My wife's a young woman – we hope to have children in the nursery one of these days – which would mean carrying meals upstairs. My own clothes and shoes, and my guests', would need valeting to the highest standard. Shall I continue?'

'Yes, please.'

'I don't want references. I know enough about you to be prepared to offer you a contract. Your initiative deserves reward. Don't thank me yet! I have no time to prevent or correct the mistakes of others – I'm hard at it trying to correct my own. Your contract will give me the right to sack you with a week's wages in lieu of notice. If you sign on, you risk losing your job and the roof over your head at any moment. I'm sorry – that's how I operate and manage to give employment – and you'll have to take it on trust that my wife and I aren't as tough as our lawyers. If we can stick to one another for two years, you would begin to have some legal say in your destiny. That's my offer. Maude and I would be delighted if you saw fit to accept it.'

Six months elapsed. It was December, the Wednesday of the week leading up to Christmas. The time was four o'clock in the afternoon, the twilight of a clear still winter's day, and the scene the exterior of the vicarage at Measham. The front door was open, light emanated from it, and the bright windows of ground floor rooms also helped to illuminate the assortment of cars parked in the driveway. Figures were emerging from the house, two little boys aged seven or eight, a woman arm-in-arm with an older man, and another man bearing a carrycot: the Milsoms, Melanie with Willo, and the new baby.

The occasion was a family lunch party with traditional Christmas fare, organised early in consideration of the fact that Willo would be on duty throughout the festive season, and presided over by Josh, who was pleased to repay the similar hospitality he had received at The Court.

Guests had begun to leave. Melanie wanted to get the children home to Sprocketts, and Edgar, who had taken the middle of the working day off with difficulty, was keen to look in at his office before closing time. William and James swung plastic bags of presents at each other, giggling.

Their father's mild rebuke also paid tribute to the mood that had prevailed indoors: 'Steady on! We've all had the greatest fun – don't spoil it!'

Melanie turned by the bigger and better car that went with Edgar's more important job, and, holding Willo's hands and keeping her distance for a change, studied his smiling face and asked: 'Truthfully, Dad, do you love being at Waddington as much as you've been saying indoors?'

'Truthfully, yes.'

'Last year we were sitting pretty at The Court. Coming down in the world with a bump may be what we needed.'

'You haven't come down, you're on the up and up.'

'The bad things that happened to you seem to have been good for us.'

'I'd like to think that. Anyway, you're happier than you were a year ago, aren't you?'

'Thank God, yes – I've my Willoughby Milsom. It's stupid to have a William and a Willo' – she meant her eldest and youngest sons – 'but our little Willo will probably become Bill – and meanwhile two Willos are much better than one. I'm not complaining,' she said, reaching up with unwonted reserve to receive a chaste paternal kiss. 'You are rather a marvel, Dad,' she added, and climbed into the back seat of the car beside the secured carrycot.

Willo leant in to pat his youngest grandchild, then clumsily embraced the other two, and had his hand shaken with firm professional sincerity by Edgar.

'How's the insurance business managing without my involvement?' he asked.

'Business is never good,' Edgar replied, laughing at the old chestnut. 'But it could be worse in my own experience.'

'I hope you're not ashamed to have a father-in-law in service.'

'No – you've set us a constructive example. Well – happy Christmas!'

Edgar slid into the driving seat and started the car and rolled off smoothly as if to a triumphant chorus of goodbyes.

Willo waved, while a small person wearing trousers, a leather bomber jacket, scarves and a crash helmet strutted briskly out of the house.

'Do you need to go, Barbara?' Willo inquired as she began to tinker with the lights on her bicycle.

'I should have left long ago – it's darker than I thought it would be. The party was nice, Willo – thanks for including me.'

'How's Honeysuckle Cottage? I haven't had a chance to ask you.'

'Oh yes – I want to talk about something – another time maybe.'

'Why not now?'

'All right. Would you object to Roger moving in?'

'Good gracious!'

'What's so surprising? Don't tell me you've got moral objections.'

'I just thought Roger had been studying for all these years in order not to be dependent on his mother or anyone, and to stand on his own feet.'

'I'm not like his mother, Willo.'

'No – of course not – sorry! I'm afraid I've some catching up to do. I'm not even sure that Roger's graduated. Are you going to marry him, Barbara?'

'We don't hold with marriage. Yes, he has graduated, he did brilliantly, he got a second. But he can't settle for any job, like you. He can't throw himself away.'

'I see.'

'That's not meant to be rude – I don't underestimate your achievements.'

He shrugged his shoulders. Other voices issued from the house, other people were appearing in the doorway.

He said hurriedly: 'You're free to do exactly as you please – my only wish is that you should be happy.'

She replied, mounting her bicycle: 'I'm much happier, Willo – and I hope you are.'

'Wait a tick! Speaking of freedom, what about divorce?'

'Do you want a divorce now?'

'Don't you? Both of us might as well be prepared for emergencies.'

'Very well – I'll tell my solicitor to get a move on. Goodbye!'

He had to shout his thanks after her as she wobbled into the darkness and her red tail-light faded from view.

His sister Mandy and her daughters Muriel and Desirée were singing in unison as they came across to bid him goodbye: 'We wish you a merry Christmas!'

Desirée had audibly put mumps behind her and regained her strength; but her father was in the grip of yet another mysterious indisposition, and had not been feeling well enough to come to the lunch party. The four other Wriggs issue, Jim, Alice, Cathy and Peter, having flown the nest soon after Willo began to be a butler, were unexpectedly turning honest pennies in various parts of the globe.

[171]

Mandy, obviously not short of party spirit, sang out: 'Oh my beloved little brother, I can't bear to think of you becoming a flunkey.'

He corrected her vocabulary and kissed her and his nieces goodbye.

Mandy hugged him again by the ever more battered Wriggs Volvo and said in maudlin accents: 'You haven't only robbed me of my darling old home, you've robbed me of my babies, four of them – who were inspired by you to go and do unpleasant things in faraway places for filthy lucre. I should be cross with you, Willo, though you have borne up and turned the tables on your beastly poverty. But it's Christmas – and Theo's all for forgiveness – so I hereby absolve you of your sins.'

The girls in the car chorused: 'Come on, Mum!'

'There!' Mandy exclaimed, patting Willo on the shoulder and giggling. 'I lead a dog's life – or should I say a bitch's? Goodbye, Will, God bless!'

She got into her car and drove off.

Prue, carrying her overnight bag, joined Willo.

'What a lovely visit I've had!' she said, smiling up at him indistinctly through her specs.

'I wish we had longer,' he returned. 'But it was much better than nothing – and the party went well, didn't it? Here, let me have your case. I hate you having this long drive in the dark.'

She had motored from Penzance, arriving the previous evening, and was now about to motor back. The reunion of father and daughter after six months had been on the hectic side: they had prepared the food for today's lunch. Although he had thought she looked tired, and was afraid that helping him in the kitchen would make her tireder, she insisted that driving did her good and that cooking in his company was fun. She was laughingly impressed by the domestic skills he had acquired since she saw him last, and praised him more seriously for having the nerve to be a butler. He tried to satisfy her curiosity about life at Waddington, and steered clear of questions that might detract from the apparently mutual happiness of their being together again.

But now one anxiety, that she had to drive so far at night, seemed to summon another, as a result of which he said: 'I haven't had time to ask you anything important.'

'No – but it doesn't matter, Dad,' she replied in a slightly repressive manner, removing her overcoat and throwing it into the back seat of her Mini.

Willo said: 'Shall I put your case in as well?'

'Oh yes.'

He did so, saying: 'You haven't met a nice new friend by any chance?'

'No – not to speak of.'

'Are you still missing John Seward?'

'Yes.'

'You're not in touch with him?'

'Oh no – never again! And you're better, Dad – which is the best news – I've never seen you so perky.'

'What's happened to me – just up to this evening – I can't speak for the future – is really too good to be true.'

'But it is true – and wonderful.'

They kissed each other goodbye and she sat in the driver's seat. The interior light was not working – standing by the open door of the car he could scarcely see her.

'Drive carefully, darling,' he said.

'Yes,' she replied, and then: 'Dad, it was such a relief not to have secrets from you any more.'

'What?' He was taken aback by her announcing it so abruptly and in the past tense.

She continued: 'I don't want to keep secrets. I've had a bit of trouble and I'm having it treated – nothing much – but I want you to know. Please don't say anything to Melanie or anyone. I haven't told Mummy.'

After a pause he asked: 'What sort of trouble, what sort of treatment?'

'Radium therapy or whatever it's called.'

'Where's the trouble?'

'The usual place – and it was minuscule a month ago and is responding to the treatment – and the doctor seems to be fond of me – I'm in good hands – there's absolutely nothing to worry about.'

'I'm not worried,' he claimed. 'You've done everything right – you'll be as right as rain – I know that. But when can I ring you for bulletins? I do my best not to bother you with telephone calls.'

'Ring me in a week. Early in the morning might be the easiest time for you. I'm always awake by half-past six.'

'Okay. About Christmas: are you sure you'll be happy with your mother?'

'It'll be a change – but yes.'

At this point Prue got out of the car, embraced Willo again and said: 'Thank you for being so calm and confident – I hoped you wouldn't get in a flap.'

[173]

'Certainly not – most people have had a spot here or there – I'm glad the doctor appreciates you. Have you been working, are you able to work?'

'Of course. I'm not ill, Dad.'

'No – I can see that. Promise to contact me whenever you feel like it – you can get messages to me via Josh if need be.'

'Cross my heart,' she said, back in the car and starting the engine.

He leant in and kissed her and closed the door.

'Lights,' he reminded her.

She laughed and switched them on – they were both laughing and waving as the car moved away.

Willo remained where he was for a few minutes. The moon had not yet risen or was invisible, and breezes rustled the last dry leaves on trees. He shivered and walked in, closing the front door.

In the kitchen Josh said to him: 'Have they all gone?'

'Yes,' he replied, taking off his jacket and rolling up his shirtsleeves, preparatory to helping his friend to do the clearing and washing-up.

'The party was a success – more successful than last year if I may say so – largely thanks to you,' Josh said.

'No – not true – I've succeeded at nothing – Prue's having radium treatment.'

'Oh!'

Josh sat down on one of the assorted chairs crowding round the kitchen table, on which wine glasses with the lees of wine in them, half-full glasses of orangeade, coffee cups and bottles still stood amongst the paper hats and pulled crackers.

'She just sprang it on me out there. I thought she looked tired. Because of not having The Court to come to, she finished with John Seward and fled to Cornwall – and the shock of separation after ten years, the wrench, must have done something bad to her health. It's my fault.'

'Clever Willo, to have discovered the cause of cancer.'

Now Willo sat, confessing: 'I was feeling stupidly complacent before she let on – I was patting myself on the back for the way everything's turned out – pride comes before a fall.'

'What did Prue say?'

Willo answered the question and Josh commented: 'It doesn't sound that bad to me – I believe Prue and I trust her to pull through.'

'I hate her being so much alone in strange surroundings.'

'Nonsense – we're all alone – forget you're her father and remember and respect her independence.'

'I can't forget how much I care for her.'

'No. It's hard on you too. And I'm sorry I can't stop preaching nowadays. Shall I shut up?'

'No, Josh.'

'Well – let me pat you on the back – you've remade your life in record time – you say you're happier than ever in your work – you're even interested in a new lady-friend, this secretary at Waddington Hall. Judging success or failure is not our business – nevertheless what's clear for all to see is that you've adjusted to change with remarkable grace. But change refuses to be a singular experience. Life equals changes in the plural. You thought Prue was perfectly fit ten minutes ago, you know she isn't now. And you love her, and it's sad. You've another change to adapt to, Willo.'

'You adapted to it, didn't you, with Clare?'

'Clare's illness was never nothing, and getting a little worse was the death of her. It was rare and incurable, whereas Prue suggested hers was common or garden and can be and is being cured. You have to have faith that Prue will soon be well.'

'Did you have faith?'

'I've had to have faith that my religion would keep its promises.'

'In respect of life after death?'

'Yes.'

'Apologies for the pessimism, Josh, but I've always had difficulty with the idea of resurrection. I'm too earthbound – or probably not good enough – heaven seems damn far away – in circumstances similar to yours I couldn't begin to adjust as you have.'

'Who knows? You didn't give up the ghost when you lost all your money – I don't believe you'll ever give up on Prue, whatever happens.'

'I must say, God asks a hell of a lot of us.'

'Poor God's out of favour these days – He's mocked and sworn at – and His religion seems out of date and beside the point and useless – and too much effort and altogether too difficult. But it's designed to make living and especially dying easier or more bearable. And it can, believe me – don't forget Trooper Biggins.'

Willo glanced at his wristwatch and said: 'Time's flying – I promised to be back at Waddington by six. Thanks, Josh, for counselling me – Barbara once told me I needed counselling – she may be a counsellor one day and make us all better. And thanks again for entertaining me and my family. Come on, let's get things straight.'

He stood and began to collect the debris of the party.

Josh joined in and remarked: 'I can't think why I've been preaching at you – it's impertinence – you put it all in a nutshell by word as well as by deed.'

Half an hour later the two friends parted by the front door.

'Thanks for everything,' Willo said.

'Not everything – give credit where it's due.'

'Yes – I have done and I do.'

'Happy Christmas and new year, Willo.'

'Same to you.'

'Will you be all right now?'

'Definitely.'